IT'S COMPLICATED

CAMILLA ISLEY

Boldwood

First published in Great Britain in 2024 by Boldwood Books Ltd.

Cover Design by Alexandra Allden

Cover Photography: Shutterstock

A CIP catalogue record for this book is available from the British Library.

Paperback ISBN 978-1-83533-640-3

Large Print ISBN 978-1-83533-641-0

Hardback ISBN 978-1-83533-639-7

Ebook ISBN 978-1-83533-642-7

Kindle ISBN 978-1-83533-643-4

Audio CD ISBN 978-1-83533-634-2

MP3 CD ISBN 978-1-83533-635-9

Digital audio download ISBN 978-1-83533-637-3

Boldwood Books Ltd
23 Bowerdean Street
London SW6 3TN
www.boldwoodbooks.com

If the song "The Way I Loved You" by Taylor Swift feels like the soundtrack of your life, this book is dedicated to you...

1

LORI

The moment I flip through my mail and find an ivory wedding invitation, my heart cracks in my chest and my mind snaps back to a spring night of fourteen years ago when I could've stopped it all and didn't.

My two best friends and I were at a home party, junior year of college at Urbana University. I can't remember much about that night, whose house it was, what day, or even what I was wearing. But I do remember the drinking game we were playing: Never Have I Ever. At least Aiden and I and his then girlfriend were playing. Jace was somewhere probably being hit on by all the single women at the party.

I'd already taken quite a few shots. One for losing my virginity. One for breaking a bone in the fifth grade. One for googling myself —I know embarrassing. One for crashing a party—we were probably crashing that party as well. One for reading an entire book in a day—duh, how are there people who've never done that? And one for giving out a fake number—not cool, I know, but I'm not big on confrontations, even for something as small as telling a stranger

I don't want to give them my number, so I always choose the path of least anxiety.

I'd just downed the shot for the fake number, when it became Tracy Dillon's turn to speak.

A textbook mean girl in our year, she locked eyes with me as she spoke, "Never have I ever..." she paused for suspense, studying me with a malicious glint. "...Been in love with my best friend!"

A dare.

And it must've been the six shots I already had in me that made me accept the challenge. Because next, I looked Aiden straight in the eyes, not even caring that his girlfriend was sitting right next to him, and downed the seventh shot of the night.

I drank.

He didn't.

I don't know why my mind flies back to that night of so many years ago as I trace a finger over the expensive cotton fiber paper of the envelope. Maybe because my subconscious knows better than I do that something could've changed that night. Or maybe it's just the usual wishful thinking on my part. I can still remember the dumbstruck expression on Aiden's face as I downed the shot. And the closed set of his jaws as he didn't touch his. Or the way he frowned as strong arms hooked under my armpits and scooped me up from the floor. Next, I was in Jace's arms, and he was carrying me away from the game.

"You've had enough to drink for tonight, Lola," my other best friend said, using the nickname he always called me. "I'm taking you home."

"But I was having fun," I protested.

"Trust me, you're going to thank me tomorrow."

Too drunk to object, I waved at Aiden over Jace's shoulder as we left whoever's house we were at. I don't remember how we got to my dorm. I probably fell asleep in Jace's arms on the way. But the morning after is another one of those moments that will remain forever etched in my memory.

Aiden knocked on my door bright and early, looking all serious while he asked me if we could talk. That was my moment. I had broken the eggs the night before and I should've made the omelet that morning, aka confess to Aiden my undying love for him. Instead, I chickened out saying that if by talking, he meant he wanted to feed me pizza and one of his famous hangover-crushing smoothies I was game because, seriously, I'd never felt more under the weather and couldn't remember a thing from the previous night. Had the party been any good?

Gosh, how I hated myself at the relieved expression on his face.

Crisis averted, I guess. No one had to deal with silly old Lori's unrequited crush and unwanted feelings. We could all go back to being The Three Amigos, a trio where I was considered a sort of asexual being—not exactly a man like the other two, but also not someone either of them would ever date. In all the years we've known each other, neither Jace nor Aiden ever went for anything more risqué than a hug with me. No matter if I was in sweats watching a movie, or out clubbing in a miniskirt, or even sharing a bed with one of them on a trip. Nothing ever happened. I was friend-zoned from day one.

Now, crushed under the weight of the posh envelope, I lean against the front door for support—I sure didn't expect such a bomb to come out of my mailbox when I got home after a long day at work.

I shouldn't feel so blindsided, but I do. It's too soon to send out wedding invitations. Aiden proposed to Kirsten only a few months ago. And even if I saw the ring, the engagement posts plastered all over Instagram, and have been to the engagement party, a small part of me still hoped he wouldn't actually marry Kirsten.

I'm an idiot.

Of course, Aiden would marry Kirsten. She's the ideal woman—beautiful, posh, funny, with her head on her shoulders, and from a good family. She has everything.

But me? I'm a hot mess. I can't keep a boyfriend for more than a few months—being secretly in love with your best friend will derail most relationships right from the start. And my hobbies are spilling all over the place—none of them are suitable for a wife.

As new cracks spread down my heart, I want to rip the letter into a million pieces. Instead, I let it fall to the floor, holding on to the walls for support as I head for the safety of the couch. To reach the living room, I have to meander through the piles of old novels littering my apartment—inconvenient hobby number one: I rescue books from destruction.

Why do certain books need rescuing? Because when sales of a novel slow and not even a prolonged sojourn in the bargain cart can make copies shift, the unfortunate volumes are returned to the printing facility and destroyed through a process called "pulping."

I shudder, thinking of the piles of books stripped of their covers and munched into the recycling machines. I can't stand to fold a book's page and do my best never to crack the spine while reading, so witnessing the book pulping process scarred me for eternity.

How did I get into this hobby? The manager at one of these printing facilities is a patient of mine—I'm a family doctor, the only accomplishment of my life—and he lets me save some of the volumes destined for the paper grinder. The liberated novels then move in with me and litter my floor until I manage to resell them online or at garage sales. Some I donate to little free libraries. But most just keep on not selling and end up camping in my apartment for a very, *very* long time.

I dodge another leaning tower of neglected dystopian novels and make it to the open space living room. Four cats await me sprawled on the couch—inconvenient hobby number two: I also rescue animals. The addiction started with cats and expanded to chickens when I moved into my industrial loft that has a cozy backyard. I've always been a cat person, but the extension to chicks came after I saw a traumatizing documentary on chicken factories, which also converted me to being a vegetarian.

Unlike books, I have to set strict limits on the pet population I'm allowed to keep. At any given time, I can't house more than four cats and six chickens.

I wiggle my butt on the couch, plopping down between Leia, a tawny tabby, and Chewie, my ginger, long-haired stud. Sitting down doesn't help calm my nerves. My mouth is still paper-dry and my heart pumping in my chest on the verge of a full-blown panic attack. I drop my head in my hands, folding my torso over my knees and taking a few deep, hopefully calming breaths.

The Christmas tree lights blink in my face from a corner of the living room. And while I usually enjoy their bursts of colored joy, now they're making the anxiety worse. Sure, the holidays are over. I just didn't get around to taking the tree down yet. I'm not in a hurry to do it, either. I love Christmas and the warmth the tree lights sprinkle on the house.

I bet Kirsten is one of those people who take down their Christmas trees on 26 December.

Shudder.

And perhaps that's what's better for Aiden. Someone organized and efficient, who doesn't come with the baggage of approximately a thousand books, four cats, and six chickens. Maybe seeing him getting married and hearing him promise his eternal love to another woman will finally cure me of loving him. A disease I've carried with me for my entire adult life.

From the moment I met Aiden in college, I knew he was The One, but I have never confessed my feelings. I even encouraged him to date Kirsten at the beginning, when he thought she was too posh for him (I totally agreed and still agree with that assessment). The only reason I told him to go out with her was that I figured she was entirely wrong for him and that they wouldn't last past a couple of dates. I'm such a fool and such a coward.

I've been a wimp since the winter of freshman year when I first fell hard and fast for him.

Aiden was in one of my classes, Introduction to Undergraduate Biology Research, the weirdest class I had that quarter. The professor, George Quilliam, was unconventional and, on the first lesson, he lectured us on how scientific research is 90 per cent rule-following and 10 per cent rule-breaking. He then asked who among us had a problem breaking rules. Aiden and I raised our hands. Jace didn't.

Bioresearch wasn't the first class I'd had in common with them, seeing how all three of us were bio pre-med students. But we weren't friends back then. They were the cool kids, totally out of my nerdy league. Wherever they went, their then-duo made heads turn. Jace and Aiden had to be the hottest freshmen on campus. Both tall, athletic, and broad-shouldered. Jace, dark-haired, with eyes the color of a glacier, and a chiseled profile that would've made Michelangelo's David hide in shame. With his full lips constantly upturned in a lopsided, confident smirk, he was the essence of casual, endless charm. And Aiden, fair, blond, everybody's All-American dream. His face beautiful, elegant, and ageless—in a hanging on the walls of a museum kind of way. But his expression was never arrogant and his blue eyes were always gentle and warm. Jace was the personification of danger and excitement. Aiden, an angel fallen on Earth.

So, yeah, I'd noticed them before. But despite our many shared classes, they'd never spoken to me, and neither had I to them. I've never made friends easily, and after four months of cohabitation I was barely getting comfortable around my dorm roommate, so I wasn't about to approach the two coolest guys in my year with some embarrassing, never-show-your-face-in-public-again line.

But that first day of the spring quarter changed everything. The course was elective and smaller than usual, with only ten students. So, obviously, that had to be the class where I picked a fight with the professor. Academic contexts are the only ones where I have no problems stating my opinion or openly disagreeing with someone —especially if it is to fight for one of my patients. But, as that day showed, my academic confidence isn't always a plus.

Quilliam studied us law-abiding losers with our hands raised and smirked. "Very well, class. For your first homework assignment, I'm going to send you on a little rule-breaking quest. The Garden Gnome Liberation Front recently broke into my backyard and depleted my collection. So your first assignment, due next class, is to steal me a garden gnome."

Students looked between themselves with a mix of amused expressions and is-this-guy-for-real frowns. But of course, I had to be the jerk who raised her hand and asked, "Excuse me, professor, but what do garden gnomes have to do with biology?"

"Ah, Miss..." He paused to check the class roster and confirm my name. "Archibald. As I said, no great scientific discovery was ever made without breaking a few rules first."

I pouted, and he called me out. "Something you'd like to add?"

"Yeah, even if we bring you a gnome, what would make you think we actually broke into someone's garden to steal it and didn't simply order one online?"

"Excellent point, Miss Archibald. Express deliveries *are* a plague of these times. Let's agree each of your gnomes must look properly timeworn, then." He peeked at us from under his spectacles. "And in case you were thinking of fabricating the distress I should warn you, I also hold a degree in applied chemistry and will be able to tell."

That statement earned me a lot of glares from my classmates, so I refrained from commenting I could just order an old gnome from eBay.

It turned out that I couldn't. By the time I got home that evening, and on my computer, four out of the five gnomes available for sale that would reach Urbana in time for the next class were already sold. The remaining one had reached a four-figure price tag that was way above my college allowance. Apparently, flexible pricing was another plague of the times.

That's how the following evening I ended up dressed in all black, complete with a black beanie and black running gloves, strolling through the residential neighborhoods of the small college town in search of garden gnomes to abduct. I was walking alone in a side street, trying to act inconspicuous, when Jace and Aiden overtook me from behind. Jace stole the beanie from my head and twirled it on a finger.

"You're going to get us caught by stalking the streets dressed so suspiciously. You have garden gnome thief written all over your face, Archibald."

"I do not," I hissed as I tried to rescue my beanie.

But Jace snatched up his arm, bringing it out of my reach.

Aiden smiled. "You do look a little suspicious, Lori. Could you at least lose the gloves?"

I was flabbergasted that he knew my name—that they both did —and blabbed, "I didn't want to leave fingerprints and it's cold."

Jace smirked. "I promise you, a crime scene investigator won't be involved in a case of gnome grand larceny."

I glowered. "You the expert?"

That's when Aiden ruffled my bangs—also a thing back then—and I was a goner.

"Are we doing this or not?" he asked. "Jace and I scouted the perfect house filled with creepy dwarfs."

Jace put on my beanie and started jogging backward, preceding us. "Do you think we'd get extra points for stealing Snow White?"

By the next class, we'd stolen three hideous lawn ornaments. We handed them in, got the bonus marks we were promised, and that was the beginning of our friendship. For shy, self-conscious me it felt inexplicably easy to hang out with them. I just fitted with Aiden and Jace in a way I'd never belonged with anyone before.

Probably because I hadn't known them growing up. To them I was just Lori Archibald, the nerdy, rule-abider in their pre-med classes and never the "silent girl" I had been in Sarasota, the Florida town where I grew up.

I was born with a very small cleft palate that didn't extend into a cleft lip and ironically, made the birth defect a hundred times more difficult to discover. Kids in pre-school made fun of me for my nasal voice and things got worse in grade school where I entered the first grade being practically mute for fear of being made fun of.

It was only when our old G.P. retired and we had to switch to a new general practitioner that I was diagnosed. That woman changed my life, she's the reason I've always wanted to become a family doctor growing up. To change lives in return. I had a small surgery and solved the defect. But I still was made fun of as I was behind with my speech development and had a slight lisp, which turned me into an overly shy kid without many friends. And even years later, now my speech is perfectly normal, I sometimes feel like I still haven't found my voice. At least if my fear of confrontation is any indication.

Anyway, the night of our gnome grand larceny made me feel for the first time like I belonged. Sadly, that's also the night that stuck me in the friend zone forever. With Jace, it's never been a problem. He's always been too wild for me. But Aiden, poised, sweet, caring, fun, gorgeous Aiden, is my soulmate. Only he doesn't know.

Palpitations make my heart throb again as my mind goes back to the ivory envelope adorning the hall floor. I can't be alone in my apartment with the dispatch from heartbreak central. And I sure as hell can't open it by myself.

I roll a finger inside the neck of my blouse. I need air. I need to get out.

I stand up, top the cats' water and food, fill the hens' feeder, collect their eggs that I'll sell at Saturday's farmers' market, grab my keys, and get back out of the house merely twenty minutes after getting in.

2

JACE

Long day. I pull up into my building's underground garage an hour later than I'd planned after having handled a last-minute walk-in with an upper respiratory tract infection. I kill the engine and debate if I can still squeeze in a quick workout in the 24/7 fitness center or if I should ditch the training for tonight and go for a run in the morning.

I get out of the car and take the elevator one floor up to the lobby, checking the weather forecast for tomorrow on my phone: 21 degrees with a chance of snow.

Oof.

Gym it is. Chicago's winters and outdoor training don't mix.

Before I can put the phone back in my pocket, it pings with a text.

FROM ZOE:

Want to hang out tonight?

The message is from Zoe. A woman I see occasionally. She's often away for work, isn't interested in a serious relationship, and doesn't expect anything from me. In short, perfect. Still, the idea of another meaningless hookup feels as appealing as being stuck in traffic right now.

I shoot her a short text as I exit the elevator.

TO ZOE:

Sorry, I'm busy

In the hall, Denzel, the night doorman, greets me with a polite, "Good evening, Dr. Barlow. I have your mail."

He hands me a stack of envelopes and I shuffle through them on the ride up to my apartment. Utility bill. Credit card offer. Medical insurance renewal notice. Wedding invitation.

I low-whistle as I spot the fancy ivory envelope sealed with a pearly wax seal, the letters A and K monogrammed in the middle.

If Lori has seen this, she will have blown a gasket.

I enter my apartment, dropping my keys, wallet, and phone on the foyer console, then hang my coat in the small entrance closet. Next, I take off my shoes, stacking them in the built-in cabinet at the bottom of the closet—I hate to bring the dirt from outside into the house. I set down my unopened mail on the kitchen counter and walk down the hallway to my bedroom. I've just changed into basketball shorts and a T-shirt ready to hit the gym when my buzzer goes off.

What now?

With a groan, I throw my dirty clothes in the laundry basket and rush back toward the entrance to answer the intercom.

"Yeah?"

"Good evening again, Dr. Barlow." Denzel's voice comes distorted through the speaker. "Dr. Archibald is coming up to see you."

Ah.

"Thank you, Denzel."

A heartbeat later, three quick knocks come from the other side of the door.

When I open it, Lori storms into my apartment, cheeks red from the cold, chestnut hair tousled and falling in her face, beige coat billowing behind her. The scent of Chanel Coco Mademoiselle follows her, delivering the usual punch to my gut.

"Lori." I close the door with a sigh and turn to her. "What's—"

"Did you see this?" She brandishes an ivory envelope identical to the one lying unopened in my kitchen, flapping it back and forth.

I jerk my chin toward the counter. "Got mine today, too."

Lori shoves one hand through her hair and huffs. "Why did he blindside us like this? We saw him, what, less than two hours ago at work, and he couldn't have bothered telling us our invitations were coming in today, or that they'd picked a date?" Next, she points an accusing finger at me. "Did you know they'd set a date?"

"No, Lola, I didn't. Maybe Aiden didn't tell us we'd get the save-the-date cards tonight because he wasn't sure when they'd be delivered. And I wouldn't call this being blindsided. You knew this wedding was happening. The proposal and engagement party should've been strong enough clues. Hasn't Kirsten already picked a dress?"

Lori waves me off dismissively as she paces around my living room. "Insignificant details. Twenty per cent of all engagements get called off—I checked the statistics."

I follow her into the living room. "Which means the other 80 per cent don't."

Lori stops and faces me, her eyes wide as she throws up her arms in exasperation. "I always try to see the glass half full."

"The optimistic part being Aiden's engagement falling apart?"

"Or at least not being the shortest in history. Some engagements last for years. What's the rush? I bet she's the one pushing to move the date forward." Lori grabs her chin as if pondering Kirsten being pushy, then she takes in my sporty clothes and asks, "Were you about to work out?"

"No, just ready to chill at home," I lie, pointing at the invitation in her hands. "Have you opened it yet?" I can't see if the seal is torn.

"No, have you?"

"Nope."

"Should we do it together?"

I nod.

Lori drops her invitation and bag on the coffee table and takes off her coat, draping it on the backrest of the couch.

I grab the coat and make to hang it in the closet by the door. An unforgivable move, apparently.

"Can you pause your neat-freak habits for a second?" Lori scolds me. "I'm dying here."

I put the coat away all the same and come back into the living room. "Sorry, Lola, not all of us thrive among clutter."

And I must've said the wrong thing because her brown eyes widen and her lower lip trembles. "Do you think that's why Aiden never liked me that way? Because I'm such a mess?"

Before she can start to full-on cry, I pull her into one of the rare hugs I allow myself to give her. "You're not a mess, Lola, just a little *messy*."

She hangs on to me like a stranded baby koala. I drop a kiss on top of her head and hate myself when I can't resist smelling her hair. Coconut and shea butter. "Any guy would be lucky to have you."

Lori pulls back with a glint in her eyes and a little smirk. "Even neat freaks like you?"

"Totally," I say.

"So you wouldn't mind me hogging the bathroom counter, or

leaving dirty dishes in the sink to wash later, or forgetting food in the fridge until it rots?"

I struggle not to shiver at the list of capital offenses. "Nope, not a problem." For her, I could overlook anything.

With a flash of challenge in her eyes, Lori leans into me, whispering in my ear, "Not even if I left wet towels on the bathroom floor?"

It's been years since she's been so close. Years since I've wanted to kiss her so badly. I push her back and turn her around, gently shoving her toward the couch. "Come on, Bridget Jones... enough with the smart talk."

Lori sags on the cushions, pouting. "I prefer to picture myself as Julia Roberts in *My Best Friend's Wedding*."

I raise my eyebrows at that and drop down next to her—but at a safe distance. "Didn't she lose the guy in the movie?"

"At least she fought with honor. Me? I haven't done a single thing to stop this dreadful wedding from happening."

"Would you really want to jeopardize Aiden's happiness?"

She unzips one boot, kicks it under the coffee table, and moves on to the other one. "You want the honest answer or the politically correct one?"

The second boot joins the first, and she sits on the couch in a butterfly pose.

"You know you can be your horrible self around me, Lola."

Lori throws me a pillow and exhales a long, hard breath. "Honestly, I don't know, Jace. I have nothing against Kirsten personally, but she's so... I don't know... shiny?"

I scowl at her. "What's wrong with shiny?"

She laughs. "Nothing, I'm just saying she's like a shiny new toy. Come on, did you see her shoes the other night?"

I can't help but laugh, too. "Her high heels are the least of Aiden's problems, Lola."

I hate how eager her face becomes. "Why? You have some dirt on her?"

"Nope, just agreeing she errs on the high-maintenance side."

"So why does he put up with her?"

"Because he loves her?"

Lori hurls the remaining pillow at my head. "Now you're just being vile."

I shrug. "Oh, you know me. I'm always the villain in every fairy tale."

Lori rolls her eyes. "Yeah, that's why we get along so well."

I glance over at her and recognize the sadness in her eyes that she tries to hide with humor.

Lori smiles. She's even more beautiful when she does. But the smile doesn't reach her eyes, she's only putting on a brave face. And I wish I could be the one to make that beautiful smile reach her eyes, the one to make her happy. That's when I realize how badly I want to kiss her—*again*. Proximity isn't good for me.

I want to press my lips on her neck and wipe that heartache away forever. I want to drag my mouth up along the curve of her jaw to whisper in her ear how special she is, how badly I want to kiss her, but there's no way she'd reciprocate.

Struggling to keep my impulses in check, I scoot further down to my side of the couch. Lori steals back one of the pillows and settles down, a hand on her chest as she hugs it for comfort.

"Thank you," she whispers, looking at me with Bambi eyes.

"What for?"

"You're the only person in the world who could've made me smile today." I want to tell her I can see through her fake smiles, that I know I'm not who she needs but wish with everything I have that I could be.

Instead, I do what I always do. Keep quiet. Keep my feelings to myself. Play aloof. Always the villain never the hero. "Careful there, or my reputation will get a hit."

"Don't worry, I won't tell any of the ladies you're not really the dangerous bad boy they want you so hard to be."

I chuckle, but the sound is bitter. It grates on my throat. None of the women I've been with have ever meant anything.

She tilts her head. "So, has Aiden ever complained about Kirsten's excess primness?"

And we're back at it. "Aiden's a grown man, Lola," I say, doing my best not to lose my shit completely. "He can make his own decisions."

Her smile dies. Lori bites her lower lip as if to stop a retort from coming out of her mouth. Her eyes fleet back to the coffee table and the ivory envelope resting on the dark wooden surface. She reaches for it and cradles the missive in her lap. Lori looks down at the letter and hands it to me, whispering, "You open it, I can't."

I take it from her and carefully tear the seal.

A single piece of ivory cardstock rests inside.

"With great pleasure," I read aloud, "Dr. Aiden Jackson Collymore and Kirsten Ann Cunningham invite you to join them in the celebration of their marriage..."

I turn to Lori, who's staring out the window.

She scoffs. "I bet Kirsten insisted on putting the doctor in. Come on, rip the Band-Aid. When is it?" Her voice cracks over the question.

"Soon."

Lori turns to me, eyes teary. "How soon?"

I make to put the card away. "Maybe we should do this another time."

Showing the reflexes of a panther, Lori snatches the invitation from me and reads it.

"WHAT?!"

Here we go...

"They're getting married in a month? That must be the shortest engagement ever. And the wedding is on Valentine's Day no less? Who gets married on Valentine's Day? It's so cheesy. They're clearly compensating for lack of real romance in the relationship."

"Clearly."

"Are you making fun of my misery?"

"I wouldn't dare. Listen, did you have dinner? Because I'm starving. How about I make us something?"

I stand up, my gaze landing on the boots scattered onto the rug.

Lori tracks my stare. "Those discarded shoes are killing you, aren't they?"

"Nope."

Lori picks them up and stands. "I'll put them away if you promise to make your mac and cheese. I need comfort food. And wine, plenty of wine." She walks toward the hall.

I move into the kitchen and search the cabinets for the ingredients. "You're the worst doctor—I hope a bowl of cholesterol and plenty of wine isn't the dietary advice you give my patients when I'm away."

"Don't worry, most of your patients don't come to the practice when you're away. My face isn't pretty enough."

I'm already at the stove when she hugs me from behind, pressing her cheek between my shoulder blades. "Jace?"

I try my best to stay relaxed. "Yes?"

"Can I sleep here?"

"Won't all your pets die if you abandon them?"

"No, I've already fed them and the girls must already be in bed by now."

"Sure, then."

"Thank you. I didn't want to be alone tonight." She squeezes me harder for a second and then lets go. "You're the best friend in the world."

Kill.

Me.

Now.

3

LORI

The next morning I wake up sprawled in the middle of Jace's California King bed in a starfish pose while my best friend is relegated to a tiny corner of the mattress curled up in the fetal position —keeping as far away from me as he always does when we share a bed.

I never understood if he's afraid I might try to cuddle him—Jace doesn't exactly strike me as a cuddler, or if he just values his personal space too much.

I search the room with my eyes, not exactly sure what woke me until his buzzer goes off again.

"Jace."

No answer.

"Jace, someone's at your door."

He sleep-mumbles something unintelligible and turns onto his back, his head lolling toward me on the pillow. He looks cute with the hair falling on his forehead and the stubble darkening his square jaw. Jace lets out a loud snore, making me giggle.

"All right, buddy, I'll go see who it is."

I throw the blankets away from my body and shuffle barefooted to the entrance hall.

I press the intercom button. "Yes?"

"Oh, good morning, miss, are you a guest of Dr. Barlow?"

"It's Lori, Peter, good morning."

I greet the day-shift doorman.

"Ah, Dr. Archibald, hello. Just a heads up, Dr. Collymore is on his way over."

"Thank you, Peter."

Aiden is coming over? Shoot. What do I do? How do I look?

I check my reflection in the hallway mirror and it's not good. My hair is a bird's nest. I'm wearing one of Jace's oversized T-shirts, and icky, crusty mascara is smeared all over my face. A knock on the door makes me jolt, then panic. I lick a finger and furiously try to remove the worst black stains.

I'm not ready.

I put a hand in front of my mouth and exhale. Eww. I need to brush my teeth. But I can't, not enough time.

Aiden knocks again. "Jace? Are you there?"

Crikey, crappity, crikes.

I've almost resigned myself to welcome Aiden into the house with morning breath when my eyes land on a tin of mints resting on Jace's hall console. I grasp the metal box to get one, but of course, in my clumsiness, the lid pops free and all the breath mints tumble to the ground, except for one.

Yeah, score! I pop the white candy in my mouth and fling the door open, leaning against it sideways in what I hope is a sexy-casual pose.

"Aidenberry."

My other best friend and love of my life is standing on the other side, fist raised, primed for another knock, looking painfully handsome in a stylish blue coat.

"Lori?" For a moment he frowns as if unsure he's got the right house. Then he looks past my shoulder at the world-class city view of Chicago and his brain must compute that he didn't come to my back-alley-facing industrial loft. The scowl deepens. "What are you doing here?"

Aiden's gaze drops to the floor. "Are those breath mints?"

"Yeah, sorry, I knocked them off on my way to the door. I was still sleepy."

I step aside to let him in and before he can notice I'm sucking the last mint, I swallow it whole. Except, the treacherous piece of menthol confectionery gets stuck in my throat and I have to rush to the kitchen in a coughing fit.

And now I can't breathe.

I turn on the faucet and try to gulp down some water, but the liquid doesn't make it past the mint and dribbles down my chin.

The short-winded rasps I'm making force Aiden to catch up. "Gosh, Lori, are you choking?"

My wannabe negative, nonchalant reply comes out as a strangled death rattle.

The doctor in him takes over. Aiden is behind me in a few quick strides and lowers me down toward the sink to administer five blows to my back with the heel of his hand. And I swear, whenever I imagined Aiden bending me over fixtures, this wasn't what I had in mind.

When the gentle approach still doesn't work, he goes full Heimlich on me. He wraps his arms around my waist, makes a fist just above my navel, and, grabbing the fist with his other hand, he pushes it inward and upward at the same time. At the second abdominal thrust, the mint flies out of my mouth and goes to decorate Jace's kitchen wall.

I'm still sputtering and spattering when Aiden lets me go.

I'm fine, I want to say, only the phrase comes out still wheezy and as if I was talking in a monster voice, "I'm fhhhooine."

Aiden opens the fridge and pours me a glass of water.

I sip it while I try to regain some dignity.

When I feel like I can talk in a normal tone again, I ask, "Hey, what are you doing here this early?"

Aiden's brows shoot high in his forehead. "Are you all right?"

I wave him off. "Sure, I'm fine. Crisis averted. We're all doctors here, no need to worry. I'm great." Except for the humiliation, maybe. My reddish-blue, mascara-streaked, almost-just-choked-on-a-mint face must look especially attractive. "So, why are you here?"

Aiden is flabbergasted. "Why am I here? Why are *you* at Jace's place?"

"Oh, I slept here last night."

His jaw tightens. "With Jace?"

"Yeah, with Jace, it's a one-bedroom apartment last I checked. You're acting weird this morning, Aidenberry."

"I'm acting weird?"

"Yep." I turn to the coffee maker and grab a new filter. "You want coffee?"

"No, I want an explanation."

I turn back to him. "An explanation about what?" Aiden looks handsomely broody and I cave. "Okay, I confess. I didn't want to answer the door with morning breath, so I grabbed Jace's mints, no big deal. But, of course, I knocked the box to the floor and all the mints fell out except for one, which I ate and then proceeded to almost choke on two seconds later. Thanks again for saving my life, by the way."

"That's not what I'm talking about. I want to know how long it has been going on?"

"My mint-popping habit? Only twenty minutes, I swear, it's already a thing of the past."

"No, how long have you been sleeping with Jace?"

"Oh."

Ooooooh.

I see now how my words could've been misinterpreted. I'm about to clear the waters, telling him how wrong he is when I notice the look of distress on his face. Aiden seems really to dislike the idea of Jace and me... *canoodling.* My heart leaps in my chest. Is he jealous? Oh my gosh, he *so* is. Is me pretending to date Jace what it'll take Aiden to finally realize he belongs with me? I mean, Taylor Swift said it.

I know what I'm about to do is stupid, *really* stupid, but I can't help myself. This is one of the few, I-can-count-on-one-hand reactions I've got out of Aiden in over a decade that has made me feel seen as a woman—and not just his bestie. So I shrug. "Oh, you know, not that long."

Aiden's face darkens still, sending a thrill of excitement down my spine. He really isn't happy about this.

"Gosh." He rakes a hand through his perfect blond locks and takes off his coat. Aiden folds it on the backrest of the couch and sits at the kitchen bar, head in his hands. "How did it happen?"

How did it happen? Fair question. With no actual answer. Think, Lori, *think.*

I turn again toward the coffee maker and fiddle with the pot. I have the worst lying face. "Oh, you know... it just happened?"

"How?"

How? How? How? I summon one of my million fantasies about how Aiden and I would eventually get together that is time-of-the-year appropriate for a fairly new tryst. "Erm, I got stood up on a blind date one night and Jace was in the same bar by chance having catch-up drinks with his b—" Aiden has a brother, Jace has a sister. "Sister. He was having a drink with Jessica."

"Yeah, I know the name of Jace's sister," Aiden comments curtly.

"Sure you do. Anyway, long story short. I joined them. We had a few drinks. Then Jessica left, and Jace offered to drive me home, saying I shouldn't wait for the train at a freezing station in the middle of December. He was very sweet and looked at me funny. And I don't know, it must've been all the Christmas decorations because he kissed me and confessed how he's always been secretly into me." Okay, I could've left this last part out, but in my fantasies, Aiden would always confess to loving me from afar for all these years. "Anyway," I chuckle nervously, "the rest is history."

"And why did neither of you feel the need to inform me of this new development?"

I add two sugars and a splash of milk to his coffee and hand it to him.

"You were busy with the wedding. We didn't want to distract you or steal your thunder or anything. Plus, it's so new, we don't even know what we're doing..."

I hide my face behind my mug and take a sip.

"So, you and Jace?"

"Yep, me and Jace."

Our eyes lock, and Aiden's are intense. Oh my gosh, what is he going to do? Will he beg me to choose him? Swear he'll cancel the wedding, but could I please be with him?

Instead, he just presses his lips together. "That's a lot to take in. Is Jace even alive?"

"No, I killed him with too much sex last night."

Oh my gosh, will I shut up?

Aiden positively winces.

"Too soon?" I ask.

He nods.

"I'll go wake him," I say.

And I also have to convince him to go along with my crazy story.

4

JACE

Lori wakes me, straddling me in bed. My eyes fly open and before I can say anything, she puts a hand over my mouth. "Don't talk."

For a moment, I think I'm still dreaming, that this is one of my fantasies coming to life, but her weight on me feels too real.

Further confirmation this is not a dream arrives when Lori opens her mouth and vomits a torrent of definite real-life verbal nonsense on me. "Aiden is in the kitchen. I don't know why he came to visit you this morning, but I went to open the door because you wouldn't wake up." Easy to believe. Last night, with her sleeping next to me, it took me forever to fall asleep. I stared at the ceiling for hours, listening to her regular breathing and all the cute sleep sounds she made, imagining how it'd feel if she were in my bed as my girlfriend and not my friend. I was exhausted by the time I passed out.

"And when he saw me wearing your T-shirt," Lori continues, "Aiden asked me if we'd slept together and I said yes because, technically, we did sleep together. But he understood it in the other way—the naughty way," she clarifies unnecessarily. "And he seemed really jealous about it, so I might've… umm… not corrected him."

"WHAT?" I try to say under the muzzle.

"Shhh, shhh. Now, you can't go out there and contradict me or it'd make me look like the most pathetic human being in the history of all pathetic human beings. Even more pathetic than Aiden having to save me from choking to death on one of your breath mints."

Since I can't speak, I frown.

"Don't worry, he Heimlich-ed me and aside from the humiliation, I'm going to live. And clear your floor from all the mints…" She frantically waves her free hand in the air. "Later. In fact, if you do this for me, I'll clean your house for an entire year. Please?"

We stare at each other for a long moment until she realizes I can't answer her if she keeps me muzzled.

"I'm going to let you speak now, but please don't scream or get mad."

Slowly, she removes her hand.

"We can't do this," I hiss. "I can't lie to my best fr—"

The hand is back over my mouth. "Hissing your refusal is also not allowed. What do you want me to do? Confess I made up an entire relationship between us? What if he asks me why? What would I say?"

I raise an eyebrow in a permission-to-speak way.

Lori lets me.

"A relationship? So it isn't just a hookup you want me to lie about?"

"Sort of." She gives me details about drinks with my sister and Christmas lights.

"You actually told him I've been into you since college?"

"Don't worry, you came off really sweet."

"I'm not sweet."

"Except when with me, your secret love?" Lori bats her lashes at me. "Please don't rat me out. Please?"

She looks like Princess Ariel when she begs Sebastian not to go tell on her to King Triton. Pouty lips and big eyes. Except Lori's hair and eyes are brown.

"This is insane."

"I know, but you'll do it for me because you love me despite all my weirdness."

I push her off me and get out of bed. "You owe me, Archibald, big time. As in, you'll take all my walk-ins from now till the end of times."

Kneeling on the bed, she nods. "I know."

I pull on a pair of sweatpants and shuffle into the kitchen.

Aiden is seated at the bar, looking very put-together in beige chinos, and a light-brown sweater. Yeah, very self-possessed—except for his expression.

When our eyes meet, he stares murder at me—as he should.

"Hey, man." I give him a fish-eating grin. "What's up?"

"I don't know," he says, voice cold. "You tell me, *man*."

"Guys, guys." Lori shuffles between us. "Leave the testosterone out of this." She points at Aiden. "You don't need to defend my honor." And then at me. "And you don't have to be the alpha."

It would help if she was wearing something other than one of my T-shirts.

Aiden seems to agree because he scoffs. "Can you go put some pants on?"

"Actually, I need to get dressed and go home to change if I don't want to be late for work." She theatrically rolls her eyes. "My partners can be real pains in the ass."

I glare. She'd better not leave me alone with Aiden.

Our friend snickers. "Jace hasn't given you a drawer yet?"

Lori puts her hands forward. "As I said, still very new, still very undefined."

Aiden stands up. "I've got to go, too." He grabs his coat from the couch and pulls it on in a jerky, angry move. "See you both at work."

And he would've made the perfect stormy exit, if not for all the mints littering the entryway slowing him down, forcing him to slalom. He makes up for it with a spectacular door slam.

I turn to Lori, pointing at the door with one thumb. "That makes you happy?"

She chews on her lower lip. "He was pretty mad."

I make a duh-uh face.

"But why else would he be mad if he weren't jealous?"

"Oh, let me see. Aiden could be angry because he thinks we've kept this from him. Or because he's worried about our relationship going sideways and things getting weird at work, or about our group dynamic changing."

Lori scoffs. "In case you hadn't noticed, Kirsten already bulldozed our dynamics, and you don't have the best track record with relationships."

"Are you seriously giving me this right now?"

"No, what I'm going to give you is space." Lori grimaces apologetically. "I'll go home to change and feed the flock and cats, and we're going to talk again once you've calmed down. How does that sound?"

"Akin to a root canal."

Lori's grimace turns into a full-on smile as she points to the bedroom with both her thumbs. "I'm gonna go now."

* * *

I wait all morning for the knock on my door. Still, when it comes, I'm not any more ready for it. I don't receive patients on Thursday mornings, so I know it's Aiden.

"Come in," I call.

My best friend since junior high walks into my office, looking no more pleased with me than he did this morning at my apartment.

He takes a seat in front of me, and we stay quiet for a long time.

Aiden breaks first. "So, you and Lori?"

"Right, me and Lori?"

"Seriously, man, is that all you're going to give me?"

I wouldn't know what else to say, so I play my jerk-of-the-group role. "You want a play-by-play, or what?"

Aiden winces. His self-control greatly exceeds mine. If the roles were reversed, I would've already punched him. "Don't be like that. The tough-guy act doesn't work with me."

"Okay, dude, what do you want me to say? Lori and I are dating, is that such a big deal?"

"Yeah, it's a big deal. What happened to the pact?"

I roll a pen between my fingers. "I thought it lapsed when you got engaged."

"The pact was never about one of us getting Lori."

"What was it about, then?"

"All that crap you fed me when you made me swear never to sleep with her, or kiss her, or even look at her as if she were a woman. In your words, how our friendship was too good to risk for a horizontal hula."

"Man, that was what? Fifteen years ago? We were just a couple of dumb college kids. Of course, one of us would've ruined it with her. We're all adults now."

"And you won't ruin it now?"

"I don't plan on it."

"Are you kidding me? You're what? What? You're going to marry Lori? You? The guy who can't stay in a relationship more than a few weeks?"

For the first time, I suspect Lori might've had a point in saying Aiden was acting jealous. I never thought he had a thing for her. I've always assumed I was the only one... but could I have been wrong all these years? And could the only thing that ever kept Lori and Aiden apart be that stupid oath I made him swear freshman year? Shoot. I hope not. Or Lori would kill me—if she ever found out, that is.

"Gosh, man, relax, okay?" I say. "What does it matter to you, anyway?"

Aiden's lips press into a thin line. "You know what."

No, I honestly don't. I raise my eyebrows interrogatively.

Aiden stands up. "Forget it, it's too late now anyway, isn't it?"

He makes to storm out of my office but I call him back. "Don't go, man, we can talk this out."

"Oh, now he wants to talk. Sorry, this morning has already been too weird."

Which makes me think. "Why were you at my place at seven in the morning anyway?"

His expression darkens. "I wanted to ask you to be my best man."

The words are a blow. That he would ask me instead of his brother. "I'd be honored," I say. "And I'm sorry."

Aiden doesn't respond, he gives me a quick nod as his jaw clenches and then he slips out of my office.

I let him go this time. I sag back in my chair and massage my temples, wishing I'd said yes to last night's booty-call text from Zoe. If Lori hadn't found me home, now I wouldn't find myself in the middle of the most insane love triangle in the history of *ménage à trois*.

* * *

I spend the rest of the day holed up in my office, either doing paperwork in the morning or receiving patients in the afternoon. I don't get any last-minute appointments or walk-ins, so I'm ready to leave early. Still, I'm the last one to go. Aiden receives patients in the mornings on Thursdays and then prefers to work from home. Lori has her patient appointments in the afternoon like me, but she must've finished earlier than I did.

I close our joint practice, hoping these walls aren't about to crumble in on themselves. What Lori, Aiden, and I share is too good. We've been friends through college, med school, and our residencies. All three of us have always wanted to be family doctors and, once we got our medical licenses, the next logical step was for us to open a practice together. Our patients love it because they're basically always covered. Even if one of us is sick or on vacation, the other two can take over, providing round-the-clock care.

And the dynamic has always been weird in a I was secretly in love with Lori, while she was secretly in love with Aiden way. While Aiden was supposed to be the one above it all. But now I wonder if I was the only odd man in the group. The outsider who kept them apart.

When my phone pings as I walk to my car, I half hope it'll be Zoe again. But of course, it's Lori.

FROM LORI:

Talk tonight? Can you come over?

I really don't feel like driving all the way to Lincoln Park and then back to Streeterville. Also, I'm not that keen to talk to Lori right now.

TO LORI:

If you want to talk, why don't you come over?

FROM LORI:

The cats are already mad at me for leaving them alone last night

TO LORI:

And how do you manage when you go on vacation?

FROM LORI:

Do you have any idea how long it takes to make them purr back to me?

Please come?

We need to talk

I'll make you dinner

TO LORI:

That might actually be an incentive to stay away

FROM LORI:

Then I'll order Mexican from that place around the corner you love

Pretty please?

Lori adds a googly-eyed emoji.

TO LORI:

I'll be there in twenty

FROM LORI:

And I'll have the fajitas ready

5

LORI

Since the king of neat spaces, minimalistic furniture, and bare walls is coming over to my place, I decide to clean. I can't give him the full, unfiltered Lori home experience or he'll go into anaphylactic shock. To free some space on the floor, I stuff my bookshelves with as many volumes as they can hold and readjust the piles still littering the hardwood to make them slightly less precarious. Then, in the little time I have left, I also manage to vacuum about 90 per cent of the cat hair dusting my furniture, order our food, and even set the table, adding some fake lilies as a final touch.

When the doorbell rings, I'm not sure if it's Jace or the food.

I go to open the door.

It's Jace.

He's frowning and… "Wow," I say. "The broody look really suits you, you're hot."

Jace's eyes widen. "You always blab the first thing that crosses your mind?"

"To you? Yes. And you love me for it, or at least you're going to pretend you luurve me for the next three to four weeks."

Oh, oh. The frown is back.

I'm saved from hearing Jace's sure-to-be-lectury response by the delivery guy arriving with our food. His hurried approach to the front steps forces Jace into the house. I grab the food, tip the guy, and close the front door with a backward kick.

Jace is removing his coat and looks uncertain about where to put it. In theory, I have an entryway closet similar to the one at his house. But of course, mine is blocked by three turrets of old novels. I'm not even sure what coats or bags got trapped in there. One day, I'll finally move the books and go on a treasure hunt inside. I won't have seen the clothes and accessories locked in for so long that they will seem like brand-new additions to my wardrobe—or totally out-of-style goodwill candidates. Only time will tell. I'd say it's a fifty-fifty chance. But I tend to buy items of clothing that are more timeless than on-trend, so there's a good chance I'll still want to wear whatever is inside that closet.

Anyway, I quickly deposit the food on the kitchen table and grab Jace's coat from him. "I'll put this away."

But where? The back of the couch wouldn't be safe from one or more of the cats taking a nap on it, leaving behind copious shedding. Not an option. I consider the other hook-y surfaces in the house and settle for hanging the coat on the corner of a tall bookshelf.

Jace tracks my movements but abstains from commenting.

When we sit at the large, round kitchen table, Leia, Ben, Chewie, and Han Solo each claim one of the four empty chairs.

The cats sit, immobile, Egyptian-statue-like, and observe us.

Jace is at the end of his quirkiness rope.

"Do they always act like that?" he asks.

"Yep, they're passively-aggressively pressuring you into sharing your food with them. They've stopped with me, but since you're new, they're testing you. Don't budge."

I seldom invite people over to my place, even my closest friends —for obvious reasons. When we hang out in my neighborhood we eat out, but I didn't want to discuss secret, fake-relationship stuff in a crowded restaurant where anyone could hear us.

Jace gives me the first half-smile of the night. Lopsided, teasing, his eyes crinkling at the corners. "Did they stop asking because you're such an accomplished cat trainer, or since you've gone vegetarian and stopped eating anything they might like?"

My expression is outraged. "I'm not dignifying that question with a response."

I open the delivery bag and hand Jace his fajitas, then unpack my cheese quesadillas and cauliflower tacos.

We eat a few bites in silence until Jace says, "Aiden came to see me today."

My pulse immediately picks up. "And?"

"You might've been right. He acted a little territorial, which I wouldn't have guessed, to be honest—"

"That's amazing. You think my plan will work?"

"No, your plan is the dumbest idea ever."

"But you said he was jealous!"

"Even if he were, he's never going to act on it. Aiden is more loyal than a Labrador. He would never leave Kirsten at the altar, especially not to steal a woman from his best friend. You basically dug yourself into the only position worse than him being engaged: Aiden still being engaged and you becoming 200 per cent off-limits."

My cheeks heat. "Whatever you say," I mutter, taking a few small bites of my food.

Jace regards me for a moment. I'm sure he's about to lecture me about my selfishness again, but he says, "Plus, I don't want to lie to him. I already felt awful today."

"What are you suggesting? That we tell him we broke up one day after confessing we're together? Because I'm not going with the truth."

"What's the alternative?"

"You fake date me until the wedding for moral support. I don't want to go single."

Jace finishes chewing before saying, "You know you'd technically still be single."

"But I'd feel a tiny bit less pathetic." I take a bite of a quesadilla and add, "Should we set down a few basic rules?"

"I haven't agreed to anything yet."

"Okay, but you can either pretend-dump me or pretend-date me because I'm not telling Aiden I made everything up, period."

"Why can't *you* pretend-dump *me*?"

"Because you're not the getting-dumped kind of guy, while I get dumped all the time."

"That's ridiculous. You have to dump me."

I drop my food and square off to him, arms crossed over my chest. "Or else?"

"Or else Aiden will beat me to a pulp for hurting you."

"Yeah, I could see that. Remember how you guys wanted to beat up Blaine Brown in sophomore year?"

"That guy had been a total jerk to you."

"And you went alpha best friends on him. You terrified him so much he didn't show his face around campus for the rest of the quarter." I sigh. "Okay, I see why you can't dump me. Can we make it a mutual thing? We tried being in a relationship and then realized we're really just friends?"

"No one ever believes in the mutual break up. It has to be you."

I roll my eyes. "Okay, you're such a wuss. Gosh, it's only a fake break up. I'll do it."

"Okay, we should tell Aiden, tomorrow."

"What? No! We can't do it tomorrow, it'd look too suspicious. You have to fake date me for at least a couple of weeks." I add a little pico de gallo to my tacos, and ask, "Should we move on to the rules, then?"

6

JACE

"What rules?" I ask, stoically accepting my destiny.

Lori smirks, aware she's won. "First off, we should be fake dating exclusively."

I raise an eyebrow.

"I know it might be difficult for you."

"Gosh, Lori, thanks for the vote of confidence."

"I meant no offense, just saying that I'm aware this arrangement will affect you more. I haven't been on a date in three months while you're a single, healthy man who's very sexually active. Nothing wrong with that."

Lori blushes and I can't help but tease her a little. "Exactly how sexually active do you think I am?"

The blush deepens. "Ha-ha. I'm referring to the fact that you could probably get any woman you want."

Not the only one I care about.

"You assume I'm a player?"

She shrugs. "I'm just saying. When was your last serious relationship?"

"I dated Michelle for four months."

"Your girlfriend from three years ago?"

"Yeah."

"Exactly." Lori plays with her hair like she does whenever she's nervous. I enjoy making her flush. It makes her even cuter. "My point is, can you fend off women's advances for the next month so that from the outside it'll look like we're in a committed relationship?"

I smirk. "I'll see what I can do, Lola."

Lori rolls her eyes.

"Any other rules?"

"Not really. Just please, for the next few weeks, pretend you find me irresistible."

Ah! Not gonna have a problem with that. "You're my goddess, and I worship at your altar. Got it."

"Great." Lori smiles, then as if we hadn't been discussing me pretending to be in love with her for the near future, she asks, "You want another Coke?"

"Sure."

She stands up and opens the fridge. "Shoot, I'm out. I'll grab one from the basement."

While she's gone, one cat, the tabby silver one, stretches a paw over the table, enormous eyes boring into me.

"Okay, but be quick." I pick four slivers of pork and give each of the cats one.

By the time Lori comes back, they've finished the contraband meat and are sitting straight-backed in their chairs again.

Lori drops the Cokes on the table and freezes. "Did you give the cats food?"

"Just a little pork," I confess. "They looked so hungry and it seemed mean to eat a full meal in front of them."

Lori laughs at this. "Oh, poor baby, they'd just had a double serving of their favorite dinner." She caresses my cheek. "They tricked you. What did they do? Purr? Gave you the puss-in-boots eyes?"

I glare.

"You're cute," Lori teases.

"And you're a gigantic pain in my—"

"Language, Dr. Barlow." She gestures at the cats. "Not in front of the kids."

Lori never calls me Dr. Barlow, and it's a good thing because the words send a shiver down my spine.

"You think you're so funny," I say, opening my Coke.

"I'm pretty hilarious, actually." She opens her can, too, and takes a sip.

Whatever comment I was about to make dies on my lips as I get distracted by the movement of her throat as she swallows.

The skin of her neck is so smooth, so... bitable.

Lori takes another sip and smirks. "What's up, Jacey Pooh? The cat got your tongue?" She winks.

I throw my napkin on the table. "Well, thanks for dinner and for trapping me in a fake relationship, I'm gonna go home now."

Lori stands, too. "No need to be such a sour*puss*."

"Make another cat joke and I'm out."

"Of the house or the fake relationship?"

"Both."

Lori comes over to me and hugs me. "You'd never do that to me, you're too good a friend."

No, I'm a patented idiot, that's what I am.

* * *

By a stroke of luck, I manage to avoid seeing both Lori and Aiden all of Friday. Quite an accomplishment, considering we share a lobby, a secretary, a nurse, and a lab. But then I make the rookie mistake of wanting to leave work at the end of the day and bump into both of them at the same time, with the awkward addition of Aiden's fiancée, Kirsten. In a freakish coincidence, we all get out of our offices at the same moment. Except for us, the lobby is empty, as it always is at 6 p.m. on a Friday.

Aiden's office is the middle one while Lori and I are at the extremities. For an awkward moment, we all stand still. The green pastel walls Lori insisted on having to make the ambience more welcoming are the only witnesses to the uncomfortable silence. The situation becomes even more embarrassing when Lori blushes and, eyes on the floor, crosses the space to come by my side and clumsily hold my hand.

Aiden pouts while Kirsten's eyes fly wide open.

She turns to her fiancé. "Did I miss something?"

Aiden scratches the back of his head. "Apparently, these two started dating and forgot to tell me. I found out yesterday."

Kirsten unleashes such a bright smile, her pearly veneers threaten to blind us all. Next, Aiden's fiancée squeals in delight, as if she couldn't believe her luck. "But that's amazing, you guys. I want to know everything."

Lori squeezes my hand as if in warning, then she makes a dreadful attempt at casually flipping her hair backward. "Oh, you know, it just happened. One day we were best friends and the next, we were knocking boots morning, day, and night."

Aiden's eyebrows disappear behind the perfect golden locks covering his forehead and this is my cue to make an intervention.

7

LORI

I can't believe I said knocking boots morning, day, and night in front of Aiden. My cheeks are on fire and I'm internally hyperventilating.

Things get worse when Jace pushes my hair aside and leans in to loud-whisper in my ear, "Maybe that's too much information, babe." Then he kisses me just over the jugular.

The touch of his mouth on my neck is searing. The softness of his lips mingles perfectly with the gentle scraping of his stubble.

I fight to stand still as my knees go weak. Gosh, the man really has got game.

"Sorry, guys," Jace says, pulling off his effortless charm. "We weren't ready to share our news with the world, and Lola is still a little nervous."

"This is fantastic news," Kirsten shrieks.

She trots toward us in her stiletto boots and hugs Jace. I'm next. Before I know what's happening, I'm being squashed by five-feet-eight of former cheerleader in a bone-cracking hug. In the three years I've known Kirsten, the extent of our bodily interactions can be summed up by the half-hearted handshake we shared the first time we met and a few accidental shoulder brushes. The enthusiastic hugging takes me by surprise. All I manage to do in response is awkwardly pat her back until she finally lets me go. But apparently, the eagerness isn't over.

"Guys," Kirsten says when she pulls back, still lingering too much in my personal space. "We have to go out for drinks." She checks her watch, talking to Aiden. "We have to meet my parents at Morton in one hour and a half for dinner, but we have time for a quick cocktail. We can go to the bar down the block. What do you say, guys?"

Aiden, Jace, and I all stare at each other, none of us keen on the idea of going for drinks, each for our own reasons. But Aiden's fiancée is one of those don't-take-no-for-an-answer people. It's how she force-convinced me to be a bridesmaid at her wedding when it was literally the last thing I wanted to do in life. Now we all know better than to interfere with her cocktail-hour plan. A weird situation considering how until today, Kirsten has done her best to cut Jace and me out of Aiden's social life completely.

I sigh. At least, if they have a dinner appointment with her parents, the torture will be short-lived.

* * *

And short-lived it might be, but the next hour is excruciatingly painful. I have to simultaneously invent answers to Kirsten's one million questions about Jace and me, and try not to short-circuit every time Jace lays a finger on me, all the while avoiding meeting Aiden's gaze altogether.

Surprisingly, the middle part of the equation proves to be the most difficult. I mean, it's easy to avoid looking at Aiden when his fiancée fires one question after the other at me. She's monopolizing my attention. As for the answers, I have years of unfulfilled fantasies about Aiden and me I can pick and choose plausible explanations from. But Jace touching me? That's not something I'm prepared to handle.

It's not like he's being grope-y or creepy, but I'm not used to him being physical with me. He's always been sparse in his interactions over the years. I might get a hug every once in a while—I got one when Aiden got engaged and one the night we received the wedding invitations, but I can't remember the last hug before then. And even after years of sleepovers, we've barely ever shared *any* body contact.

But tonight it's different. *He*'s different. There was that kiss on the neck in our lobby that made me short-circuit. Then, when he wrapped an arm around my waist as we walked out of the office and toward the bar, pulling me against his solid, muscular side, my skin broke into the worst case of goosebumps. I shivered and heated at the same time. And when we got to the bar and he let go of me to open the door, I understood what real cold feels like for the first time in my life. I bet that if I joined the Chicago Polar Bear Club and took a dip into frozen-over Lake Michigan, I wouldn't feel that cold.

Then Aiden and Kirsten walked past us into the bar, and before I could follow them, Jace pulled me back, cupping my face. For a CPR-inducing moment, I thought he was about to kiss me. My hands went all sweaty, and I had trouble swallowing. I stared into his ice-blue eyes, wondering why I've always thought of Aiden's baby blues as more soulful. Jace's gaze on me stirred something deep in my belly that felt suspiciously like a kaleidoscope of butterflies was having a carnival dance party in there. As his face drew closer to mine, my gaze dropped to his full lips, the thump-thump-thump of my heart echoing the pulse in my ears.

But all he did was kiss me on the forehead, a soft, chaste kiss that left me confused and a little disappointed.

"It's going to be fine," he whispered. "Just relax and act normal. You're being too fidgety."

At that moment, I forgot how to swallow. I only nodded and followed him inside on wobbly legs.

Throughout the night, he kept doing other little things that pushed me off balance. The way he held my hand as we walked to the bar, or how he ordered my favorite drink for me and the extra-large portion of nachos I was craving without me having to say a thing. Or how he kissed my temple when I had to go to the ladies' room with Kirsten.

If he's not straight-out holding me, he's touching me in some other way, brushing a finger on the back of my shoulder, or playing with my hair—the *exact* opposite of what I'm used to from him. And he smiles every time he catches my gaze. We're sharing a booth and he's sitting so close to me the heat of his body seeps into my skin through our clothes, causing sweat beads to dot my forehead. Each small interaction brings my body temperature up a notch. And he's charming and funny, making Aiden and Kirsten laugh at his jokes and blush at his compliments.

The attention he pays me confuses me. I know we're fake dating. But it doesn't feel fake. Either he's the best actor on the planet or…

What?

I don't know. But one thing is certain, my reactions are as real as it gets.

By the end of the night, I'm so dizzy and confused that I'm unable to form a single logical thought in my head. Thank goodness that's also about the time when Kirsten remembers they have to go.

When we say goodbye outside the bar, Kirsten pulls me into

another hug, chirping, "Remember, we have an appointment at the bridal shop tomorrow for dress fittings."

I had actually forgotten about tomorrow's appointment. Or rather, my the-love-of-my-life-is-marrying-another-woman traumatized brain had tried to shield me from the prospect of a preview of Kirsten in her white gown and selectively erased the memory.

"Sure," I say.

"And we have to get dinner together afterward, the four of us, I insist."

"Oh, well, Jace?"

I look up at him, silently begging him to get us out of it.

Instead, he drops an arm on my shoulder. "Sure, you want to go for sushi since you're going for steak tonight. I've heard the place on Clark is good. And the vegetarian menu is supposedly great, too." He smacks a kiss on top of my head. "So it should be perfect for you, too, babe."

The sound of the word *babe* on his lips is pure sin. I'm an emancipated woman, I should deplore such monikers. But my fluttering heart is apparently still stuck in the Regency era.

Jace smirks down at me, and I stare daggers at him. So much for getting us out of it.

Across from us, Kirsten's smile in response to our confirmed dinner plans is blinding. All that fake ceramic in her mouth should come with a potentially-damaging-to-the-eye warning.

We say our goodbyes, and the moment Aiden and Kirsten have turned the corner, I get away from Jace and the arm he still has wrapped around my waist. That leaves us awkwardly standing on the curb a foot apart. For the first time in my life, I feel self-conscious around him. We stand in silence for a few seconds, looking at each other.

Jace's eyes dance with that mischievous, boyish twinkle as he asks, "Do you think I've sold them on being helplessly in love with you?"

My stomach bottoms out. I don't know about them, but I'm sold on the Jace Barlow experience.

Unsure how to answer that question, I choose to be flippant. "I don't really get the helpless part, but tonight, you were the perfect, attentive boyfriend every woman dreams of."

The lopsided grin that cracks his lips is disarming. Again, I've seen it a million times. Even weaponized against innocent, unsuspecting women. And I've always rolled my eyes at it. But tonight I'm suddenly not immune anymore.

Jace makes a mock bow and whispers, "I live to please."

And is it just me who's reading double meanings in everything he says? To be cautious, I bring the conversation back to safe ground.

"Did you see Kirsten tonight? What was up with all the hugging? I thought she hated me."

Jace gently taps the tip of my nose. "You're so clueless it's cute."

I cross my arms over my chest. "Please explain the way of life to me, oh sage one?"

Jace scoffs, fake-annoyed. "Until a few hours ago, in Kirsten's mind, you've been Aiden's hot, single friend. A potential threat. But now you've suddenly become my girlfriend, aka the most untouchable woman on the planet for her fiancé."

Did he say *hot*, single friend? I think he did.

I roll my eyes. "Please, you seriously expect me to believe perfect, posh Kirsten saw me as a threat? In what universe?"

"I'd pick you over her a million times."

The statement puts an incredibly silly smile on my lips. And I feel an almost imperceptible shift in my gut. But I refuse to acknowledge the fact that his words have affected me more than I'd like to admit. "You're saying that just to stay in character."

"That of your besotted boyfriend?"

"Yep."

"What can I say? Maybe the performing arts were my real calling. As soon as I've repaid all my student loans, I'll leave medicine behind and become a street artist."

"You're forgetting the mortgage on the office."

"Gosh, Archibald, you're such a buzzkill." He inches his chin toward the garage in front of the practice where we have reserved parking spaces, both for us and our patients. "Walk you to your car?"

"Sure," I say.

Our parking spots are in the same order as our offices. Jace's sleek Mercedes on the left, Aiden's now-missing, luxury SUV in the middle, and my Tesla on the right.

Jace walks me all the way to the driver's door.

"Guess I'll see you tomorrow at dinner. Have fun trying on dresses and send me pictures."

He jokingly waggles his eyebrows.

Still, a tingle of excitement zaps down my spine at the idea of posing in front of a mirror for him.

"You want to tag along? I'm sure we could find a cute dress for you to try on."

"I wouldn't want to upstage the bride—or the bridesmaids."

Barely able to suppress a smile, I roll my eyes and open my door. "Guess I'll see you tomorrow night, then."

I get in the car.

"Sweet dreams, Lola," Jace says, closing the door for me.

His last words are kind of prophetic. At home, I curl into bed, slithering under the covers in a position that won't disturb any of the three cats currently occupying the bed—Chewie opted to sleep on the couch alone.

As I settle in, I'm still a little over-excited from the night's happenings but also bone-tired. I crave an undisturbed sleep, but as soon as I close my eyes, the sexy dreams start. And for the first time in fifteen years, they're not about Aiden.

8

LORI

The Perfect Day. Even the name of the bridal shop is cheesy. I lock my car and sigh, preparing myself to enter enemy territory. I don't have many female friends, the few I made in college and that I still keep in touch with, have scattered all over the country after graduation. And with Aiden and Jace both here in Chicago with me, I got lazy and never saw the point of branching out.

Plus, men are simpler. Less easily offended, more straightforward, less complicated. And I'm not a tomboy, but I'm not that girly either. On a scale of one to ten, my femininity is at a solid six, seven when I make an effort. Kirsten is an eleven. Kirsten and her bridal party combined are six figures.

I push the door of the shop open and my entrance is announced by the tah-dah-da-dah notes of the wedding march, immediately followed by a high-pitched screech that quickly reaches dog-hearing-only frequencies.

"Lori," Kirsten greets me. "You made it."

As if I had a choice.

The bride-to-be loops an arm with mine and leans in conspiratorially. "Everyone's so jealous of you."

"Me?"

"Yah-ah girl, all my friends had their eyes set on the best man, my sister, too."

I don't even have to fake the cringe reaction.

"And now he's taken!" I reply, unable to keep a little venom from spilling into my words.

I've never considered myself possessive, but apparently, I was wrong.

Kirsten chuckles. "Yeah, don't worry, hon, I told all my friends Jace is off-limits. A few hearts broke, but that's life. Come, we have a private room"—she pulls me along—"I want to introduce you to the others."

She must mean the lovely women who are after my boyfriend. *Fake* boyfriend. Whatever.

We turn a corner and enter a small suite equipped with a rose-velvet couch, an armchair in the same material, a pedestal, and, behind it, a human-sized trifold mirror. Two other women are already inside, sipping champagne out of crystal glasses.

Kirsten lets go of my arm and heads toward them to make the introductions.

"Ladies, this is Lori, one of Aiden's best friends." The women in the room smile at me tentatively. "Lori, this is Britney, my maid of honor."

A slender blonde waves at me. I wave back.

Gosh, this is excruciating.

"And this is Erin," Kirsten continues, probably oblivious to my deep discomfort. "One of my bridesmaids."

"Kirsten and I have been in the same class since kindergarten," the woman says. "Nice to meet you."

I'm about to say nice to meet you, too, when a tall brunette enters from the other side of the room, carrying another bottle of champagne.

"Score," she announces.

I take in the newcomer's features, and I'm taken aback by her resemblance to Kirsten. Same bright green eyes, same pouty lips, same flawless skin. Kirsten and the newcomer are identical except for a few minor details: the unknown woman's hair is a dark shade of brown and has longer layers, tumbling down in soft waves, and she is significantly taller than Kirsten. And most of all, her face is too smug. She must be the lovely sister of the bride.

Kirsten rolls her eyes. "And this is my sister, Kendall."

Yep. And they've all got K names like the Kardashians.

I wave. "Hi."

Kendall pours a glass of champagne and hands it to me. "You're late, dear." As I take the flute from her, she studies me. Like a cheetah would study a gazelle she can't wait to eat alive. "So *you're* Jace's girlfriend?" Her eyes narrow still—apparently she really had her sights set on him.

"Yeah, we're dating," I say. I raise my glass in a mock toast and take a sip of champagne. Heaven knows I'll need the booze to survive this.

Kirsten hops onto the pedestal. "Girls, now that we're all here... you want to try your dresses first, or should I show you mine?"

I do my best not to roll my eyes at the fakeness of the question and join the enthusiastic choirs of, "You go first."

Yay.

"All right, girls, you take a seat and drink a little more bubbly while I go change," Kirsten suggests.

Like good troopers, the bridesmaids all sit down. Kendall claims the small armchair while Britney and Erin sit on the couch next to each other. I instinctively perch on the armrest as far away from them as possible.

"We can squeeze," Britney offers.

"No, thanks," I say. "I'm fine. This is the coziest armrest ever."

To shut me up before I blab some more nonsense, I take another sip of champagne.

"Kirsten has told us you have a lot of pets," Erin says.

"Yeah, four cats and six hens."

"Eww," Kendall comments from her solo seat. "Aren't chickens gross?"

I try to keep my smile in place. "Not to me."

"But why would you keep chickens in a city?"

"I saw a documentary on chicken farming and it broke my heart, so I decided to save as many of the poor birds as I could."

"That's very sweet of you," Erin says.

Kendall's pouty lips become poutier. "But don't those factories process, like, thousands of chickens? What difference do six make?"

All the difference in the world, I want to say, but I'm spared having to further argue by Kirsten's voice calling from the distance, "I'm coming, ladies... close your eyes."

The other bridesmaids all oblige, so, feeling none the less silly, I close my eyes, too.

I can hear the soft clack of Kirsten's heels as she enters the room and the rustling of her skirt on the carpet, followed by another set of steps—she must be with a shop assistant. A pause. Then she announces, "Okay, you can open your eyes now."

The bride-to-be is standing on the pedestal, looking positively radiant while a shop assistant fans out her train.

Kirsten is facing us, but the trifold mirror behind her doesn't spare me any details of her utter perfection. The dress is a mermaid cut that would turn me into a bad-shaped pear, but on her, the effect is stunning. The strapless top flows into the mermaid-cut skirt, which is emphasized by a long train the shop assistant is showcasing to all its impressiveness.

My gaze travels away from the train to the sheer fabric of the bustier that hints at what's underneath, hugging the bride's curves in all the right places. A sweetheart neckline accentuates her prosperous cleavage. Her back is almost completely bare while the bodice makes her waist look tinier than ever. The whole dress is covered in an intricate lace pattern.

The woman herself is a vision. Her skin is flawless and her eyes shine with happiness. The absolute picture of the perfect bride.

Kirsten beams at her bridesmaids. "What do you think?"

The bridesmaids all ooh and aah and gush over how beautiful she looks, but I can't form a single word. Staring at Kirsten, imagining her walking down the aisle while looking so beautiful to marry Aiden, *my* Aiden, makes my mouth go dry.

I don't care how it looks, I throw my head back and chug the rest of my champagne in one long sip. As I straighten my neck again, I make the mistake of looking around and meeting Kendall's eyes. The bride's sister raises an eyebrow at me. I try to smile, but it must come off as a grimace.

The shop assistant that's been fussing over Kirsten, says, "And now the final touch." She brings out a long veil and places it on top of Kirsten's blonde locks.

"Isn't she the most gorgeous bride?" the woman asks.

I want to die.

Another woman enters the suite, a seamstress judging from the needle pincushion wrapped on her wrist, making the small room suddenly very crowded. To distract myself while the seamstress prods and pinches Kirsten with needles to make sure the dress fits her even more perfectly, I take out my phone and shoot a quick text to Jace. I need the distraction.

TO JACE:

So sorry I ruined all your chances at action for the wedding

FROM JACE:

Oh?

TO JACE:

Apparently the bridesmaids were ready to wrestle in the mud to win your favors

FROM JACE:

fearful face emoji

Glad we're fake dating then

TO JACE:

Although, if we fake break up, they still might brush up their shiny leotards and fight valiantly to comfort the handsome, brokenhearted best man

FROM JACE:

We might have to extend the terms of our agreement, Lola

TO JACE:

I knew I should've never started fake dating you, you're so clingy it's embarrassing

FROM JACE:

eye-rolling emoji

I forgot you're an insufferable sassy texter

TO JACE:

Gosh, you really have it bad for me, Barlow

I get a double eye roll this time, followed by a change of subject.

FROM JACE:

How's it going?

Still lost in Bridaland?

TO JACE:

Yes, and it looks like it's going to take a while still

On the bright side, we have a brilliant, Kirsten-full night to look forward to afterward

FROM JACE:

Don't worry, I'll be there to hold your hair up should you feel sick at any point

TO JACE:

At the pace I'm downing bubbly that might actually be a necessity

FROM JACE:

You have booze? Why are you complaining then?

TO JACE:

Kirsten has a sister named Kendall, who's the snottier, meaner version of the bride

She's single, by the way

smiling devil emoji

FROM JACE:

You deserve all the ruffles coming your way

I chuckle out loud.

"Texting Jace?"

I look up from my phone and find Kirsten hovering nearby.

"Yeah, how did you know?"

Aiden's fiancée smirks. "Because of the loved-up smile on your face, and it's the third time I've called your name, but you were completely lost in your world."

"Oh, yeah, sorry about that."

"Don't apologize. Those first months are the most precious. Even if I'm not sure how that translates for you guys, since you've known each other for so long."

If the butterflies in my belly last night were any indication... "Oh, it's the same, but better," I add. "No chances of nasty surprises."

Kirsten smiles. "That's so true. Would you like to join the others and try on your dress?"

I take in the small room and notice for the first time that I'm alone with Kirsten and a different shop assistant.

"The others already went to change," Kirsten explains.

I drop my flute on a small glass table and follow the sales assistant to the fitting rooms.

Just as I'm about to put my phone away, another text arrives:

FROM JACE:

Remember to send me a pic

9

JACE

I send that last text—I probably shouldn't have—and put my phone away in my gym bag. I definitely shouldn't have sent it. Shaking my head, I enter the indoor basketball court, ready for my weekly one-on-one game with Aiden.

Should be interesting today.

My friend is already warming up with dribbles.

When he spots me, he stops the ball. "You made it, man." Aiden throws me the ball in a fast pass. "I thought you were too busy knocking boots morning, day, and night."

I toss the ball back to him. "Don't give me that, dude! You know Lori becomes such a goofball when she's under pressure."

The ball flies back to me and, raising his hands, Aiden says, "Hey, I just hope you have enough stamina left to play."

I study his teasing smile. It seems genuine—no hints of scorn. "I take it you're good with me and Lori dating?"

We stare at each other and a million unspoken words pass between us, until Aiden says, "Took me a minute to digest the news. But after a couple of nights to sleep on it, I'm happy for you guys."

"Really?"

"Yeah, you're my two best friends. I couldn't wish for a better partner for either of you. Just don't screw it up."

"I won't, man." Even I should be able to not screw up a fake relationship.

"Ready to roll?"

Aiden tips off the ball, and the game is under way.

We play hard, driving to the basket over and over.

Aiden scores the first three points.

"Hey, man, did you forget to bring your game?"

I have the ball. "Got it," I reply, not breaking stride. I drive to the basket for a layup when Aiden falls for a left fake. And dunk.

We alternate scoring until our hour is almost up. Aiden is up by one point. I've got the ball again, and shoot from outside the paint to sink a gorgeous, deep three-pointer.

Aiden catches the ball as it falls from the hoop and dribbles it toward the basket, unsuccessfully hiding a smirk.

I go after him.

Aiden feints right, left, and right again. "Fast break," he says, bullying his way toward the hoop one last time.

And it's game over. A tie.

Aiden pulls up his T-shirt to wipe the sweat from his face. "Good game, man."

I hold out a fist and Aiden gives me a pound.

"Sauna?" he asks.

"Nah." I slip on my sweatshirt and pull up the hood. "I've fallen behind on my running. I'm just going to jog home."

"Too busy bonking, I take it?" Aiden's grin is merciless.

"At home, I have a notebook chock-full of wedding night jokes. Should I pull it out and work some into my best man speech?"

"Sure, get all the pointers you can. I've got a feeling you won't be too far behind me in tying the knot. See you later, man."

"Later." I mock-scold him.

I put the gym bag away in my locker and grab my phone to pull up a running playlist. Instead, I find another string of texts from Lori.

One is a selfie.

10

LORI

"Please follow me." The shop assistant ushers me out of the suite. "I'm sorry, but all the fitting rooms on this side of the shop are taken by your friends." They're not my friends, I want to say. "But we have a space for you this way."

The lady shows me to a pretty room fitted in pastel pink, like the rest of the boutique, with a silver quilted pouf in the middle and a giant mirror at the back. My zipped-up gown is already hanging from the rack on the side wall.

"Let me know if you need help with the zipper or anything. A seamstress will be with you shortly for the fitting."

I'm relieved to be in a completely separate area of the shop from the others. At least this way I won't have to go stand on that stupid pedestal while the other bridesmaids watch.

I'm about to close the fitting room tent when I catch the shop assistant eyeing my feet dubiously.

"Something the matter?" I ask.

Her eyes snap back to mine. "Err, sorry, did you bring the shoes you're going to wear the day of the wedding for the seamstress to do the hem on the skirt?"

A vague memory of Kirsten mentioning shoes when she gave me the bridal shop's address crosses my mind, but it's another of those things I blanked out and then forgot. Also, none of my fancy footwear—mostly sensible black pumps, practical but not overtly fashionable—would pair well with the silvery light-blue tulle A-line dress with boho dropped sleeves, shirred bodice, and flowing, floor-length skirt Kirsten has picked for her bridesmaids.

"Err, actually..."

The shop assistant smiles. "Or if you're in the market for new shoes, we offer a wide selection."

"Yes, please."

"Should I bring you a few options while you're changing? Or would you like to browse?"

A keen fashion sense isn't exactly my strong suit. "Options might be better."

"I'll be right back."

While the shop assistant is gone, I shift out of my clothes and pull on the dress. I stare at myself in the mirror, kind of mesmerized. At least Kirsten knew what she was doing when she picked this dress. Her level-eleven girlishness has its uses. Also, I suppose she couldn't put me in the bridesmaid dress from hell or her other bridesmaids would've killed her—especially her sister. See? Everyone has their purpose.

The shop assistant is back a few minutes later.

"I've brought some shoes," she calls from behind the curtain.

I pull the heavy drapery aside, and her eyes widen. "Wow, you look gorgeous in that," she says, balancing a stack of shoe boxes in her arms.

"Thank you."

"I have three options for you." The shop assistant drops the boxes on the floor and opens the top one. "Beaded pumps?"

I make a nah face and shake my head.

"Next, I have a pair from a few seasons ago. I only have a size eight left; what size are you?"

"Eight."

"I thought so." She puts away the beaded monstrosities and shifts their box to the side. Before opening the next box, she gives me a few more selling points. "These are Sergio Rossi originals and come with a hefty price tag, but since they're the last pair and from a few seasons ago, I can give you a good discount. They'd be gorgeous with your dress. Plus, the quality is stellar, Italian leather soles, laminated hammered leather, metal inserts with the logo..."

The sales pitch is becoming old fast, but when she finally lifts the lid and uncovers the marvels underneath, I'm left speechless, and a squeal erupts from my lips.

She has brought me the most gorgeous pair of metallic silver pumps I never knew I needed. The shoes are classy and elegant, but also have a sassy kick.

"Can I try them on?"

"Sure." She nods enthusiastically and frees the pumps from the paper padding, turning them toward me.

I slip them on, and, oh my gosh, they're even comfortable. I wiggle my toes, satisfied.

"How much are they?"

The sales assistant gives me the exorbitant figure, and I groan a little as I say, "I'll take them."

Between the dress and now the shoes, I don't know if this wedding will end up costing me more financially or emotionally.

"Fantastic," she says. "As soon as the seamstress is finished with your friends, she'll be right with you."

As I wait, still admiring myself in the wide mirror, Kendall's voice filters down from the vent on the side of the wall. "Where has our mother hen gone?"

"Shhh. Lori could be back at any moment," Kirsten chides her sister.

"Defending her? I thought you hated her."

Aha-ha, I knew it!

"I never said I hated her. I've only always been worried she was after my man."

Inner groan, *she also knew*.

"But now that she's dating Jace, I've nothing against Lori. I actually kind of like her."

"That woman? She seems so uptight."

"She's more serious than us, that's all."

"I wouldn't have pinned her down as Jace's type."

"And who'd be his type?" Kirsten's voice comes off a little condescending.

Kendall doesn't pick up on it and gives a smug reply. "Someone fun, gorgeous, and with a sense of style?"

"Are you describing yourself?"

"Your words, not mine! No, seriously, how are they together?"

"Eh..."

Eh? What does she mean, eh?

I get my answer pronto.

"The relationship is supposedly new. Anyway, we went out last night, and Lori seemed a bit on the stiff side."

"Stiff how?"

"She sort of jumped like a bunny whenever Jace touched her, and they didn't kiss once."

"Oh, you think she's one of those sexually impaired women?"

"Now you're just being mean."

"Am not. You said she couldn't stand to be touched."

"I only said she seemed a little skittish. But we were in a bar for less than an hour. Maybe they argued before. But tonight we'll be together for an entire dinner so I'll know more by tomorrow."

"Please report first thing in the morning."

"Why the sudden interest?"

"Human cases fascinate me."

A beat of silence follows, in which I assume Kirsten must make a face. Then she says, "Enough gossip, get out of that dress before you stain it with champagne."

"You're the one to talk, still wearing your wedding gown."

"Then we don't need to be the Pot and Kettle sisters. I'll go get changed, too."

In the silence that follows, I take out my phone and shoot a couple of venting texts to Jace.

He doesn't respond. So I send another one:

TO JACE:

I can't believe it, not two days of fake dating and you're already ghosting me

I have to put the phone away when the seamstress arrives. Despite my protests, she has me standing on a pedestal while she pulls the waist of the dress in by half an inch and the bust area by a lot more inches—not everyone was blessed with Kirsten's or Kendall's generous cleavages.

Once the bodice is taken care of, the seamstress moves on to the skirt. She pricks my hip with a needle, but I don't say anything. I hate any form of confrontation with strangers. I'm the best customer you'll ever have. My motto is "the seller is always right." And I don't know if it is for the fact that I didn't manage to speak normally until I was ten. But I've never been able to stand up for myself. Also, I hate being put on the spot, and loathe even more doing it to others.

But when the seamstress accidentally pricks me a little harder, I involuntarily jerk my hips away.

"Oh, I'm sorry, honey, did I stab you with my needle?"

"It's nothing," I deflect.

"I'll be more careful, but please let me know if I do it again by accident."

There'd be a better chance of me passing from the blood loss of a thousand pricks before I'd say anything.

Thankfully there are no more unintentional stabbings and, after what feels like forever, she announces I'm free to change if I want to.

As I return to the fitting room, my fingers are reluctant to pull down the zipper. Instead, I lift my hair and turn sideways to see the rear of the dress.

Not Bad.

On instinct, I grab my phone and take a picture of the gown in the mirror in this half-turned position. I take a few others from the front. Then I scroll my camera roll to pick the best one. The shots from the front are okay, but the one from the back makes me look sexy. And I don't know what's gotten into me today, why I want Jace to find me sexy, to fully see me as a woman—maybe because Aiden already rejected me in a way, or because I just want to feel desired, or because I'm just tired of being invisible to everyone—but that's the picture I pick and send to Jace captioned:

TO JACE:

This is what you're missing out on, ghoster

Still no reply.

With a shrug, I put the phone away, preparing myself for one last interaction with the Cunningham sisters. Then I'll be free of Bridezilla for all of three hours.

11

JACE

Instead of jogging home, I end up walking at a leisurely pace—despite the biting cold—as I read Lori's texts.

FROM LORI:

So I'm standing in a changing room with an air conditioning vent that's treating me to an unfiltered eavesdropping of the Cunningham sisters talking about me behind my back

You seriously have nothing to say to that?

I can't believe it, not two days of fake dating and you're already ghosting me

The next text is a picture of her in a shimmering silver gown. Lori is turned half-sideways toward the mirror so that I can see both the front and the back. She's holding her hair up with one hand while angling her phone down with the other to take the picture.

I shake my head, smiling as I read the caption of the pic.

FROM LORI:

This is what you're missing out on, ghoster

Then I stare at her image some more. I know we're fake dating, but this is not the kind of selfie you'd send to a *fake* boyfriend. In the picture, she's staring at the mirror with a twinkle in her eyes and a little mischievous grin. A far cry from the crossed-eyes, silly faces, and tongue-out poses she usually sends me.

There's something about this picture that's different.

My heart does a little somersault in my chest, then I drag a hand over my face. This fake-dating thing is going to be the death of me. For the first time in my life, last night, I was free to act around her like I actually want to. Touching her, every part of her—her hair, her waist, her hands, her arms—keeping her close, making her mine. But there'll be a price to pay for every single one of those stolen touches. I've managed to keep myself in control for years, and now the fake dating is my enabler, allowing me to lose it all at once.

And this picture isn't helping.

Well, you asked for it, buddy.

I did, and now I'm about to ask for some more punishment.

Next, my thumbs fly on the virtual keyboard of my phone.

TO LORI:

Okay, Lola, replying to you in no particular order

I wouldn't say not texting back for 45 minutes qualifies as ghosting

Lori's reply comes in before I can finish answering the rest.

FROM LORI:

I was the ghosted one, so let me be the judge of that

Where were you?

TO LORI:

At the gym, shooting hoops with Aiden

FROM LORI:

Was he cool?

TO LORI:

Actually, yes, he said he's fine with us dating as long as I don't screw it up

Sorry your plan didn't work

FROM LORI:

I'm over the plan

I've spent the last fifteen years of my life pining over him and I'm tired

Plus, if he likes a woman like Kirsten, he could never be into me

I hate myself for the hope her words bring. Could she really be getting over him?

FROM LORI:

Although, after today I might have to bump up my girlishness score to a solid eight

TO LORI:

What was your previous score?

FROM LORI:

Between a six and a seven

TO LORI:

How would you justify a seven?

FROM LORI:

I like vanilla lattes, pastel pink bookshelves, and I live with four cats?

TO LORI:

The cats shouldn't count, they fit more into the crazy cat lady category

FROM LORI:

Fair point

Anyway, today I spent 400 dollars on shoes (that was the sale price, BTW) and I felt like a boho princess in that dress

TO LORI:

Aww, look at you, getting in touch with your femininity

Should I buy you a set of glitter bubble-bath bombs for your birthday?

FROM LORI:

The fact that you even know glitter bubble-bath bombs exist is scary

Do you use them often?

TO LORI:

Why? You want to get into my tub action?

FROM LORI:

If it involves glitter bubble-bath bombs, sure

Before things get too far and I straight-out start flirting with Lori. I pivot the subject.

TO LORI:

You never told me what the Cunningham sisters said about you

Only nice things, I suppose?

FROM LORI:

They called me uptight

And hinted I might be sexually impaired

TO LORI:

That's some serious Mean Girls territory

I pause in the lobby to wave at my doorman, then get straight to the elevator. The brief no-signal interruption gives me a moment to collect my thoughts. I shouldn't ask, I'm flying straight into the danger zone... still, as I unlock my apartment door and plop down on the couch, I type another question.

TO LORI:

Why sexually impaired?

FROM LORI:

Apparently last night I jumped like a bunny whenever you touched me

And we didn't kiss

So tonight we're going to have to bring our A-game

TO LORI:

As in?

FROM LORI:

You have to kiss me

I knew I shouldn't have asked.

FROM LORI:

And not just any kiss

I need you to give me a performance worthy of Hollywood

So go grab a teddy bear and go practice your smooching skills

TO LORI:

I find your supposition that I own teddy bears quite offensive

FROM LORI:

Why? They go perfectly with glitter bubble-bath bombs

TO LORI:

All right, Lola, I'm at home and in serious need of a shower

FROM LORI:

A shower, as if

You're probably filling the tub as we speak

Picturing you in a pink bubbly bath surrounded by unicorn glitter

TO LORI:

Why unicorn glitter?

FROM LORI:

Cause you're worth it, baby

I roll my eyes.

TO LORI:

You want me to pick you up before dinner?

Look more couple-y?

FROM LORI:

Nah, I'm on the opposite way

Thanks for offering, but I'll see you at the restaurant, Cupcake

TO LORI:

Calling me Cupcake is taking it a step too far

FROM LORI:

All right, Stud Muffin, I'll ease you into the nicknaming phase of our relationship more gently

PS. Did you like the dress?

My thumbs hover above the virtual keyboard forever until I type:

TO LORI:

I love it, Princess

12

LORI

I stare at the text, mesmerized. The word princess in particular. Was he just playing on the nickname quip? Or referring to my earlier self-description as a boho princess? Or what?

Good thing it was a goodbye message and I don't have to reply. But now I have to get ready for tonight's dinner.

My girlishness score bumps up to a nine as I stand in front of the mirror, wondering what to wear. I have the perfect new shoes, but I suddenly don't like any of the clothes in my closet.

I take out one hanger after the other, discarding the garments on my bed.

Now I wish I had more women friends who could help me with this. But all my doctor friends would probably suggest a psych-eval if I face-timed them with a wardrobe emergency.

The only other girlfriend I could call is Jessica, Jace's sister. We're pretty tight, especially since Jace, Aiden, and I all volunteer at her free clinic. But if I called her out of the blue on a random Saturday to get fashion advice, then I'd have to explain who I want to look pretty for, and I'm not sure I know the answer.

Only one option left. I have to go buy a new dress—no matter that my credit card is already simmering after the shoe shopping. But if I go to a department store, a shop assistant can help me choose, and getting professional help might actually be my best option.

I shower, flat-iron my hair in some sort of style, and apply basic makeup—I'm not the best at maquillage either, and I'm already doing enough experiments for today.

I dress in jeans and ballet flats and drop the Sergio Rossi shoebox in a tote bag—not confident I could drive in stilettos.

For my impromptu shopping spree, I choose a department store not too far away from my apartment. The mall is busy on a Saturday, and the parking lot is full. I circle it twice before finding a spot. I exit the car and walk to the women's section. I'm supposed to be at the restaurant in an hour. If I want to be on time, I have to make this expedition into fashion really efficient.

Before I make it to the women's fashion floor, I have to ride two escalators. As soon as I arrive, a shop assistant immediately comes my way.

"Hello, can I assist you with anything today?"

My typical response would be to avoid eye contact and mutter, *"No, thanks, I'm just browsing."*

But today, I'm a woman on a mission.

"Yes, please, I need to find a dress for a date."

"Any style you're looking for?"

"I want to be sexy, but still elegant."

"Absolutely... let me walk you to a fitting room and I'll bring over some options. Any color schemes you were considering?"

"No, but I already have the shoes."

I take the box out of the tote bag and show her the pumps.

"Oh, gorgeous. I've got a couple of dresses in mind that would be perfect with those."

That's how fifty minutes later, I walk out of the mall wearing my very first little black dress.

From the moment I saw the sheath dress, I knew it was the one. The neckline is a cross between a sweetheart and deep V with bare shoulders and long sleeves that start about halfway down my biceps—it's still winter in Chicago, I need some sort of sleeves. The hem is way shorter than what I'm usually comfortable with, not mid-thigh but definitely above the knees. To make the outfit a little less serious, I bought a pair of silver-on-black polka-dot sheer tights.

The shop assistant also convinced me to get my makeup retouched at one of the booths on the first floor, which also compelled me to buy a new mascara, blusher, eye shadow, and contouring kit. I would've felt awful letting the makeup artist work on me for twenty minutes without buying anything. Also, when she kept pushing stuff in my hands that I "absolutely needed," I couldn't say no. I told you. Best. Customer. Ever.

But at least, as I stare at the final result in the car's rearview mirror, I can honestly say it was worth every penny. The makeup lady has done a smoky eyes thingy that makes my gaze go POW!

As I turn on the engine, I'm glad I'm wearing a long down jacket. The polka-dot tights are super thin and it's freezing—the car heating will take a while to kick in. To drive, I still wear the flats and switch to heels as I get to the restaurant. Since I'm already late, I hand my car keys to the valet.

I'm not a fashionista or a diva, but, as I walk into the restaurant, I can't help the surge of satisfaction at the stares I get.

The hostess asks me for the name on the reservation and informs me my party is waiting for a table at the bar. I step into the lounge, scanning the room for any sign of Aiden or Jace.

And then I see him.

Jace is seated at the bar, dressed in dark jeans and a baby blue button-down shirt, a navy-blue sweater tossed on the backrest of his stool. He's alone, drinking an Old Fashioned—his favorite drink. His dark hair is a little mussed and gleams in the dim lights of the lounge, making my heart squeeze a little. He's the most gorgeous man I've ever seen. It's hard to explain, but it's like I've only just met him. In the past fifteen years, I've basically been immune to his rogue charm—I was too busy chasing after Aiden to notice, but now I'm like any other of the many women who have fallen at his feet.

I watch him take another sip of his drink, following the movement of his throat as he swallows. And I'm not sure when swallows became as contagious as yawns, but I find myself needing to swallow as well—*hard.*

For some inexplicable reason, I get a thrill watching him while he's unaware of me. I don't know how to describe it—maybe anticipation about this evening. We're going to kiss after all. And before tonight, I've never wondered what kind of kisser Jace is, but now... I've become curious—intrigued. And, anyway, I suspect he's the toe-curling type.

Jace turns around, and a grin lights up his face as he spots me. An unfamiliar wave of electricity goes through my body, warming me and making me feel powerful. He moves to stand up and I make my way to him, my eyes never leaving his.

That's when his gaze drops lower. I can feel his eyes roam over my body, appraising me, and I smile inside at the knowledge that I look hot.

When our gazes meet again, a twinkle sparkles in his.

Jace stands up and reaches his hand out to me. When I place mine in his, a jolt zips through my body.

"You look incredible," he murmurs.

"It's to help you pretend you find me irresistible," I reply, shrugging my shoulders.

Jace brushes my hair back, baring my neck and shoulder. "No need to pretend when you're like this."

A tingle runs down my spine. But I try to act cool and unaffected as I say, "Good, because we have to convince Kirsten that I'm super sexual and we're the king and queen of bonking."

Jace throws his head back, laughing. "If you want to keep things sexy, please don't say bonking ever again."

I mock-frown. "Where are Aiden and Kirsten? The hostess said I was the last one to arrive."

"A server came a few minutes ago to bring us to our table, but I waited for you."

I smile, even more heart-warmed by his gesture. "Thank you."

Jace pauses, letting his gaze rake all over my face. The way he's looking at me makes me feel hot—searing.

"I mean it, Lola. I've never seen you as beautiful as tonight."

The fluttering in my stomach gets out of control at his words. But I retain enough of my wits to come back with a sassy retort. Thinking of the plaid fleece PJs I was wearing the other night when we had Mexican at my place, I ask, "You mean you don't find me attractive when I wear checkered onesies?"

Jace chuckles again. "No, you're always beautiful, but tonight you're also sexy as hell."

Here comes the need to swallow again. If Jace keeps looking at me like that, the makeup is going to melt right off my face, and I spent too much on it to put it to waste.

I clear my throat, trying to sound composed. "Let's go," I say.

Steering me with a hand on my lower back that causes all kinds of hot-and-cold sensations to run up and down my spine, Jace guides me into the restaurant.

Aiden perks up from his seat when he notices us. He's dressed in a navy V-neck and dark jeans. When he takes in my dress, his eyes widen and he half chokes on his water.

Kirsten doesn't recognize me right away, but once she zones in on Jace next to me, her gaze whips back to me and she positively gapes.

Sexually impaired, my foot, I want to say.

Aiden's fiancée is quick to recover from the shock. She stands up from her chair to greet me. "Lori, you look spectacular. I love your dress."

"Oh," I reply, fake surprised. I peer down at my new outfit, then back up at Kirsten, who is dressed as fashionably as always in a caramel velvet dress. Her blonde hair half falling on her shoulders in beachy waves and knotted at the top. Jace, who's holding my hand, gives it a little squeeze and I'm grateful for the reassurance. "Thank you," I say. "You look amazing, too."

Aiden soon recovers and stands up too, side-hugging me. "I'm glad you made it. Was the traffic bad coming down from Lincoln Park?"

I wave a hand dismissively. "The usual."

Aiden smiles. "When will you cave and come live closer to the office?"

"If you find me an affordable brownstone in the Gold Coast with a small garden for my chickens, I'll be happy to take it."

Before I can do it myself, Jace pulls the chair out for me to sit. Broody, smoldering hot looks *and* impeccable manners... Well, considering the number of hearts he's broken over the years, I shouldn't be surprised.

The table is round, so I end up sitting in the middle between Aiden and Jace, with Kirsten in front of me in a perfect male-female balance. A server comes over immediately to take our drink orders. Aiden picks the wine and, as soon as the server leaves, he and Kirsten start discussing their champagne selection for the wedding.

Apparently, they couldn't get enough bottles of their preferred vintage, and Kirsten is all stressed out about finding a replacement. I tune them out, especially since Jace hasn't taken his eyes off me for a second since we sat down. Not even to look at the menu. His eyes trace my lips and the curve of my bare shoulder. I can feel the heat radiating off him, even if we're seated too far apart to touch.

I've never wished for a booth table more than now.

The server comes back with our bottle of fancy Chardonnay and pours us each a glass before taking our food orders.

Once the server is gone, Kirsten puts on her best serious face, and, staring at me, raises her glass. "A toast."

We stare at her interrogatively, wondering what we're toasting to.

"To romance," Kirsten says. "Aiden and I are getting married. And now you and Jace are together." She looks at Jace, her eyes appraising. "Guys, you're the perfect couple. You must be the talk of the office."

Jace and I share a look, and I even manage to say something. "Well, I'm not sure Eloise and Betty know," I say, referring to our nurse and receptionist.

"Oh, they know," Aiden says.

I gape. "How?"

"I told them."

"But why?"

"Why not?" Aiden shrugs. "Is it a secret?"

"To romance," Jace interrupts, clinking his glass with Kirsten's and then mine and Aiden's last. We all toast and take a sip of wine. Mine probably a little longer than everyone else's.

Jace leans into me and brushes the skin of my neck with his lips. To the others, it'll look like a casual kiss on the neck, but he whispers, "Relax, we've got this."

Relax?

How am I supposed to relax when his lips must've left blisters on my skin?

And yet, I feel slightly less on edge. Jace is right. We're going to rock this dinner. I'm sure I'm blushing when he pulls away, but I give him a smile of encouragement. Jace smiles back and takes my hand over the table, then he leans forward to listen to Kirsten and Aiden's wedding plans. I have a hard time following the conversation. I'm too busy with the way Jace's thumb is casually circling the inside of my palm.

When the food arrives and he has to let go of my hand to, you know, eat, I feel the loss keenly.

The server drops the plates in front of us, repeating the name of the dishes. When my turn comes, he announces, "Teriyaki tofu with charred spring onions with a side of cremini mushrooms."

I try to keep my face neutral as he places the wrong side dish in front of me. I had ordered the Japanese mushroom rice hot pot, but whatever.

"Please let me know if you need anything else." The server leaves.

I grab my chopsticks and move one mushroom aside.

"Is everything all right?" Jace asks.

"Yeah, the server got my side wrong. It's no big deal."

"What?" Kirsten intervenes. "No, you have to call him back and have him change it."

"No, no," I insist. "It really doesn't matter."

Aiden cleans his mouth with his napkin before saying, "Lori hates calling out servers when they make mistakes."

"Ever since she spent four years in college part-time waitressing," Jace concludes. He knows the full, couldn't-talk-until-she-was-ten sob story, but I never told Aiden because I didn't want to look lame in his eyes, so Jace is covering for me, at least in part. Because it's also true that being a server for four years made me sensitive to how hard the job is, especially when dealing with complaints.

I shoot him a glance of gratitude before saying, "Aww, look how cute you are, finishing each other's sentences."

"Excuse me." Kirsten has her arm up in the air, ignoring the entire conversation.

Our server hurries to our table immediately. "Yes, ma'am, how can I help?"

"My friend had ordered a different side," Kirsten says.

"Oh, I'm so sorry. What did you have?"

Mortified, I look up at him. "The mushroom rice hot pot."

The equally mortified server takes the cremini mushrooms away, saying, "I'll be right back with the correct order on the house."

"Thank you." My voice comes out sort of strangled.

Kirsten smiles. "See, that wasn't so bad."

"No," I agree, still wishing she'd kept quiet.

Jace leans into me. "Don't worry, I'll tip him 30 per cent."

The promise makes me smile for two reasons. First, because it's exactly what I would do, and second, because he's just offered to pay. As if we were on a proper date. And I know we're supposed to keep up appearances, but the gesture still makes me feel all ridiculously warm and fuzzy.

The warm sensation crashes as Kirsten opens her mouth again. "Why would you tip him so generously for bringing the wrong order?"

I could point out that now he has to give us my side for free, the total check will be lower and that to compensate we're going to increase the tip, but I'm not sure Kirsten would get it. Her first job probably started the day she joined her father's law firm with no student loans on her shoulders. So, there'd really be no point in trying to explain how a few bucks could make a lot of a difference to someone for whom every dollar counts.

Instead, I shift the conversation back to the only topic sure to distract her. "You said you're going to have your tasting menu for the wedding reception tomorrow?"

"Oh, yes, what a nightmare. Can you believe they're only letting us choose three appetizers?"

I take another sip of wine to hide my incredulity. Trying to keep a serious face, I ask, "Why? How many did you want?"

"At least five, but in smaller portions."

I smirk at Aiden from across the table. He must hate this entire process.

Unfazed, he raises an eyebrow and asks, "But enough about us old, quasi-married folks. Let's talk about you young people falling in love."

My cheeks flame red and I glare at him. "Last time I checked, you were the baby of the group."

"Only according to the registry office, Jace is clearly the least mature of the three of us."

Jace theatrically puts his hands over his ears. "LALALALALALALALALALA CAN'T HEAR YOU, DUDE."

"You guys are hilarious," Kirsten butts in.

No matter how hard I try to like her, Aiden's fiancée makes the job really difficult. We don't click. Kirsten is like this foreign body, trying to force herself into our previously perfectly balanced ecosystem. Well maybe not perfectly balanced, seeing how I've been spinning on my unrequited-love axis for fifteen years, but at least we had a certain harmony, until she showed up. Kirsten just isn't one of us.

"Have you guys picked a honeymoon destination yet?" Jace asks, switching subject again after probably noticing how I'm staring daggers at the bride-to-be.

"Yeah," Kirsten says. "We're going to Anguilla for two weeks of sunshine and relax..."

As we listen to Kirsten list how many pools and restaurants the resort has, and all the excursions she's planning for them, I try really hard not to do a mental rain dance targeted at the Caribbean island for the second half of February. But gosh, if I can't hear the drums in my head.

The bride-to-be monopolizes the conversation for most of the dinner, allowing me to get away with only making a polite comment now and then, and mostly tuning out what is being said. I wouldn't be able to concentrate even if the topics being discussed were more interesting. Not when Jace can't stop watching me. I catch him looking at me, and I can't help but stare back. Funny thing how my eyes keep dropping to his lips.

The lips that are supposed to give me a goodnight kiss.

I look back up again, and Jace has his eyes locked on my face. Did he catch me staring at his mouth? His gaze is so intense that I suspect he might have. My heart thumps in my chest. I panic and excuse myself to the restroom.

When I return to the table, the server is already clearing our plates. I sit down, looking at my lap just as the server's hand reaches down to pull up my skirt. I jump out of my chair and almost slap his hand away. Too late, I realize what's really going on as the server eyes me perplexedly, holding my black napkin in his hands. This must be one of those fancy places where they fold your napkin when you go to the bathroom and place it back on your lap when you come back.

"Is everything all right, ma'am?" the server asks.

"Yes, yes, sorry," I say, getting back in my chair. "I was just err..." That's when I make the mistake of meeting Jace's eye. He smirks and raises an eyebrow teasingly as if to say, I want to see how you're going to end that phrase.

"Never mind," I say. And sit rigidly as the server finally places the napkin on my legs.

Job completed with no further incidents, he asks, "Would anyone care for dessert?"

While he rolls out the options, Jace leans in and asks, "Were you about to slap that poor server?"

"Shut up," I hiss. "I thought he was lifting my skirt."

"Falsely accused of being a perv. Oh my gosh, how much do I have to tip him now?"

"Keep being such a smarty pants and that'll be the least of your problems."

When the bill finally arrives, I have mixed feelings about leaving. Between the bridal shop and the restaurant, I'm maxed out on my Kirsten tolerance levels. But I want the Jace part of the night to continue.

We get our coats and are about to leave when Kirsten announces she needs a last-minute bathroom run.

"I'll wait for her," Aiden says. "You guys go ahead."

The temperatures outside are freezing, but at least there's no wind. To keep warm, I sneak my hands under Jace's unbuttoned coat, lacing my fingers on the small of his back like I've done a million times before. Only tonight it feels different. Instead of accepting my embrace like a rigid rod as he usually is around me, Jace hugs me back. My long down jacket is zipped up, so he places his warm hands on the small of my back.

I gaze up at him. In the dim light of the streetlights, his eyes are the color of dark ice and they're smoldering. Jace stares hard at me as if trying to figure something out. Can he sense the shift between us, the same as I do? I've always been pretty much able to guess what Jace was thinking, but now I can't. I can't even decipher my own thoughts anymore, let alone his. The only thing I'm sure of is that I want him to kiss me, and not just to prove Kirsten wrong.

I bite my lower lip and he steps in even closer, his eyes traveling down to my mouth as if he were thinking the same thing.

I lean in slowly, giving him a chance to turn around, but he doesn't. Even when my nose brushes his, he doesn't take a step back. Our lips are so close I can feel the heat rolling off his body, the scent of his cologne filling my nostrils. I close my eyes and make that last inch of distance between us disappear, brushing my lips against his, softly.

I pull back and open my heavy lids. This is when he should make a move. He doesn't, though. He just keeps looking into my eyes, his lips parted slightly. I close the distance between us again, this time my kiss firm and deliberate.

Jace doesn't return the kiss, but he doesn't reject it either. He lets me brush his lips with mine a few more times before I'm forced to pull back.

That's when the restaurant door opens and Aiden and Kirsten shuffle out.

Okay, maybe Jace doesn't want to kiss me for the sake of it, but he must at least fake it in front of them. Eyes pleading, I pull closer once again, whispering, "Jace, please, just for tonight, can you pretend you find me irresistible?" And then I press my lips back to his once more.

13

JACE

All right, I'm not a saint. Only so much restraint I can muster before instinct takes over. I can no longer hold back. I don't care if it's not wise, or that I'm surely going to regret it later. I pull her firmly into my arms and kiss her back.

It takes Lori a few seconds to catch up that the kiss is happening, but when she does, she doesn't hold back either. The kiss is deep and searing. Lori returns the hug, her fingers twisting into the fabric of my sweater.

My brain goes haywire. Is this really happening? I'm kissing the woman I've loved for years and she's kissing me back. I want so much more, but I don't know if I'll get it. She's not mine. This is just a ruse for her. And the way she's been flirting is probably just Lori being on the rebound from Aiden getting married. But do I care? No.

Because right now, right at this moment, she's mine. I kiss her like I'm drowning, I kiss her like I'm starving, and I kiss her like I'm about to die. Lori's lips are warm and soft, and her mouth tastes like mint and strawberries. With her body pressed against mine, the scent of her hair fills my senses. It's just her and me and nothing else exists.

Only when Kirsten whistles behind us, do we tear apart from each other.

"Bravo!" Aiden's fiancée applauds. "Gosh, you guys, go get a room."

Lori and I break apart. She looks at me, almost startled, and then her eyes fly to Aiden. Next, Lori's gaze drops to the ground, her cheeks a deep red. Of course, I have to remember her heart doesn't beat for me, it never has.

To make things less awkward, I do what I do best, and pretend I don't care. "That might actually be a good idea before we all turn into popsicles."

The goodbyes are slightly stilted after that. Kirsten gives us both a hug while I think Aiden looks at me oddly, but I can't be sure.

We finished the wine halfway through the main course and didn't order another bottle. So we're all good to drive at this point. We give our keys to the valet, but thankfully, Aiden's SUV arrives first.

He and Kirsten get in, and then it's just me and Lori again. We keep silent until the driver comes back with her Tesla.

Lori is looking uncertain, too. "Look, Jace..."

Nuh-uh, whatever she's about to say—thanks for the kissing, what a show you put up, or worse, she could ask me why I just kissed her like I'm really in love with her—I take the keys from the valet, round the car, and open the driver's door for her.

Lori follows me but hesitates to get in. "Listen, Jace..."

"It's okay, Lola," I interrupt again, kissing her on the forehead. "We don't have to make a big deal out of it." I wink at her and add, "Drive carefully, text me when you get home."

I'm the image of insouciance, like that kiss didn't affect me at all. After years spent practicing the attitude around Lori, it comes to me as second nature.

Looking disappointed, Lori gets into the car. "Goodnight, I guess."

We say goodbye and I close the door on her, both literally and figuratively.

Then her car pulls away and disappears into the night.

Despite acting completely unaffected in front of her, on the drive home, I can't help replaying the kiss in my head over and over again. But allowing myself to fantasize Lori and I could actually become more than friends is a huge mistake. Lori is in love with someone else. Maybe now that Aiden is getting married, she's trying to convince herself that she's over him, but it can't have happened overnight. She's doing what she can to survive, even if that is experimenting with me.

Because she thinks of me as this womanizer bad boy she can't hurt, if only she knew. But she doesn't, because I never told her.

I don't regret kissing her, though. It was one hell of a kiss—the kind you want to remember for the rest of your life. I brush a hand over my mouth, remembering the sensation of the lips of an amazing woman pressed to mine. I don't care if it wasn't real.

The streetlights blur past my car window as unfocused as my thoughts until I pull up into my underground garage and step out of the car. My steps echo on the concrete as I head to the exit.

As the elevator climbs up, I can't stop wondering what Lori wanted to say to me after the kiss. Why did I shut her down? Because I'm such a coward.

I get into my apartment and it's dark and quiet and so darn lonely, just like it's been for years. I flop down on my couch, put my feet up on the table, and pull out my cell phone. Why? I don't even know what I want to do—write to her?—when the screen lights up with an incoming text from Lori.

FROM LORI:

I'm home safe

Glad to hear it, I type. Then I fidget with my phone and, going against every self-preservation instinct I have, I add:

TO LORI:

Did you want to talk about something earlier?

I hit send and wait for her response. It doesn't take long.

FROM LORI:

You mean when you all but shoved me into my car?

TO LORI:

Yes

My fingers tap against the screen, my heart pounding as I wait for her response. It only takes a few seconds.

FROM LORI:

No, I just wanted to thank you for being such a good friend, I know I've put you in an impossible situation. I'm sorry

My eyes widen and my stomach drops.

Such. A. Good. Friend.

The words haunt me from the screen. That's all I'll ever be to her. An effing friend.

I drop the phone on my couch and don't respond. These last few days I let my guard down and acted like an idiot. I can't flirt with her, I can't touch her, and I sure as hell can't kiss her. Not if I want to keep my sanity, my heart whole. Not if she keeps telling me what a good effing friend I am.

The madness stops tonight. From tomorrow on, I'll go back to my old ways of keeping a healthy distance between Lori and myself. We only have a couple more wedding-related events to push through before Aiden is off on his honeymoon and we can call this whole farce off.

I only have to survive another month before the wedding and then I'll be free to go back to my old life of solitude and evasion.

14

LORI

Jace's not going to reply. If he didn't in the last five minutes or so, he's not going to. I know him too well, I'm too used to his disappearing acts. He pulls them on me every once in a while. Ghosts me for no apparent reason.

Only maybe tonight he has a reason.

I shouldn't have told him thanks for the kissing, telling him what a great friend he is. That was a cop-out.

But what was I supposed to say? Thanks for sweeping me off my feet? Thanks for kissing me like I'm the most desirable woman on the planet? Thanks for frying all my brain cells with your deft lips?

Gosh, his mouth. I can't stop thinking about the feel of his pillow lips pressed on mine, the graze of his teeth over my lower lip, the way he gently bit down on it before deepening the kiss.

It was pure fire, pure electricity, pure Jace.

But now he's gone radio silent. He's mad at me. I know it, even if he won't say it. He's probably mad that I forced him to kiss me and is sitting in his apartment, brooding and counting off the days until we can end this whole fake-dating sham.

I stare at my phone, willing him to respond, to say something, anything. But the silence is deafening.

After another five minutes of silent treatment, I drop the phone on my nightstand and go back to staring at the ceiling. I'm laying starfish-style in bed silhouetted in cats—two under my arms and two alongside my legs—and while I usually enjoy the companionship of my feline friends, tonight I'm feeling claustrophobic. Like I need to move.

I'm itching all over, except for my lips, which are still tingling from Jace's kiss.

I close my eyes and try to relax, try to will the memories away. But they're burning through my skin and mind as if they were seared onto both by a raging wildfire.

All I can think about is the kiss.

Kissing Jace was… uh… kind of earth-shattering. Sexy, hot, tingly, a bit of a punch in the gut?

I get it, he's a really hot guy. Objectively gorgeous. But he's my best friend, he's like my brother.

Well, that's not how kissing your brother should feel like. Not unless you're Cersei Lannister, which I'm most definitely not.

It's weird. I've never seen him this way, like us potentially being more than just friends. It's always been Aiden.

But now… now Aiden is getting married and Jace has gone from being a block of ice with barbed wire wrapped all around himself and warning signs plastered all over with "I do not cuddle" written upfront, to being a flaming inferno of a guy who set ablaze every nerve ending in my body with his sexy mouth.

What do I do now?

I can't go from being in love with one best friend to lusting after the other. Plus Jace doesn't do relationships. And while my track record with dating isn't stellar either, it's only because the only guy I've ever wanted has never been available. I would want a stable relationship. While, for Jace, I suspect being a bachelor is more of a lifestyle choice. I'm not sure.

Jace and I have always been able to talk about everything except his love life. Whenever I tried to talk to him about any of his flings or short-term girlfriends the barbed wire would come up, and he'd change the subject so fast I'd get whiplash.

I should try to get some sleep. I scratch the heads of the cats closer to me and, slowly, their purring lulls me into a slumber. I can't toss and turn—as per the feline silhouette I'm confined into—but when I wake up the next morning I feel like I've spent the entire night thrashing about, tormented by sexy dreams mixed in with even sexier memories.

I get out of bed and decide to treat myself to store-bought coffee, and since I'm in a particularly despondent mood, I go to my favorite bookshop that doubles as a café.

I order my breakfast and peruse the bookshelves for something to read. I end up reading the first few chapters of an enemies-to-lovers fantasy romance that does nothing to help me get a grip on my raging lust.

I finish my breakfast and put the book back on the shelf, ordering an e-book copy from the bookshop website. I love paperbacks, but I literally can't fit a single extra one into my loft. The rescue books take up all the available space and then some. But my e-reader can support my hoarding tendencies like a champ. No storing limits there.

I browse the shelves a little longer and download a thriller that comes with a handwritten cardboard recommendation from one of the store clerks. Yeah, maybe reading a steamy romance isn't the best way to cool off, but if I stick my head into a deep conspiracy mystery thriller maybe I can get out of the lust funk.

After the bookshop, I drop off my chicken eggs at the farmers market stall where I donate them to be sold off for charity. The little money they make goes to a rescue that saves animals from food factories.

I'm back in my loft before noon, and all I want to do is curl up on the sofa for an afternoon of reading. But I can't. This afternoon I'm on duty at Jessica's free clinic. It's going to be Aiden and me today.

A week ago, I'd be ecstatic I'd get to share an entire Kirsten-free afternoon with him. Since they started dating I never got alone time with him any other way.

But dare I say I'd rather it be Jace today? Yeah, because I don't like this tension between us. And whether or not I've fallen in lust with him, I can't stand for him to be mad at me.

I sigh. But that's not how life works. You get A when you want B, and when you stop wanting B, that's when you're going to get it.

Have I stopped wanting Aiden?

I don't know. Maybe? If nothing else, this afternoon will help me clarify that point.

Even if it's a little early for my shift, I put my coat on and get into the car. I turn the music on, loud enough for me to forget about everything as I sing my lungs out to "Speak Now" without even starting the car. I'd be lying if I said standing up at Aiden's wedding at the ominous "speak now or forever hold your peace" beat hasn't been my secret dream since he got engaged. Only today, I have more details placed into the fantasy. I know what Kirsten's dress will look like, I have faces for the other bridesmaids and maid of honor.

I grab the wheel and close my eyes; the image is so clear in my head it almost feels real. And it goes like always. Aiden and Kirsten at the altar about to exchange vows, the preacher asking if anyone has objections, me catching Aiden's blue eyes and seeing the doubt in them. I step forward about to speak, only this time I get distracted by icy-blue eyes in the background as Jace subtly shakes his head at me from his position next to the groom. He's a vision in a tux and... my eyes fly open.

What the heck was that?

Why is Jace suddenly interrupting my wedding-wrecker fantasies? Gosh, that kiss really scrambled my brain.

I shake my head and put the car into gear, pulling onto the street and changing song to "Blank Space," that's more of a Jace song.

Traffic isn't bad on a Sunday and I reach my destination a little over ten minutes later. The free clinic is a dingy gray building, but it houses so much warmth and love inside that I always feel uplifted when I come here. We do our best with whatever limited resources Jessica manages to put together.

Despite the emotional roller coaster I'm in, I smile as I push through the glass entrance doors and enter the lobby. And, judging from the number of chairs already occupied by waiting patients, I didn't get here a minute too soon.

At the back of the large room there's a small glass booth where patients have to register, then a set of double doors that lead to the open-space visiting room, which doesn't look much different to an ER with twin rows of hospital beds pushed against the far walls and curtains to separate them if a private examination is needed.

I greet Rue, the nurse sorting admissions behind the glass booth, with a bright smile and drop my jacket and purse in the locker behind her, grabbing a white coat.

Once I'm changed, I ask, "What do you have for me today, Rue?"

The black woman smiles at me before perusing her admission book. "I already gave Dr. Barlow a nasty eye infection, you can get the ear one." She hands me a wooden clipboard with the patient data.

"You meant Dr. Collymore, right?" I take the clipboard as my heart thu-thumps a little at hearing Jace's name.

"No, I—"

The double doors fly open and Jace enters the lobby. Our eyes meet through the glass of the booth and the thumping in my chest worsens.

"Dr. Barlow is on duty today," Rue repeats. "You can give him his next case." She hands me another medical file and after taking it, I circle the booth to go meet Jace.

"Hey," I say, smiling tentatively.

"Hi, Lori." His face is a mask of polite friendliness and I. Hate. It.

"Wasn't Aiden supposed to come today?"

Jace's brows pinch. "He had the tasting menu with Kirsten and asked me to cover for him."

His reply feels clipped and my smile falters. Gosh, I've never felt this nervous around him. Usually Jace is my safe place, my go-to confidant whenever I need someone to talk to, the calm in the midst of a storm. But today, the air is thick with tension.

"Oh right, the tasting." I try and fail to sound casual. Jace is about to side step me when I block him. "Are you sure we're okay? You didn't reply last night."

He shrugs. "I fell asleep." He's *so* lying.

"Really? So having to kiss me didn't freak you out? I know it's weird for us to kiss but—"

"This is not the place, Lori." He makes to turn away again, but I grab his forearm, stopping him.

"I just want to make sure kissing me didn't gross you out."

He stares at me, inscrutable, the only movement of his features a ticking in his jaw. "Not. The. Place."

"All right. What time do you get off?"

He takes a look at the crowded lobby. "I think we're both in for overtime."

He's right, we're not getting out of here any time soon.

"Don't go home without saying bye, promise?"

He gives me a stiff nod.

I grab the patient file Rue gave me and scan it quickly before handing it to him. "In that case, I have a wonderful suspect UTI for you." I hand him the file and beam.

He takes the folder from me and turns on his heels without another word.

Uh-oh.

15

JACE

"You have to be more careful in this weather, Mrs. Parker," I tell the old lady I'm treating for a mild case of frostbite in her distal phalanges.

"Sorry, Dr. Barlow, I got my gloves wet and I didn't think my fingertips would freeze so fast."

"The wet clothing probably didn't help, and it's January in Chicago." I catch a blur of Lori passing by and make a conscious effort not to look at her. I already hate how hyperaware I am of wherever she is in the room. But then I hear her laugh, and I can't help myself, I look up.

And there she is, lighting up the entire room with her infectious smile. I feel my heart lurch in my chest, and I turn back to Mrs. Parker, trying to focus on her condition.

But every time Lori laughs or talks, my concentration falters. I finally finish to re-warm Mrs. Parker's hand in a warm bath and loosely wrap her fingers with sterile dressings to protect the skin.

When I hand her a prescription for antibiotics should the area get infected, she takes it, staring at me keenly.

"You have some other health concerns you wanted to have checked out today?"

"You know." She tilts her head, still studying me. "If you're in love with the beautiful doctor across the room, you should tell her."

I hardly suppress a grin. "What makes you say that I'm in love?"

"Ah, young man, the longing in your eyes whenever they dart toward her—which is an awful lot—is not that hard to spot."

I clasp my hands in my lap. "And why do you suppose that I haven't told her?"

"It's the indecision on her face whenever she looks over when she thinks you're not looking, like right now."

I snap my eyes up and lock gazes with Lori across the room. She quickly looks away and goes back to caring for her patient, but I can still spot the faint coloring in her cheeks.

The blushing sure is new.

Mrs. Parker pats my hand as she gets off the examination bed. "If you love her, tell her."

Ah, easier said than done.

What's the point when I already know she doesn't feel the same.

I inwardly cringe picturing the way Lori's face fell when she saw it was me here today and not Aiden. Not to mention how she keeps repeating what a good effing friend I am and how weird it is for us to kiss.

I give Mrs. Parker a nod while mentally shaking my head. Lori is a lost cause; she'll never see me as anything other than a friend.

I exhale heavily before turning to my next patient. It's a little girl, no more than six years old, with a cough and fever. She clings to her mother's hand, looking up at me with big, scared eyes.

"What seems to be the problem?" I kneel down in front of her, trying to be as reassuring as possible.

The mother babbles on about how her daughter has been sick for a few days now, and the girl coughs weakly into a tissue.

I examine her quickly, taking note of her symptoms and vital signs. "I think it's just the flu," I tell the mother. "But we'll do some tests to be sure."

The little girl looks up at me again and tugs on my sleeve. "Will I be okay, doctor?"

I smile at her gently. "Of course you will be okay. We're here to make sure you feel better."

She nods solemnly before resting her head on her mother's shoulder.

As I run through all the basic medical checks, I try to shake off the thoughts of Lori. I can't keep dwelling on something that will never happen.

My mental vows are interrupted by the sound of Lori's voice. "Hey."

I turn to see her standing next to me, holding two cups of coffee. "I figured we could use a caffeine boost," she says, handing one cup to me.

"Thanks," I say, taking a sip. The warmth spreads through me, both from the coffee and from being near her.

She looks at me expectantly. "So, how's your last patient doing?"

"Oh, she'll be fine. Just a little case of the flu." I take another sip and look back at her. "How about yours?"

Lori's face falls. "Not good. Possible sepsis."

"Anything I can do to help?"

"Yeah, don't be mad at me, please?" Her eyes get even bigger than usual if that's even possible. "The medical work I can handle on my own."

As if I could ever be mad at her. My resolution to keep my distance begins to crumble. "I'm not mad, Lola, I promise."

Her expression relaxes considerably and she goes in for the kill, wrapping her arms around my waist.

I keep my hands to myself, I'm not a complete fool.

"You know," Lori says, snuggling her face even more into my chest. "It'd help show how not mad you are if you hugged me back."

I can't, I want to scream. I won't.

"Please?"

And that's all it takes for my good intentions to fly out the window. I drop the coffee cup on a nearby mayo stand and wrap my arms around her, pulling her close. She fits perfectly in my embrace. I drop my chin on top of her head, inhaling the sweet scent of her shampoo.

For a fleeting moment, everything feels right in the world. My heart beats faster against my chest as I hold her tight. I can feel her warmth seeping into me, making me forget about everything else.

But as soon as she pulls away and flashes me a smile, my doubts come rushing back. I'm just her friend, after all.

"Thank you," she says, before heading off to take care of her patient.

I watch her go, feeling more confused than ever.

Maybe Mrs. Parker was right. Maybe I should just tell Lori how I feel. But what if it ruins our friendship? What if she doesn't feel the same way?

And that's not even a what if because I already know. She's in love with Aiden. I need to drill that fact into my brain and stop imagining things that aren't there.

I survived my feelings for over a decade, I can keep doing it. Even if now I have to pretend to love her while pretending *not* to love her.

But it gets impossible only when we're with Aiden and I have to put on a show. And I've checked our schedules, they don't exactly align for the next few weeks, which means not many lunches together. Kirsten keeps Aiden very busy with all the wedding planning so he's not around the office to hang out that much.

The only truly dangerous moments are going to be the meet and greet for the wedding party Kirsten insisted on having for bridesmaids and groomsmen to get to know each other before the wedding. It'll be at a cool bar slash club downtown. And then there's the three-day bachelor party in New Orleans, where Lori will be joining the boys as she refused to attend the bachelorette—first time I ever saw her put her foot down so adamantly over something.

It's easy, it's only three nights. I can do it.

16

JACE

Two weeks later

It's not easy and it's not only three nights. Now that Kirsten is sure Lori isn't after her man, she's constantly inviting us out.

It was lunch last week. I spent the whole time in a booth with Lori's side pressed into mine, one arm draped over her shoulder as I twirled a lock of her silky hair around my finger. I just couldn't help myself, now that I briefly get permission to touch her, I can't control the impulses. And Lori didn't help things along. Throughout the lunch she kept leaning into me, shooting me these looks, with her big brown eyes sparkling up at me.

Then it was another dinner out and a casual outing at the movies. And I swear, it took all the self-restraint I had not to pull a move on her in the dark movie theater while she snuggled against me for the entire duration of the action flick.

Then came the weekend and another invitation to scout a new, posh rooftop bar. Dark lighting, fancy cocktails, and Lori in a dress. A recipe for disaster in short.

I swear sometimes it feels like she's doing it on purpose. I'm not used to seeing her in sexy clothes. And maybe it's a last-ditch effort to seduce Aiden before the wedding, but the way she looks at me sometimes, like she's trying to tell me something without saying a word, drives me crazy. But I've no idea what she's trying to say, if anything. We don't talk much. Other than when we have to pretend in front of the others, I try to avoid her as much as possible.

But having her so close while still keeping my distance is chipping away my soul one stolen touch at the time.

Well, at least I managed not to kiss her again.

But tonight is the first real test. The meet and greet for the wedding party. An entire night in a club with loud music, too many drinks, not enough inhibition, and too much temptation.

It's okay. I can do it.

When I take a cab to the club downtown, it's already past the agreed meet time. But arriving as late as possible without passing for a total douche is part of my survival strategy. Even shedding a mere half an hour of pretending off my sentence will do great things for my mental health.

Yeah, who am I kidding? The moment I enter the club, my eyes immediately snatch onto Lori. She's talking to Aiden's brother, a cocktail in her hands, her head tilted backward as she laughs.

Her hair is up in a high ponytail. No dress tonight. Just black jeans and a plain tank top, which in a way is worse. Because this is the Lori I fell in love with, the goofball who wears minimal makeup and dresses comfortably. And my heart aches when I think about how I will never have her.

Mrs. Parker's words play in my head, *"If you love her, tell her."*

What the heck, maybe I should just tell her.

I take a step forward and freeze on the spot just as fast as a memory slams into me. That of the first night I wanted to tell her...

It was a little over a month after we'd started hanging out after gnome night. Aiden was out on a date, which meant I had our shared dorm room all to myself. I'd invited Lori over for a study session slash movie night slash woo-her night.

We'd started with studying, but soon enough, the textbooks were forgotten, and we were cuddled up on the bed, watching some horror flick. She kept burying her face in my chest at the most frightening scenes, and I was sort of sweating cold but it had nothing to do with the scary movie. I'd been working up the courage to kiss her all night.

When the movie ended she looked up at me, with those impossibly big brown eyes and said, "Jace, can I ask you something?"

"Sure."

"Do you and Aiden date a lot?"

Yep, I thought, she wants to date me but she isn't sure if I'm the serious-relationship kind of guy. And to be honest, I wasn't back then. But for her, I would've been.

"Define a lot," I teased.

"How many girls have you slept with since college started?"

It was two, not a wild number, but I wasn't about to disclose that information. "Yeah, hard pass on that answer."

Lori bit her lower lip. "If I tell you something, will you promise not to tell Aiden?"

That should've been my first clue, but I was still being too naively optimistic to catch up. "Yeah?"

"I think I like him."

That's when it all came crashing down. At that moment, a lot of her reactions over the past month began to make sense. How she seemed shier around him. How she'd light up whenever he walked into a room. Her constant blushing.

I felt like an idiot for not seeing it earlier. For thinking that maybe, just maybe, Lori might feel the same way I did.

In response, I scooted to my side of the bed, listening to her gushing about how perfect Aiden was, and I've kept my distance ever since.

And tonight, as I watch her laughing with Aiden's brother, I realize that nothing has changed. Except now, it feels like the world is closing in on me. Like I'll never be able to escape this feeling of wanting something I can't have.

I take a deep breath and shake my head, trying to clear away the memories that are clouding my mind. This is not the time or place to be having these thoughts.

But then she turns her head and our eyes meet across the dancefloor, and I know I'm toast no matter what I do.

17

LORI

I'm fake dating Dr. Jekyll and Mr. Hyde only Jace is Dr. Sizzle and Mr. Frost. In the past two weeks, he's gone hot and cold on me so many times I've lost count.

Whenever we're in character around someone, he can't let go of me. He touches me constantly, keeps me close, plays with my hair, and the looks he gives me—those are enough to make me melt. And they don't feel fake at all.

But the moment we're alone, he shuts down completely, barely even speaking to me. He turns back into an ice block. The barbed wire comes out along with the "Keep Out" signs and a chasm spreads between us.

It's like he doesn't want to be anywhere near me. Every time I try to start a conversation with him, he either changes the subject or makes some excuse to walk away.

I'm so confused and so tired of pretending. First pretending I didn't love Aiden, then pretending I love Jace, and now I don't even know what's real and what's pretense. To hell with them both. Tonight I came dressed just for me in comfortable clothes—low-heel ankle boots, jeans, and a tank top—and I'm just going to have fun and not try to seduce any of my best friends or try to sort out my feelings for them. Especially not Mr. Frost—that is if he ever shows up. Jace is late.

Mr. Neat Freak is never late. And his tardiness is pissing me off way out of proportion. Or maybe it's more the fact that he didn't want us to come together or that he's been so distant lately or that he hasn't texted me to let me know where he is. I feel like he's deliberately ignoring me, and I don't understand why.

In the midst of my mental rant, I try to keep up with what Aiden's brother is telling me while also giving appropriate answers in return. And I'm mostly succeeding, at least until I feel a prickle in my scalp and turn my head, meeting Jace's eyes across the club. I lose track of whatever I was saying, the words getting stuck in my throat. All my good intentions of keeping to myself and of not having feelings for any of my best friends vanish into thin air because that man staring at me from across the dancefloor is not Mr. Frost, he's very much Dr. Sizzle.

Jace looks unfairly hot in a pair of simple jeans and a black T-shirt that hugs his toned chest in all the right places. His dark hair falls in messy waves around his face, adding a touch of reckless sex appeal to his features.

And I don't know how I should or shouldn't feel, but I can certify that after he kissed me, I can state with 100 per cent certainty that I don't see Jace as just a friend anymore.

In fact, I can't tear my eyes away from him. I watch as he moves through the crowd of people, his eyes never leaving me. My heart beats faster as he approaches, and I can feel my body responding to him in a way that it didn't use to. These reactions are all very new. But I can't help it. He's just so damn attractive.

"Hey," he says as he reaches us, flashing me a small smile.

I nod, not trusting myself to speak.

"Hey, man," Aiden's brother says, then, probably noticing the heated way Jace and I are staring at each other, he excuses himself.

"I was beginning to think you weren't coming," I say to him finally, trying to sound nonchalant, while feeling both relieved and irritated at the same time.

He shrugs. "Sorry, lost track of time at the gym."

I roll my eyes. "Couldn't you have texted me to let me know?"

"I didn't think you'd miss me that much."

That's a passive-aggressive response if I've ever heard one.

I study him, trying to read his expression. He looks like he's trying very hard not to let something show, but I can't quite put my finger on what it is.

"Is everything okay?" I ask tentatively. "Are we okay?"

Something flares behind his eyes, blue fire, and as he opens his mouth to speak, I brace myself for whatever is about to come.

But of course that's when Kirsten barrels into us. "Hey, what are you guys doing here on your own?" She shakes her blonde locks. "Not what this night is about."

Then she grabs Jace by the arm and drags him away. "Come with me, I want you to meet all my friends."

I gape helplessly as she hauls him away toward her salivating bridesmaids. As I watch the other women drool over him, something dark twists in my stomach.

He isn't doing anything wrong, but as I watch Jace shake the hands of Kirsten's pageant-queen friends all I want to do is storm over there and claim him as mine.

When it's the turn of Kirsten's sister to be introduced, jealousy becomes a wild beast in my chest. Which is ridiculous. I have no reason to be jealous. Jace and I are just friends, we're just *pretending* to date.

"You don't need to stare murder at the other bridesmaids." Aiden appears by my side with a cocktail in his hands. "Jace only has eyes for you."

The words send me on a tailspin. Because they're not true. Because in that moment, I realize I *want* them to be true.

I stare up at Aiden in shock, even more so when the usual twinge of desire is not there—gone. I look back to where Jace is being presented like a show pony, catch Kendall casually brushing his upper arm, and I get *all* the twinges.

I raise a finger at Aiden. "I need a minute." And flee to the bathroom to lock myself in a stall.

What is happening to me?

I take a few deep breaths, trying to calm down. But no matter how much I try, I can't shake off the feeling of jealousy eating me up from inside. It's not like Jace and I have anything going on, but just the thought of him with someone else sends shivers down my spine.

As I sit on the toilet seat, trying to calm my racing heart, I can't help but feel confused. Why am I feeling this way about Jace all of a sudden? We've been friends for years and I've never had these kinds of feelings for him before. Is it because we kissed? That must be it. The kiss must have sparked something in me that I didn't even know was there.

But as I sit there, staring at the dingy bathroom stall walls, I know that's not the whole truth. Yes, the kiss was amazing and it definitely ignited something in me, but there's something else there too. Something that I can't grasp or comprehend yet, but that I'd better sort fast if I don't want to lose my best friend.

Jace is my rock. My safe place. The person I could always be myself with. The one I could tell all my secrets. And lately, I've felt like we've lost that. And I want it back—with a vengeance. I want more of him, more of us.

The realization is just as scary as the alternative—losing him. I'm just coming to grips with what the next steps I need to take are, when the restroom door swings open and Kendall's and Kirsten's voices drift inside.

"Gosh, Jace is so hot," Kendall says, and I cringe. "Are you sure he and Lori are serious."

"Very sure," Kirsten chastises.

"Bleagh, they're really not a good fit. He's miles out of her league."

"Kendall, stop it, you're being mean."

The evil sister laughs. "Come on, have you seen how she's come dressed tonight. Does she shop only at goodwill?"

Nothing wrong with shopping at goodwill, I want to yell. But all I can do is stay paralyzed in my stall hoping they won't discover me. How I wish I was a badass now, someone who wouldn't have a problem walking out there with her head held high while putting them in their place. But I've accepted a long time ago I'm not that person. Get a nickname in grade school, and if you live in a town small enough it'll follow you until graduation.

I've moved away, changed life, changed friends, but sometimes I still feel like the "silent girl" I was back then. So I keep quiet hidden in my stall and listen on as they keep on talking behind my back.

"And have you seen how she walks? Like she has a stick up her—"

"Kendall!"

"Okay, okay, I'll stop."

If I were a different me, I'd walk out there and tell them the stiff walking is for being sore after all the sex Jace and I are having. But... still me. Still silent.

So I endure another few excruciating minutes of sisterly chit-chat, and then they're out.

I let out a long breath and lean against the stall door. All right, let's focus on what really matters. Time to go out there and force Jace to have a conversation with me.

18

LORI

Only when I go outside, I find him at the bar surrounded by fake Kardashians. Britney, the maid of honor, grabs her cocktail from the bartender and leaves to rejoin Kirsten and the others, but Kendall doesn't look like she has any intention to scram.

She picks up her cocktail and sucks on the small straw while staring up at Jace from under her long lashes.

Okay, that's it. My blood boils and screw Silent Girl, I'm in for my first voluntary confrontation.

No matter that every fiber in my body is itching, begging me not to go. I ignore my prickly nerves and march across the club toward them. Without sparing Kendall a second glance, I insert myself squarely between them, bringing my back flush with Jace's front. Ignoring his jolt of surprise, I take the arm he's not leaning on the counter and wrap it around my waist, keeping it in place with my hand. Not content, I reach up with my other hand and sink it in his silky locks, tilting my head backward to plant a soft kiss on his jaw.

Then I level the bride's sister with a stare and, plastering the most fake-sweet smile on my face accompanied by an equally pretend-saccharine voice, I say, "Hi, Kendall, so nice to see you again. Did you need anything from Jace?"

Her eyes widen in surprise, clearly caught off guard by my sudden boldness. "Oh, no thanks," Kendall stammers out, clearly caught off guard. "I was just saying hello."

"Well, hello then," I say, my smile still in place.

Jace's arm tightens on my waist, and I relish the pressure.

Kendall gives me a tight-lipped smile and scurries away, her high heels clacking against the tile floor.

Jace's breath is hot against my ear as he whispers, "That was very subtle."

I spin in his arms to face him. "Should I have given the lovely sister of the bride free rein to keep hitting on you? I mean, do you like her?"

Something close to rage flares in Jace's eyes, he drops his arms from my waist and crosses them over his chest. "I don't like her."

"What do you like then?"

He shoots me a searing look and, arms still crossed over his chest, he leans forward so that his mouth is level with my ear. "Not. Her," he purrs, and then he walks away.

I go after him. He's not going to avoid me tonight.

I grab his arm to stop his retreat and tug, forcing him to face me again. "We're not done talking."

His face is an unreadable mask. "You might not be done. But what if I am?"

"Then I guess you're just going to have to deal with it," I say, my voice low and steady despite the pounding of my heart. "Because I'm not done with you yet."

Jace's eyes darken, and he steps closer to me, his breath hot against my face. "What do you want from me?" he asks, his voice rough.

"I want—what if I don't know what I want?"

His jaw sets. "Then that's too bad, try to figure it out next time before you come after me."

He makes to jerk his arm away from me, but I don't let him. "Please Jace, don't be like that, don't be mad at me. I can't stand it."

His shoulders drop.

"I'm not mad," he says, his voice softer now. "I'm just... frustrated."

"Why are you frustrated?" I ask, looking up at him with wide eyes. My heart is racing, and I can feel my palms getting sweaty.

"Because I don't know what you want from me either." His gaze drops to my mouth, but he quickly looks away.

"Do you want to kiss me right now?" I ask, forcing myself to say exactly what I'm thinking.

His blue eyes X-ray me and he takes a step closer. "What about you? Do you want me to kiss you?"

I swallow and nod, giving him the honest truth.

He grimaces. "Why? For show? So everyone can see? So you can make Aiden jealous?"

Slowly, I shake my head. And to make it perfectly clear that I mean it, I pull him behind a corner where no one can see us. I lean my back against the dark walls of the club and give another little push. "Just for me." And then I wait.

Jace's eyes widen in surprise, then darken, then it's as if a dam has broken loose.

His body slams into me, pressing me against the wall as he cups my face in his hands with contrasting gentleness. Then he crashes his mouth to mine, and it's like fire blazing through my veins.

It's like nothing I've ever felt before, this complete and utter abandon. I wrap my arms around his neck, holding on for dear life as he devours me whole.

I wrap my arms around his neck, pulling him closer to me

while his hands trail down my body, gripping my hips as he presses himself against me harder. I can feel every inch of him and it's not enough. I want more.

We break apart for a moment, gasping for air before he lowers his mouth to my neck, kissing and nipping at the sensitive skin there. I moan softly, arching into him as he works his way down.

"Tell me this is real," he murmurs against my skin, his voice hoarse. "I want you so much it hurts."

"It is real," I manage to say with the last ounce of sentient thought I have before he kisses me again.

And it's even more intense. He bites, sucks, and kisses me all the while whispering sweet nothings in my ears until I need to grab onto his strong, muscular shoulders for support because my legs won't hold my weight anymore.

And then he kisses me some more.

We pull apart only when our phones begin to simultaneously vibrate in our pockets with a string of texts. It's Aiden in our group chat.

FROM AIDEN:

You guys

Kirsten organized this night for the members of the wedding party to mingle

You're not mingling

I swear, if you're somewhere in a dark corner making out that's what I'm going to put in your wedding speech

Now, chop, chop

Get over here and mingle

Jace and I look up from our screens and smile. Then he drops his forehead onto mine and whispers, "We'd better go."

"Yeah," I agree. "But mingle too much with the sister of the bride and I'm not responsible for my actions."

He drops a soft kiss on my mouth. "You don't have to worry about that, I promise."

I flash him the goofiest smile on the planet as I interlace my fingers with his to guide him back to our table where the others are playing a drinking game. As we sit on the couch next to each other, Aiden pointedly asks Jace to switch places with him. And I feel like an unruly kid in school who had to be separated from her partner in crime.

And that's a bit how it feels to be with Jace tonight. As if we were doing something we weren't supposed to do. But doesn't it feel good?

And, separated or not, gosh, the stares he throws me from across the table are scorching. He's basically undressing me with his eyes.

But as the night draws to a close and people start to go home, I get nervous again. Especially since Jace regains a hint of Mr. Frost. I never want to see Mr. Frost ever again; I only want Dr. Sizzle.

So, as we wait outside for a cab, I keep hold of his hand, even if we're both wearing gloves. "I think we should talk," I say.

Jace looks sideways at me with an expression that if I didn't know better I'd say is pure dread.

"Not tonight, Lola."

Is it fear of this thing that is growing between us? Fear that it'll ruin our friendship? Or is it fear of commitment? What is it? I will never know if I don't ask.

"Why not tonight?"

"It's freezing cold out here and we had too much to drink, we need to clear our heads."

I nod, a little disappointed. His words make perfect sense, but I can't help but feel like he's already pulling on the brakes, and I don't understand why.

Still, I wish him goodnight with a chaste kiss on the cheek and get in a cab alone like a good girl.

I give the driver my address, but as we zoom past the tall skyscrapers of downtown, I can't shake the feeling that a piece of the puzzle is missing. That Jace is keeping something from me. And I could wait. I could give him space like he asked. Wait until our heads were clearer and we weren't still so strung up by that kiss.

But, honestly, I don't want to.

I knock on the glass separating the back seats from the driver and say, "Excuse me, I've changed my mind."

19

JACE

I crash into my apartment like a hurricane, the tipsy buzz from this evening still lingering in my body. Without turning on any of the lights, I head straight for the wall-wide windows and end up standing with an arm braced on the cold glass overlooking all of Chicago's glowing beauty.

I'm hiding. Lori wants answers, and I'm not giving them to her because the only ones I have to give are scary as hell.

What am I supposed to do? Confess everything I've been feeling for the past fifteen years? Play it cool? Act as if this attraction between us is as new for me as it is for her?

I'm not even sure what this is for her. And I'm too scared to ask. Too scared to find out she only needs me to survive Aiden getting married.

I'm digging myself into a hole and I don't care.

I punch the glass, I'm about to do it again when my phone vibrates in my pocket. It's a text from Lori.

FROM LORI:

You're a great kisser

And just like that, I can't help the smile that pulls at my lips as I hit reply.

TO LORI:

Surprised?

FROM LORI:

Actually, no

I don't suppose Nancy Powell would've super-glued your gas cap when you broke up with her in junior year if you were a lousy kisser

TO LORI:

Tonight wasn't the first time we kissed, though

FROM LORI:

No, you're right

But tonight was real

At least for me

I stare at the words not sure if I can let myself believe them. But I'm tired of fighting this. Of always having an ironclad self-control and constantly keeping myself in check. I can't do it anymore. Not when she asks me to kiss her. Not when she tells me it's real.

My thumbs fly over the keyboard.

TO LORI:

Are you still in the cab?

Tell the driver to turn back

FROM LORI:

Already ahead of you, Barlow

TO LORI:

Where are you?

FROM LORI:

Riding up in your super slow elevator *eye-rolling emoji*

My heart hammers in my chest. I cross my apartment at record speed and get to the door just as a knock comes from the other side.

I fling the door open. "What are you doing here?"

"You wouldn't let me talk earlier. And you might've had a point because it's freezing outside." Lori pushes her way into the apartment past me, losing items of clothing as she goes. "I half froze just getting out of the cab and into your lobby."

I follow her, picking up her coat, scarf, and gloves from the surfaces she's tossed them on. But when I get to the couch, she stares at the pile of clothes in my hands and takes it from me. "This is not the time to worry about the proper place where to put outerwear, Jace." Lori grabs her things and drops them in a heap on the living room armchair.

"Why are you here, again?"

Lori takes a step closer and rests a hand on my chest. "Because I really liked the way you kissed me tonight, and I'd like you to do it again?" The affirmation comes off as more of a question.

I swallow and when her hand slides up over my shoulder and into my hair, I grab her waist and pull her to me. The moment is tender and intense, not frantic like before. I ride my palms up her back and let my fingers slide into her soft hair, freeing it from the ponytail she still has it in. Then I cup the back of her head, keeping my other hand to the small of her back. We stare at each other for a few long instants before I close my eyes and press my lips to hers in a gentle brush, then another. I take my time, teasing her to insanity, just as she's done with me for years.

When I finally deepen the kiss, drawing a moan from her

throat, she buries her fingers in my T-shirt, trying to pull me closer even if it's physically impossible. Our bodies are already molded to each other. At the edge of my mind, an annoying bug is still buzzing around, screaming that this is a mistake. But I can't fight this, not anymore. I simply don't have the strength. Lori is all I want. She's all I've ever wanted. I need her. I'm drowning and she's my life raft. I could do this all night, kiss her deep and slow, and never tire of it.

Her hands keep tugging at my T-shirt, and it's not helping to cool me down. I reach lower, plant my hands behind her thighs, and scoop her up, laying her down on the couch and sliding beside her, careful not to crush her.

Without breaking the kiss, I lay my chest against hers, my hard planes molding perfectly against her soft curves. I caress her cheek and trail my hand down to her neck where her pulse is pounding harder than ever before. Lori's warm breath tickles over my lips when she nips gently on them, driving me wild like never before.

My head is in a daze; all rational thought has left me. Nothing else matters but Lori and me on this couch lost to blissful oblivion while the wind blows wildly outside my windows.

Our hands move from one body part to the next while our breaths become more labored and ragged, blending together into one erratic rhythm.

Underneath her coat, Lori was still wearing only a tank top and now she pulls it above her head, revealing the simple black bra underneath. My T-shirt goes flying next.

She pulls me back down to her, desperate to kiss me. The friction between our bodies is heaven and hell, too much and not enough.

When she arches into me I'm about to completely lose it.

"Jace, please," she moans.

I pull back to look at her. Her eyes are heavy-lidded and lust-filled, *lust* being the keyword here. She's in lust with me, not in love. This is probably just a distraction for her from the heartbreak of Aiden getting married. No matter how hard I try to ignore it, reality crashes on me like an icy wave.

I can't do this. I can't make love to her. Not when I know she wants another man and is here with me only because she can't have him. Not when she's not mine.

I prop myself up on my elbows, putting a little distance between us. Lori tries to pull me back down to her, but I resist and use the backrest to drag myself upright and scoot down to the other end of the couch.

Lori blinks at me, her gaze still a little hazed but mostly confused. "What are you doing over there?" she asks.

"We can't do this."

She frowns. "You mean kiss?"

"We were about to do a lot more than kissing." My gaze drops down to her bra.

She follows the trail of my eyes and blushes slightly, but makes no effort to cover herself. "Fair enough. Why can't we?"

"Because it's not fair on either of us."

She's obviously taken aback by my reply. "Why not?"

"I'm not the guy you want."

"You don't know that."

"You're in love with Aiden, and I don't want to be your consolation prize."

"Can we just leave Aiden out of this for a moment?" She tucks her feet underneath her thighs, staring at me with eyes bigger than ever. "I'm here with you. I'm attracted to you."

"You want to be *distracted* by me, to turn a blind eye to the fact that the man you really want is marrying someone else."

"That's not what this is, I swear." She shakes her head. "Since we've started this fake-dating thing, I've begun to see you in a different light, and I've been thinking more and more about you not as my best friend... but as a man."

I arch an eyebrow at that. "How did you think of me before? As an Ewok?"

Lori smiles. "Deflecting much? I see you're attracted to me, too. So why can't we explore whatever this new thing between us is?"

"I have my reasons."

"What reasons? Are you afraid we might ruin our friendship?"

"Aren't you?"

"Well, yes, but it seems like a worthwhile risk to take." She looks at me pensively for a few seconds. "Or are you really worried that if we got into a relationship, it'd be too serious?"

I scoff at that. "Quite the opposite."

"What does that even mean?" She tilts her head uncomprehendingly. "What is it you're not telling me?"

I stare at the ceiling for a long instant. The words are on the tip of my tongue... I've been holding them back for so long... but now they want out. Yeah, I could give Lori whatever rubbish excuse, but what would be the point?

"Jace," she pleads. "If you don't tell me I *can't* know. Let me in. Please."

I turn my head and lock eyes with her. "The way you've felt about Aiden for all these years..."

"I already told you to leave him out—"

I raise a hand to silence her. "That's how I felt about you—how I still feel about you. I'm in love with you, Lori, I have been since forever. So unless you can honestly tell me you feel the same about me, that I'm the only man you want, we can't take this any further."

20

LORI

Jace's words floor me. The wind's been knocked out of me. I'm frozen in place, my eyes wide, my mouth hanging open. He loves me? I stare at him, unable to speak, still trying to process. He's been in love with me for years? My entire world has been tilted upside down.

I open my mouth to say something, anything, but I have to close it again because how do you respond to a declaration like that?

I search the room, half expecting a camera crew to jump out from behind the couch and yell, "You've been punk'd!" But Ashton Kutcher is nowhere in sight, so I just have to assume this is real.

I focus back on the man on the other side of the couch, still not sure how to respond.

The flicker of hope in Jace's eyes fades the longer I keep quiet while the set of his jaw hardens. "That's what I thought." Jace grabs his discarded T-shirt from the floor, pulls it back over his head, and stands up. He crosses the room to go stare out the window, back turned to me.

I pull my tank top back on as well and follow him. Tentatively, I hug him from behind, pressing the side of my face between his shoulder blades. Jace goes rigid at first but then slumps, exhaling a deep breath.

"How long?" I ask him.

"Since the beginning. I knew the night you got pranked in the shower."

I inwardly cringe. That night was one of the lowest moments in my academic life. Someone stole my clothes from the shared bathroom and I had to walk back to my room wearing only a towel, which wouldn't have been so bad per se, except that it was a Saturday night and everyone was out in the halls, mingling, and then I tripped and basically flashed half the dorm.

"So, it was love at first flash?"

Jace's shoulders shake with amusement. "No, although I won't pretend that wasn't a tremendous bonus." Somehow, this conversation is easier to have face to shoulders instead of face to face. My cheeks are already burning, and I wouldn't be able to sustain Jace's stare as he reveals all this new information. "What I fell in love with was your boldness as you strolled half naked across the crowded halls as if nothing strange was happening. The way you held your head high even after you accidentally dropped the towel in front of the entire golf team."

"Then that was my best performance; you've no idea how much I was hyperventilating inside."

"But you have a way of always being able to laugh off any situation. To stay positive no matter what. And, yes, seeing you naked moved you out of the friend zone good and forever. Since that night, I have wanted you."

I shift position slightly, burying my forehead between his shoulder blades, whispering, "So why don't you want me now?"

"I don't want just your body, Lori. I want your head and I want your heart. I want the full deal or nothing at all."

"I always thought you dated those plastic sorority girls because you weren't interested in someone like me."

Jace relaxes a little more and lets out a soundless laugh. "No, I've always dated girls who I knew weren't after anything serious and that I wouldn't hurt. Because basically, I wasn't available."

"Ah, I bet Nancy Powell would beg to differ."

Jace shrugs. "I'm not perfect, sometimes I misjudged."

"I don't know what to say."

"Don't worry, I get it if you don't feel the same way." The quiet hurt in his voice destroys me.

"Jace," I whisper, and press a kiss against his warm, solid back.

"You should go," he says, but he doesn't move. "We can't do this. It's not right. I'm not the man you want."

I turn him around and cup his cheek. "But what if I want to figure this out instead? Explore my feelings for you before you decide for the both of us they don't exist?"

Jace looks at me. "And how do you propose to do that?"

"Can't we just date, like real-date, and see what happens?"

"I already told you I don't want to—"

I press a finger to his lips. "I said *date*, not sleep together, you perv. At least not until we're both sure we're all in."

His eyebrows rise in a hopeful question and I release his mouth. "And you'd be okay with not having sex?"

I bite my lower lips. "I guess the sexy *dreams* will have to do for now."

"What sexy dreams?"

"I've been having a few lately…"

His eyes darken. "And what would happen in these dreams?"

I shake my head. "Can't tell you, sorry." I kiss his jaw. "But maybe one day I'll be able to show you."

Jace buries his face in my neck. "Are you trying to kill me, Lola?"

"Yes, but softly."

He trails soft kisses down my neck to my bare shoulder. "Careful, Archibald, I can reciprocate."

"Just to be clear, what exactly is forbidden in this deal?"

Still torturing the sensitive skin under my earlobe, he whispers, "Everything beyond first base."

"For how long?"

Jace pulls back to look me in the eyes, his burning like ice. "Until you can tell me you're in love with me and only me."

I swallow. "That is the most frustrating and romantic thing anyone has ever said to me."

"Good." He kisses me on the mouth, softly at first and then more purposefully. He suppresses a chuckle when I melt into his arms. "I just want to make sure you're absolutely clear on that."

"I'm clear. So clear, I can't see straight."

Jace kisses me again before slowly backing away. "Bed? I'm not letting you take a cab home this late."

"The cats are going to kill me."

"We'll make it up to them tomorrow."

"How?"

"Extra cuddles? Food? We'll think of something." He takes my hand and leads me down the hall to his bedroom.

I stop at the foot of the bed and take in the military-grade smoothness of his sheets, inhale his scent lingering in the air, and admire the flawless white of the pillows.

"Now that I'm officially your girlfriend, do I get to use your extra toothbrush?"

He suddenly looks a little sheepish and averts his eyes. "Oh."

"Too soon for the G-word?"

Jace smirks. "You mean only fifteen years later?"

I cross the last few steps between us and take him in my arms. "I'm so happy right now, Jace," I whisper against his lips.

"Me too," he replies and kisses me.

This kiss is different, slower. The spark of desire is still alive and kicking, but there's more. Jace is no longer holding back, not now that he's free to show me what he really feels for me. And I'm tempted to throw caution out the window and just tell him I feel the same… but do I? This is all so new for me, and I owe it to him and to myself to be 100 per cent sure before I say anything.

My body, however, has a completely different mind. Before I auto-combust, I pull back. "This is going to be hard."

Jace's smile is heart-shattering. "Welcome to my world."

I change into one of his T-shirts and gym shorts and scoot into bed.

When Jace joins me under the covers, I ask, "Is spooning allowed?"

"Totally."

I turn on my side, and Jace wraps his arm across my waist, his fingers gently circling my wrist. A tingle shoots up my arm, and I become hyperaware of every cell in my body that's touching him. My skin is burning so hot I'm afraid I might catch fire.

Despite not wanting to lose contact, I turn on my other side and prop up on one elbow to hold up my head. "How are you not dying to rip my clothes off right now?"

A wicked, wolfish smirk curls his lips. "Oh, *I am*, trust me."

"And where did all this self-control come from?"

"I had years of practice."

I frown, confused.

"If you had to make an estimate…" he explains, "how many nights would you say you've spent in my bed since we met?"

I don't know the answer, but I'm sure it's a pretty high number. "A lot?"

Jace trails a finger down my arm, making me shiver. "What you're experiencing now, I've felt every single one of those nights."

"Then I guess this is all your fault."

His eyes crinkle in mock outrage. "My fault how?"

"You should've seduced me a long time ago."

"Seduced you?"

"Oh, come on, Jacey Pooh, we both know you've got game. If you'd batted your lashes and did that wicked bitey thing you did to my neck earlier, I would've succumbed in no time."

Jace chuckles now. "Forgive me for not thinking of myself as someone women have to *succumb* to. And I've already told you, if something ever happened between us, I didn't want it to be just physical."

I puff air out of my cheeks. "You're so romantically perfect, it's disgusting. Turn around."

"Why?"

"I'm spooning you instead."

"Oh, so I'm the one who's supposed to suffer now?"

"You're more practiced, as per your own admission."

"You'd better catch up soon."

"Oh, I will, trust me."

Jace drops a kiss on my forehead. "Goodnight, Lola." Then, locking eyes with me, he adds, "I love you."

* * *

The next morning, I wake up to the sound of Jace's phone vibrating on his nightstand. He shifts under the blankets and picks up with a groggy, "Hello?"

I don't understand what the other person says, but the voice sounds like an angry cartoon chipmunk speaking a thousand words per minute.

"Yeah, no, M—" Jace tries and fails to chip a few words in. The tirade on the other side continues until Jace, sounding defeated, says, "Yeah, okay, see you later."

He sags back on the pillow, letting out a puff of air and raking a hand through his bed hair. Jace turns to me and upon finding me staring, his lips curl into the most adorable lopsided grin. "We might have a problem, Lola."

21

JACE

Lori blinks at me, more curious than worried. She looks so cute when she's freshly awakened with her hair all tousled and one of my T-shirts on.

Gosh, could I really wake up to this every morning?

"What's wrong?" she asks.

"That was my mom. Apparently, Aiden has a big mouth and told his mom we were dating who in turn, told my mom."

"And she wasn't happy?"

"No, she was thrilled about you but very offended that she had to learn about her only son's love life from a friend. So we're summoned for a family Sunday lunch today."

"Oh." Lori's lips form the cutest little O shape. So cute, in fact, I have to restrain myself or I'll start kissing her again and never stop.

I scratch the back of my head. "Now, until yesterday, I would've simply explained the fake-dating situation to Mom..."

Lori quirks an eyebrow. "You would've told your mom I made up a relationship with you to make Aiden jealous?"

"Yeah, Mom's cool and she reads enough rom-coms to get your predicament."

"Okay, but she could've told Aiden's mom by mistake or someone else, and word could've gotten back to Aiden. Haven't you seen *Fight Club*? The first rule of Fight Club is: you do not talk about Fight Club. The second rule of Fight Club is: you *do not* talk about Fight Club!"

"Relax, Lola, it was just a hypothetical," I say, sitting up and shoving the covers off me.

Lori seems to get distracted in her outrage by gawking down at my bare stomach. I flex my abs a little and tease her. "You're staring like a perv, Archibald."

Lori's eyes dart back to mine. "That's because I'm not used to seeing you shirtless and wanting to..."

I bounce my pecks. "Test the goods."

"If we have to abide by your rules, you'd better cover yourself, Barlow." She pulls off my T-shirt and throws it at me.

The T-shirt hits me in the face and when it slides off, the tables are reversed because now Lori is in my bed with her black bra on and I have to muster all my self-control not to close the distance between us and forget all about my stupid rules.

My gaze must convey some of my thoughts because Lori blushes.

"What are you doing, Archibald?" I ask.

"Returning the favor?" she says, smiling coyly. Lori inches forward on the bed.

"How altruistic of you."

Lori nods and leans the rest of the way toward me. Her lips brush against mine softly. I drop my hands, clenching the sheets so hard I'm afraid I might tear them.

She plants tiny kisses across my jaw and down to my neck. Normally, I'd be all over this and we'd be ripping each other's clothes off, but now I'm fighting my body and aim to keep my hands to myself.

"Lori," I pant, "we can't."

"If I remember correctly," she whispers against my ear, "kissing is allowed."

"You're killing me."

"Good."

Her lips meet mine again and this time I have no strength to resist.

I grab the back of her neck, deepening the kiss. I rub my thumb on her cheek and kiss her jaw, her neck, and her mouth until she goes limp in my arms.

When I pull away, I straighten Lori up—all her bones seem to have melted, saying, "Should we call it even and get dressed?"

Lori smiles and I know I'm a goner. "You play dirty, Barlow."

"Oh, I play dirty? Miss Killing You Softly?"

She rolls her eyes, but she's smiling. "Can I borrow a hoodie? I only have my tank top from last night."

That might actually help me keep my sanity.

"Sure." I gesture to my right. "Mi closet es tu closet. I'll go make some coffee."

When Lori walks into the kitchen, she finds me seated at the table, cradling my phone.

"What's with the phone rocking?"

I look up and the breath gets knocked out of me. She has no right to look that stunning in an oversized hoodie. But with her legs bare, long hair falling on her shoulders, eyes still a little sleep-puffy, and a bright smile stamped on her kissed-up lips, she's beyond beautiful.

"Yeah," I say. "'Cause I just realized we have a bigger problem to solve before lunch with my mother."

Lori frowns questioningly.

"Remember that delightful story you spun Aiden about how

we first kissed on a night you supposedly got stood up by a blind date and I was out having drinks with my sister?"

"Yeah?"

"Jessica is going to know that's not true."

For a moment, Lori stares at me blankly, then sinks into the chair across from me. "And she's coming to lunch, too, today?"

"Probably. But even if she isn't today, she will eventually."

"What do you propose?"

"We have to bring her into the loop."

"You mean to tell her everything?"

"Yep."

"Oh, gosh." Lori covers her face with her hands.

"That's why lying is never a good idea."

Lori pokes her face out from behind her palms. "And she's going to cover for us?"

I sigh. "For the right price."

Lori slides off the chair and sits down on my lap, planting a quick kiss on my lips. "You mean actual cash?"

"I wish. No, it's going to be much, much worse."

"Like what?"

"For starters, she's going to saddle me with all the family duties we usually try to offload on each other."

Lori pats my shoulder mockingly. "You're old enough to bring out the trash." Then she steals a sip of my coffee and adds, "I'd better go home and feed the animals before they revolt. What time do I have to be ready?"

My parents live in the suburbs north of Chicago, so Lori's house is on the way to theirs. "I'll pick you up at noon."

"Perfect." Lori drops a kiss on top of my head. "Now be brave and give Jessica a call."

22

LORI

A firing squad of four awaits me at home. Leia, Han Solo, Ben, and Chewie are sitting in a tight line across the floor just behind the front door.

"Hello, sweeties," I greet them, pretending I didn't abandon them last night.

The cats narrow their eyes to various degrees of indignation and one by one turn to sit facing the other way.

"Well, I guess you're not interested in getting breakfast, then."

Now they get up, tails raised straight up into the air, and stroll toward their bowls, regaling me with the sight of their displeased kitty butts.

I hang my coat on a bookshelf, drop my bag on a pile of books, and hasten into the kitchen.

After a quick search of the cabinets, I fill each of the four food bowls with the sourpusses' favorite salmon meal. As much as I'd prefer to keep them vegetarian like me, the one week I tried, they went on a hunger strike, and I had to relent. Now they're pescatarian and happy.

As they eat, I stroke Leia behind the ears. She must've forgotten how offended she is with me because she purrs right away. I relax. If she's forgiven me, the rest will follow suit. Their feline society is very much a matriarchy.

Next, I grab the hens' pellets and go wish a good morning to my chicks. They don't hold grudges like their quadruped counterparts and happily flock by me, pecking the food straight from my hands. They've already laid eggs as well. I collect the eggs, go back to the kitchen to wash them, and use a pencil to write today's date on each before I store them in the fridge.

Ben jumps on the counter, then lifts on his hind legs to drop his front paws on my chest and butt his head against my chin. He's the cuddliest of my four furry babies.

"Yes, sweetie, I've missed you, too."

I pick him up and carry him upstairs with me. I deposit him on my bed and enjoy the cuddles while staring at the ceiling a little dazed.

Jace is in love with me.

It's a thought that both terrifies and thrills me. Thrilling because Jace is wonderful and being loved by him feels like the greatest gift in the world. Terrifying because a small part of me still can't believe it. He's the one person in the world who knows me, truly knows me, he's seen all the ugly and still loves me. Has been doing it quietly for all these years while I wouldn't shut up about Aiden.

I groan. Oh my gosh, poor Jace, the years of pining I've put him through. And I never knew, never suspected. He's been so good at keeping his distance. Now I understand all the barbed wire and Mr. Frost act, he was just trying to protect himself.

But now he isn't any longer. He's mine if only I want him to be.

The thought makes my heart skip a beat. I never saw it coming, but now that it's here, I can't deny the feelings creeping up inside me in response.

I replay last night's events in my mind. The way he kissed me was like nothing else mattered in the world. I roll in bed unable to suppress a smile as a warm fuzz spreads all over my body. Jace can make my skin burn even when he's not in the room. If this isn't being in love, well, then it's pretty darn close.

I allow myself a few more cuddles with Ben, then I kiss the top of his head and move into the bathroom to shower.

I don't stress about what to wear to lunch. A pair of navy chinos and a cozy sweater will do. Jace's parents are pretty laid back, and I've known them since the first weekend Jace and Aiden invited me to spend in Chicago with them.

The drive from campus took a little over two hours, hardly an adventure, but I'd hoped to crash at Aiden's place, fantasizing that would be the night we finally kissed. Instead, his brother had randomly decided to come home from Madison. With the spare room in Aiden's house suddenly taken, I ended up bitterly disappointed and sleeping in Jessica's room at the Barlows', which was pretty much always available. Jessica went to UC San Diego for college, so it wasn't like she could drive home on a whim. Still, Julia, Jace's mom, made pancakes the next morning, sweetening the deal. Now that I think back on it, I remember Jace wouldn't stop smiling that morning as I had breakfast with his family. He must've been so happy to have me there. And I never saw it, I never saw past the cocky act and the barbed wire. I've been such an idiot.

That weekend was also my first trip to Chicago, and it left me jaw-slacked and in love with the city. I'm from Sarasota, originally, and I wanted to spend my college years somewhere with seasons and as far away from home as I could. Urbana is a nice, quaint town, with a spectacular winter. But Chicago is a proper city and next-level gorgeous. And I know it's weird that I prefer to live in a city as opposed to open country considering my tendency to rescue all kinds of animals. But if I lived on a farm, I could adopt a million strays, and that would probably turn me into a full-time vet, which I wouldn't want because the only thing I care more about than rescuing pets is taking care of my patients. In a way, urban living forces me to keep a balance between the humans and animals I help, which has worked great so far.

A pang of worry courses through me as I imagine Jace having to adapt to my messy lifestyle. If things progress between us, would he ever be able to accept my baggage of weird hobbies and strays? Well, he's walking into this with his eyes wide open. It's not like I have any secrets from him. Over the years, Jace has been my confidant. I never opened up to Aiden the same way. With Aiden, I've always kept up the I-want-you-to-be-my-boyfriend-one-day filters, whereas Jace has been getting the raw, unembellished version of me since the start.

I've just finished drying my hair when a text pops up on my phone's screen. It's from Jace.

FROM JACE:

I'm outside

I hurry down the stairs and tip-toe across the entrance hall to make sure the cats don't spot me leaving again so soon. I put on my coat, grab my bag, and exit the house. On the landing, I close the door behind me as stealthily as I can and, equally carefully, slowly turn the key into the lock.

Then I spin toward the street and spot Jace waiting for me in his black Mercedes. A glint of sunlight on the driver's window masks half his profile, but that doesn't stop the fluttering that explodes in my belly as I take him in. How did I tune out his raw sex appeal for all these years? It's like I've been wearing a blindfold all this time, and now that it has come off, I can't help but look at him in an entirely different light.

I hurry across the street and mount shotgun. "Hey."

Jace smirks. "Why did you leave your house looking like a thief fleeing a crime scene?"

"I was trying not to get caught leaving again by the cats."

Jace's eyes widen. "The worst part of that statement is that I know you're being 100 per cent serious."

"How did things go with Jessica?" I ask.

"She basically owns us now."

"Pardon me?"

"We're going to have to volunteer at her free clinic."

"Don't we already volunteer there?"

"Yep, but one of her regular doctors is going on maternity leave next month, which means we basically won't have a life until next September."

I shrug. "As long as we can take our shifts together, I'm cool with that."

"I knew you'd be a glutton for punishment," Jace says as he starts the engine.

I don't mind volunteering. Plus, Jessica's free clinic is doing super important work to guarantee excellent healthcare, even to the less privileged. And if Jace and I are there together, it won't feel like work at all. A few more hours at the clinic is not what worries me.

"But your sister is sworn to secrecy?" I ask to make extra sure.

"Yep. She's going to give me a hard time about it forever, but Jessica has sworn she'll cover for us."

I let out a relieved breath.

"Especially since I've mentioned to her we might be catching feelings for real."

"And what did she say about that?"

"Told me I was cute and cooed over me like a mother hen."

"Oh, poor baby..."

Jace flashes me a crooked smile before concentrating back on the road. "Oh, you think I've had it bad? Wait until my mom starts treating you as her best chance at getting grandbabies..."

"Are you suggesting I shouldn't encourage the baby talk? Like saying I've walked past a baby store the other day and saw this cute pink onesie and"—I theatrically put a hand over my chest—"my heart swelled at the idea of holding tiny feet."

Jace stops at a red light and looks at me with pure terror in his eyes.

"I'm kidding! I'm kidding!" I say. "Plus, we're not having babies any time soon, given we're on a sex ban."

Jace laughs and shakes his head. "Maybe don't mention that either."

I make a zipper-over-mouth gesture. "Come on, your mom loves me. We'll be fine."

We arrive at the Barlows' house, and Jace parks in the driveway. He kills the engine, and we get out of the car. I follow him up the porch steps to the front door. His parents live in a two-story, farm-chic townhome in Long Grove, a suburban neighborhood on the outskirts of Chicago famous for its restaurants, historical sites, and quaint charm.

Jace opens the unlocked front door without ringing the bell and calls, "Mom, Dad, we're here..."

I follow him in and, as soon as I close the door behind me, I'm greeted by a scruffy white furball with a black patch right between his eyes.

"Oh, Crasher!" I kneel to pet the dog. He leans into me and yaps happily as I scratch him behind the ears—a valiant move on my part considering there'll be hell to pay when I come home smelling of dog. "Hi, sweetie, where is everyone?"

"They must be out back on the veranda," Jace says. He kneels to collect a tennis ball from the floor and bounces it twice, completely losing me Crasher's attention.

The dog eyes the ball eagerly.

Jace scoffs. "Oh, so now you remember about me?"

The Border collie mutt barks in response.

"All right, buddy, fetch." Jace throws the tennis ball, bowling style, gently rolling it on the floor down the long hall so as not to break anything with a flying projectile, I assume. Crasher darts after the ball, his nails making scraping sounds on the hardwood floor.

With the dog distracted, Jace guides me through the open space living room and kitchen, and out onto the veranda. This is my favorite room at his parents' house. The walls are made of glass and can be closed off in winter. While in the summer, they keep it mostly open as a sort of large covered patio.

Today, with the sun shining high above us, the room is flooded with light. Julia, Jace's mom, is putting the final touches to the table setting. She has a candlestick in one hand and is holding a flower vase in the other.

"Mom."

At the sound of Jace's voice, she unceremoniously drops both objects on the table and turns to us. "Jace." Julia gives her son a quick hug and a peck on the cheek and then focuses on me. "Lori," she says, her voice both surprised and happy as she pulls me into a bear hug. Then she pulls back, planting both her hands on my shoulders. "You always were part of the family, but now it's official."

Julia Barlow is one of those warm, nurturing people you can always count on. She has a soft, motherly smile and gentle eyes, but she can be blunt as hell when necessary. She's also a brilliant artist with a knack for portraits. Paintings of the family and of strangers adorn the entire house.

"Aw, there you are," Jace's father's voice booms across the room as the man himself emerges from the basement stairs, carrying two bottles of wine.

His wife lets me go and turns to him.

"Hunter." I wave.

Jace's dad smiles as he approaches. "Hi, Lori." He leans over and kisses my cheek.

"Hi, Dad," Jace says.

After the greetings, Jace and I help to finish setting up the table. And when everything is perfect in Julia's eyes, she disappears inside the house to bring out a tray of hors-d'oeuvres, which she offers us. "I made these to snack on while we wait for Jessica. She's always late."

Then, pointing at one side of the tray, Jace's mom adds, "This is the vegetarian side, dear."

"Thanks." I grab a carrot tart and pop it into my mouth. Even if Jace and I have been dating for less than a day, being at the Barlows' already feels like being with family. They've known me forever and I probably see them more than my own parents.

Two goat cheese croquettes later, Jessica strolls onto the veranda.

"Took you long enough," Jace says, once his sister arrives.

"I think what you meant to say was: My dear sister, I so look forward to our co-volunteering in the free clinic where we will spend hours together side by side helping the less fortunate." The threat to tell on us not too subtle in her tone.

"That's exactly what I meant to say," Jace agrees with a grin.

"Thought so." Jessica's smile is as sweet as it's evil.

"Are you getting more involved with the clinic, son?" Hunter asks.

Jessica doesn't leave him time to reply. "Devi is going on maternity leave next month, and Jace and Lori have offered to cover for her." With that, she turns to me. "Lori, you are a sight for sore eyes. I'm so glad I can openly call you my sister now."

Julia gasps at that. "You mean you knew about them?"

"Oh, please, Mom, I was *there* when it all began," Jessica replies theatrically, sticking to the fake version of how our relationship started.

If nothing else, Jace's sister is giving us bang for our bucks—or more bang for our slave labor.

With the excuse of hugging me, she whispers, "You've been naughty, darling, we have to talk soon." As she pulls back, Jessica winks at me.

Meanwhile, Hunter has been busy filling glasses with bubbly and he now distributes them around.

When everyone is stocked, he raises his glass in a toast. "To Jace and Lori, we'd lost hope we'd ever see this one settle down." Hunter tilts his flute in Jace's direction, who, in response, grimaces while still being a good sport. "And we couldn't have hoped for a better daughter-in-law."

They're getting *way* ahead of themselves, but we all cheer, drink, and then take our seats around the large table.

23

JACE

Two hours into the family reunion, Lori and I have been grilled more than a slow roasted rack of ribs. Mom and Dad have been firing questions at us non-stop. They want to absorb every detail of our relationship from the moment we allegedly kissed over the holidays to now.

Admittedly, Mom asks most of the questions. Dad tips his glass to us now and then to show us he approves.

I'm not the only one affected by the third degree. It's obvious that Lori is reaching the end of her rope, especially since we have to invent half the answers on the fly, and she's the worst liar.

I study her. Right now, it's hard to tell if it's the wine or the relentless interrogations that are making Lori blush and look at the floor as she replies to Mom's umpteenth question. "No, I haven't told my parents yet. When I went home for Christmas, the relationship was too new, and I don't want to tell them over the phone."

"Then you should both take a trip to Sarasota." Mom theatrically places a hand over her chest. "Trust me, you don't want them to learn about it secondhand."

Guess she won't drop the fact that Aiden's mom knew before her any time soon.

"Well, if you're planning a trip," Jessica chips in. "You'd better do it before Devi goes on maternity leave. You won't have many free weekends after that."

Don't I know!

Lori looks more overwhelmed by the minute.

"So," Dad says. "You two have been seeing each other for a month and a half," he summarizes. "Any plans for the future yet?"

"Enough with the cross-examination..." I finally intervene. "Can we talk about something else? We're here to celebrate."

"Fine," Mom says in a disappointed voice.

So I tease her a little. "Mom, I promise you that after today you know more about us than anyone else."

She smiles. "I guess we'll have plenty of time to get you kids to open up." Mom reaches across the table and squeezes Lori's hand. "You're going to be like a second daughter."

Jessica rolls her eyes. "Why, Mom, ain't I enough for you?" she asks teasingly.

My sister should've known better.

Mom lets go of Lori and turns to Jessica. "Oh, dear, sorry we neglected you. Did you want to talk about *your* love life?"

Jessica is the worst workaholic in the family and has literally no time for relationships.

Her face turns tomato red. "Uh, thanks, but no, thanks."

"How about we change the subject altogether?" I prompt.

"And what should we discuss?" Mom quips.

"How about your upcoming art exhibit?" I ask Mom. If anything can get her distracted from her grandkids plans, it's her art. "Is everything ready for the grand opening?"

"No. There is still much work to be done."

Mom talks on, leaving us free to relax for a minute.

Lori and I share a stare, and she mouths a thank you to me.

When Mom stands up to get dessert, Dad turns to Lori. "We should all go to the gallery opening together. What do you say?"

"I'd love to." Lori turns to me for confirmation.

And I nod.

"It's a date, then," my dad says jovially.

We eat Mom's famous Battenberg cake and homemade coffee cremino bonbons and at half past four, I dare to ask to take Lori home.

Jessica jumps at the opportunity to leave, saying her car is blocking ours, so she has to go, too.

Dad and I help Mom clear the table and do the dishes, and once everything is clean, we all get ready to go. We say our good-byes to my parents, and Jessica escorts us out, placing herself between us and looping an elbow with each of us.

"Kids," she says once we're halfway down the driveway and out of earshot of my parents. "You made me proud today. I wouldn't have been able to tell half of what you said was made up."

I roll my eyes. "Whatever, sis."

And then she actually surprises me by saying, "I'm thrilled you're giving this thing between you a real shot."

"But you're still going to blackmail us for free labor?"

"Totally." She lets us go and continues down to her car, waving back at us. "Bye, kiddos, don't do anything I wouldn't do."

Jessica gets in her car and backs out of my parents' driveway, honking in greeting as she speeds down the road.

After my sister disappears around the corner, Lori looks up at me, hugging my low waist. "Dealing with your family was so much worse than I expected."

I drop my forehead to hers. "What did you expect?"

"For it to be a little less *intense*," she says.

"Want me to take you home?"

"Yes, please." Lori pulls back and stares up at me. "Will you spend the night?"

I smirk. "I don't know. Are the cats going to accept me in their bed?"

"It's *my* bed, and they'd better get used to you sharing it."

I have to keep my emotions in check and not read too much into her words. It's just early days, and no matter how much I want it, I can't get my hopes up. Lori won't forget Aiden that easily. After all the years of secretly loving him, it won't be so fast.

I sure wouldn't be able to forget *her*.

We get into the car, and, as I reverse, I ask, "What do you want to do? Dinner and a movie?"

Lori looks at me and blushes like she just thought of more naughty activities—the forbidden kind—which makes me almost lose control of the car and reverse right into my parents' mailbox. Luckily, I hit the brakes in time.

Once I get onto the main road, Lori smiles. "I don't know about dinner," she says, patting her belly. "I'm still stuffed, but I'm definitely in the mood for a rom-com."

Mock-outraged, I frown. "*Movie*, I said *movie*. I never agreed to a rom-com."

Lori pats me on the shoulder. "But you have some catch-up to do on the fake-dating scene."

"I thought we weren't fake dating anymore?"

"We're not, but we need to put together a more detailed storyline about the first month of our relationship, so we'll be more prepared for the next grilling. A good rom-com could provide plenty of inspiration."

"How long do you think people will obsess about us?"

"Until we become old news."

"And were you serious when you said you wanted to tell your parents in person?"

"Yes." Lori nods, turning thoughtful. "But I want to wait until we're sure if that's okay with you?"

"Yep. Plus, you don't risk being ratted out like I was."

"That's why I keep a comfortable eleven-hundred-mile cushion between me and my family."

"Just in case you start fake dating your best friend and don't want to be discovered?"

"Exactly."

"Is fake dating really a thing? They made many movies about it?"

Lori mock-sighs and gently pats me on the leg. "Oh, Jacey Pooh, you literally have no clue what you've signed up for."

Maybe I don't, but I don't remember ever being more excited to find out.

24

LORI

Now that Jace and I are dating for real, Monday at work feels different. For starters I don't drive to work alone. Jace spent the night at my place yesterday and he dropped me here before going home to change.

Then as I settle at my desk to go through my emails before my first patient of the day arrives, I get an adrenaline kick when my phone buzzes with a text from Jace:

FROM JACE:

Can't stop thinking about you. See you at lunch ;)

The wink makes my heart do a little somersault. Even if it's just in a text, I can picture the real thing and, oh boy.

I smile to myself, feeling a flush rise to my cheeks. It's crazy how much things have changed between us in such a short amount of time.

Even more so when there's a knock on my door and I look up to find Aiden in the doorway, holding two cups of coffee and... nothing.

No breaths getting hitched in my throat. No quickening of my pulse. No flush to my cheeks. Just genuine affection for my best friend.

I give him a simple smile and a wave toward the empty chair in front of me.

"Good morning, Aidenberry. Coffee smells great, thanks!"

He hands me one of the cups and sits down across from me.

"So, how's life going?" he asks, sounding a little awkward.

"Never been better." I beam.

"Yeah, I can tell, you're practically glowing." He shifts on the chair and gives me another weird look before he says, "And I wanted to apologize." I frown. What does he have to apologize for? He must read the question in my expression because he elaborates, "Sorry it took me a minute to get on board with you and Jace dating. I guess I was a little shocked at first and worried about what it would mean for our friendship and, well, work..."

I stare at him a little dumbfounded. The fact that he, the guy I've lied to and forced Jace to lie to as well while I was trying to manipulate him into jealousy to sabotage his wedding, should apologize to me about it is beyond ridiculous. Aiden really is a good guy. Sweet, honest, loyal, true.

I shake my head as I look into Aiden's angel face. "You've got nothing to be sorry about. I'm sorry we didn't tell you sooner."

I'm sorry I've lied to you, I add in my head.

And even if he can't know, I don't mean just about inventing a relationship with Jace. I mean about all the years I haven't been honest with my feelings for him. If I had been, who knows, I could've discovered a lot sooner we were not meant to be, romantically, and I could've let my heart open for the other significant man in my life.

And I hate that even now, I can't tell him everything. Confess how truly new and explosive this thing growing inside me for Jace is. Ask his opinion, his counsel. But I hope that all the lies I've told will soon turn into the truth and that there'll be no more secrets between the three of us.

Aiden waves me off with a bright smile. "Oh, it's nothing, I understand why you didn't tell me right away and it's okay. I'm just glad you two are happy."

Our receptionist picks this moment to interrupt us. "Morning doctors, your first patients of the day have arrived."

"Be right there."

Aiden stands up and, on impulse, I do the same, rounding my desk and pulling him into a hug.

"What's this for?" He chuckles.

"For being the best friend in the world. Jace and I are so lucky to have you."

Aiden hugs me back but still teases me. "Already talking in the plural, you're going to give me diabetes."

"You eat too healthy for that," I joke.

Aiden pats my shoulders and then leaves. And even if I couldn't be completely honest with him, I feel better after talking to him. I'm relieved that he doesn't have a problem with Jace and I being in a relationship, that he's just happy for us. Kirsten sure is a lucky woman. No, I don't envy her anymore. I'm still not sure she's good enough for him, but if she makes him happy, I'm willing to give her the benefit of the doubt for the first time.

At lunchtime, Jace shows up right after my last appointment of the morning, looking impossibly hot and snuggly in a light-gray cashmere sweater.

My heart races as my best friend, ex-fake-boyfriend, now-real-boyfriend pulls me in for a kiss. It's only been a few hours since we saw each other, but it feels like an eternity. His lips are soft and warm against mine, sending shivers down my spine. I wrap my arms around his neck, pulling him closer as we deepen the kiss.

When we finally pull away, Jace grins down at me. "You have no idea how much I've been looking forward to this," he says.

I chuckle. "Oh, I have a pretty good idea."

He takes my hand and we join Aiden for lunch at the salad bar across the street. As the three of us eat together, it finally doesn't seem awkward. We're just us, joking and sharing medical cases. We're the same and yet everything is changed. But only for the best.

I'm happy, Aiden is happy, and Jace—he looks positively radiant. Like the broody cloud that followed him everywhere has lifted for good, the ice has melted and he's finally allowing himself to truly feel and be happy.

Our eyes meet across the table and he winks at me, and, oh gosh, the reaction the simple gesture sparks in me.

I feel a warm flush spread through my cheeks, and I know that I'm blushing. His smile is enough to set my heart racing, and I can't help but think how lucky I am to have him in my life. Aiden clears his throat and brings me back to reality, giving me a knowing look.

We all burst out laughing, and I swear I've never been happier in my entire life.

25

LORI

Thursday night I'm home alone, packing my bag for Aiden's bachelor party. This is the only wedding event I put my foot down for. I accepted my bridesmaid destiny stoically. Even when I was still fully in love with the groom, I went to the engagement party, the dress fittings, and, next Saturday, I'll attend the bridal shower —*shudder*. But no way was I going to end up stuck with Kirsten, Kendall, and their cadre of pageant queens for an entire weekend while Aiden and Jace, my real friends, were out having fun somewhere else. So, as unusual as it might be, I'm going to the bachelor party.

And dare I say that for the first time in my life I'm almost relieved Aiden is getting married. If he were still single, me dating Jace would rock our dynamics, making our three-way friendship weird, I suppose, unbalanced. But these days, Aiden hardly goes anywhere without Kirsten and, even if she'll never be part of the group, him having a wife will oddly balance things out if Jace and I keep dating.

And if we don't... my heart pangs. I don't want to think about it.

I don't see a scenario where we don't end up together, at least not at the pace my feelings are catching up to Jace's.

Anyway, for the bachelor party, we're leaving straight from the office tomorrow afternoon and heading to O'Hare to catch a plane to New Orleans—which means temperatures at least thirty degrees warmer.

I open a suitcase on the bed and turn to my closet, considering what to pack.

My new little black dress is a given, and I won't even need to wear tights with it in the mild southern weather. But I'd better pair the dress with flats. We're going to stroll bar to bar and I wouldn't last an hour walking in my new silver pumps.

I pull the dress from the hanger and fold it. But when I turn to put it in the suitcase, I find it full of cats. Leia has one side all to herself, while the other three have squeezed in the other half.

"What are you doing in my suitcase?"

The cats look up at me with big, round, innocent eyes.

"We already talked about this. Suitcases aren't for kitties."

I really hope they didn't bring me one of their special gifts—the last time I went on a trip I opened my suitcase to a dreadful smell of decay and rot, only to find a dead sparrow hidden among my clothes. I had to throw away most of what I had packed and buy new stuff. Aiden and Jace never let me hear the end of it.

Leia twitches her whiskers and stretches to the length of the suitcase.

I sigh. I pick up Ben and Chewie and drop them in the hall outside my room. Han Solo is next. But when I go back to move Leia, Ben has returned, and the other two are already jumping back on the bed.

I need a decoy and a little reverse psychology. "It's okay, you can stay, I'm going to use a different suitcase."

I grab a larger one that's too big for a weekend trip and open it in the hall. The cats ignore me at first, but as I fold dirty laundry into the case, their heads turn my way. Ben is the first to come. The silver tabby jumps into the bait suitcase, kneads the dirty laundry, and then goes to sleep.

The others follow suit, all except for Leia. Still in my trolley, she's staring at me with a challenge written all over her green eyes.

"Really?" She seems to want to tell me. *"You might trick those simpletons with your fake luggage, but you can't fool me."*

I go to the bed and pick her up. "Sorry, Smarty Paws, you have to go, too."

I drop her in the suitcase with the others and close the bedroom door. I don't reopen it until my actual bag is closed and zipped. No stinky surprises this time. When I check on them again, all the cats are curled up and asleep. I guess dirty laundry is a pretty comfortable mattress.

As the doorbell rings, I tip-toe past them and down the stairs.

I hop down the last few steps and fling the door open to find Jace on the other side, holding takeout pizza boxes. We didn't have plans to see each other tonight, but this, contrary to dead birds, is the kind of surprise I like.

Jace's smile is a killer—crooked, sexy, gets me every single time—as he says, "I thought we'd get one last deep dish before we head to a foreign land."

"I'm so glad you're here. I'm starving."

Jace raises an eyebrow questioningly.

"I got derailed packing against the cats." I wave the affirmation off to say it's not important and relieve Jace of the pizza boxes. I drop them onto a pile of books and pull my boyfriend into the house and in for a long kiss.

"Were you starving for food or for me?" Jace asks when I finally let him go.

"Both, Mr. I Couldn't Spend One Night Away From My Girlfriend."

Jace shrugs, cocky. "It's not you, I only came for your Netflix."

I smile, not even sure he's kidding. In the past week, I got him addicted to the fake-dating trope. We watched *The Wedding Date*, *The Proposal*, *To All The Boys I've Loved Before*, *10 Things I Hate About You*, and *Pretty Woman*.

Shaking my head, I recoup the pizza boxes from the book tower and move into the kitchen.

"Are you all packed?" I ask as I take out paper napkins and two glasses from the cabinets.

"Yep, got my case stashed in my trunk."

I drop the glasses on the table and grab two sodas from the fridge. "Uh-uh, expecting to be invited to stay overnight." I sit opposite Jace. "Cocky."

"Again, not you. Now that I've experienced the joy of falling asleep with multiple cats on my legs, cutting the circulation to my lower limbs, I can't go back to the discomfort of sleeping star-fished on my California King. It's just impossible."

"I bet it is." I take a slice of pizza. "Mmm, this is delicious. Where'd you get it?"

"Pizzeria Uno."

"It's a good way to say goodbye to Chicago before I have to dodge eating alligator meat."

"We're not going to the jungle. I'm sure New Orleans will have plenty of vegetarian options."

"Ready for all the debauchery?" I ask Jace.

Jace smirks in a way that punches me straight in the guts. "I thought we had rules, Lola."

I swallow, thinking of the two nights ahead of us. When we booked our trip, it seemed like a perfectly reasonable thing to share a room with Jace. We'd done it plenty of times in the past.

And no matter that we've basically slept together every night for the past week, sharing a hotel bed after we will have been out drinking and dancing all night is going to make it a thousand times harder not to break the rules.

26

JACE

We land at New Orleans Airport late on Friday night. As the arrivals doors swish open on the outdoors, we're buffeted by a gust of lukewarm, humid air, a stark contrast to the cold, clear, dry winds of Chicago. We load our suitcases into two separate cabs—we're six in total, five dudes plus Lori—and give the drivers the address of our hotel in the center of the French Quarter.

After the check-in, the guys want to head straight out to get the party started. So Lori and I barely have time to drop our bags in the room and get changed before we have to be downstairs again. And it's a good thing I don't have to dwell on the fact that Lori and I are sharing a hotel room. I've gotten pretty used to her sleeping in my bed, but a hotel setting feels different, plus, we're going to be drinking tonight—and co-sleeping, well, it'll be just torture.

Dude, you're the one who set the rules.

Right, because if I gave in and had sex with Lori, and then it didn't work out between us, I wouldn't be able to come back from that. Already I'm in too deep. It was one thing to want Lori and not have her. But to have her and then lose her, I wouldn't survive that.

I'm afraid that, already, if something goes wrong between us I'll drown.

But, gosh, the way she bites her lower lip as she stares at the giant California King bed in the middle of the room is killing me softly all the same.

"Looks cozy," she says, sounding way too casual.

"It'll be fine," I tell her, even though I know it's a lie.

Lori shrugs and goes to drop her suitcase on the bed.

"I need to get changed before we head out," she says, picking a slippery thingy out of the suitcase that looks like it'll be the end of me. Dress in hand, she scurries to the bathroom, closing the door behind her.

I drop my bag on the small couch in the corner and get changed, too.

I pull on a clean T-shirt and jeans and wait for Lori seated on the bed. I don't have to wait long—she flings the bathroom door open, and I stifle a groan as she rounds the bed to stand in front of me. Her hair is swept up in a high ponytail and her eyes are outlined in smoky eyeshadow. And the dress she's wearing hugs every single one of her gorgeous curves, and it's shorter than what I'm used to seeing on her. Pure temptation.

I drag my gaze away from her legs, up her body, and meet her eyes.

Lori bites her lip and looks at me with those serious eyes. "I'm ready," she breathes.

"Yeah, I can see. You look gorgeous."

I don't move, I can't. I'm afraid that if I get up from this bed now, I'll pull her down and spend the next two days shut in this room seeing to her.

Lori shifts on her feet at the intensity of my stare on her and awkwardly points at the door with her thumbs. "Should we join the others?"

"Don't tell me you're looking forward to all the partying."

Lori laughs. "I'm looking forward to one thing and one thing only."

"And what's that?"

"Dancing."

"I'm not going to stop you."

She lifts my hand and twirls underneath my stretched arm. "No, you're going to dance with me."

"I doubt it."

"Wanna bet?" Lori lets go of my hand and bounces on her flat heels.

I watch her for a few moments, and then I study our room. "I don't know. What's in it for me if I win?"

"What would you want?"

I stand up and stalk toward her. Lori backs away until her shoulders are pressed against the wall. I crowd her space. Lori licks her lips, and I lean in to kiss her. It's electric.

I run my hands up the small of her back and move my lips closer to her ear. "Dibs on the shower for a month."

Since we started dating for real, I spend most nights at her place and she always gets in the shower first in the morning. Aaaand she takes forever in there.

Lori pushes me back and looks up at me. "Dibs on the shower? Is that really your only heart's desire?"

I shrug. "I don't particularly enjoy taking lukewarm showers."

Her mouth gapes open in outrage. "Are you accusing me of stealing all the hot water?"

"I'm just stating a fact. I've never seen anyone take such long showers."

"Sorry." Lori bites her lip again. "I thought your super fancy apartment got an infinite supply of warm water or something. It never seems to run out."

I want to point out that it's not just at my house where we barely ever go as per her demanding pets. But she already looks distraught, so instead I tease her some more. "At least I have your celestial singing to console me."

Lori pushes me away for good now. "That, I'm not sorry for. If you don't appreciate Taylor Swift, then we can't ever be together."

I laugh. "What do you want if you win?"

I see a light flicker in her eyes.

"Nu-uh, Archibald, that's against the rules."

"I didn't say anything," she protests.

"You didn't have to."

Lori comes closer to me and wraps her arms around my waist. "I was about to propose that if I win, we shower together, so we won't have to fight about the hot water."

I take a step back after having a vivid vision of what seeing Lori naked under the shower would do to me. "Yep, totally against the rules. Think of something else, Lola."

She pouts. "You're such a party pooper."

I smile and grab her hand. "Let's go before the others begin to wonder where we've disappeared to."

* * *

The French Quarter is busy on a Friday night. It's not Mardi Gras yet, but the streets are already buzzing with all sorts of people. A man is singing to the crowd on a balcony. Below him, a river of street performers and revelers flows around us.

We follow a zigzagging path down the narrow alleys filled with tourists and shop stalls, making a beeline for Bourbon Street. Live music pours out of every bar and restaurant we pass, the fast rhythm already pounding in my chest. The guys soon tire of wandering around aimlessly and walk into a random bar. Inside, it's dark, it's crowded, the music is blaring, people are dancing, and glasses keep clinking. We're lucky to find a free table by the window, and the guys go straight to the bar where they order the first round of drinks. Soon followed by another.

Lori gulps down her second mojito and then drops her empty glass on the table and places her hands on my shoulders, steering me toward the dancefloor, where it's even darker and sweatier and louder. Lori slinks her body against mine, her head on my shoulder. It doesn't take long before I get distracted as we sway in time with the music. She smells of perfume and shampoo—I can hear my heartbeat in my ears. Lori turns, her fingers tugging at my T-shirt. She pulls my face down to hers, and we're kissing and dancing at the same time.

When we break the kiss, we keep dancing, locking eyes. It's too loud to talk, but we don't need words to communicate, we know each other so well.

She gives me a smug smirk, meaning I lost the bet.

I raise an eyebrow, signaling I still don't know what her prize will be.

Lori shrugs, telling me she will come up with something.

The beat of the music changes and a young, good-looking woman sidles up to me grinding on my side, making moves as if to push me away from Lori. But my Lola is not having it, she pulls me away and switches places with me, inserting herself between me and the woman, just like she did at the wedding party meet and greet with Kirsten's sister. My would-be suitor goes in search of a different prey.

I spin Lori round and pull her against me, back to front, whisper-yelling in her ear, "I like it when you go all possessive, Archibald."

Lori struggles to get free and faces me again. "What can I say?" she shouts back. "I don't like to share."

I can't help but grin at her fiery expression.

I'm about to pull her to me again when Aiden's brother appears next to us. "Come on, guys, we're switching bars."

We squeeze our way between the crowd and out of the bar, back onto the crowded street. We follow the others holding hands, high on the drinks, the dancing, and the kissing.

Aiden's brother leads us to a place that is more a club than a bar. Soon, we're inside, sinking into wide, comfy couches around a table, surrounded by twinkling lights, a low hum of music, and a sea of people.

We order drinks at the bar on the other side of the room. I stay next to Lori, our legs touching. I have to lean in to talk to her over the music and then, suddenly, I become hyperaware of her presence again. Her smell, her smile, that secret twinkle in her eyes. I'm drunk—not on alcohol, but on her. I'm 100 per cent gone—intoxicated.

I reach for her hand. Lori's fingers are cold despite the heat of the room. I rub small circles on her palm. Her touch is the only thing keeping me tethered to reality. I look up at her, she's looking at me, her eyes are soft and she's biting her lip in her signature nervous gesture.

"You look kind of scary intense right now," she says.

How can she always read my mind?

I move my hand from her palm to her wrist, pulling her closer to me. "How can you tell?"

Lori shrugs. "The look in your eyes."

I've never been one for PDAs, but the way she understands me makes me want to pin her against the wall and kiss her for the entire world to see.

Everyone else is already on the dancefloor, singing along to some song, and I tug Lori's hand to get her to stand up. She's still watching me with that wicked gleam in her eyes.

I lean in to kiss her. I try to make it soft, sensual, but then I get carried away and we're swirling, twisting, and twirling to the beat of the music, a dance we've perfected together, coming up for air only to kiss again. Our bodies are pressed at every angle, but it's not enough. I want more. I want it all.

But I can't have it. Not yet. Not until she's sure it's me she wants.

I have to give her time, wait, and be patient. But right now, I can't think straight. Not with her hand on the back of my neck and her lips touching my jaw and then, even more dangerously, my earlobe.

Lori smirks and whispers in my ear, "Now you look naughty intense."

I can't take it. I want her so much it's killing me.

I take a step back and basically run out of the club.

Lori follows me outside and is by my side in an instant.

"Hey, what's up?"

"Sorry." I rake a hand through my hair. "It's just that..." I cup her face. "I love you. I love you so much."

27

LORI

I want to say it back, I really do. But for some reason, the words seem to get stuck in my throat. I've never been scared of my feelings—no matter how unwanted or unrequited they've been in the past. But with Jace, everything is so different. I have no idea what to do with my heart. I want to give it all to him, but I'm scared that I won't be able to pick up the pieces if something goes wrong between us. It's as if I'm falling so hard and I can't do a thing to stop it.

I'm petrified. For me, for him. I just don't know if it's fear of hurting him or of hurting myself. I know I can trust him, but I still don't know if I can trust myself—not after all the years I've spent wanting Aiden. Can I be really over him? Just like that? It feels that way. But what if *I* end up hurting Jace?

Or maybe it's the intensity in his eyes that's keeping me frozen in place. The desperate way he's staring at me. The way his gaze makes me feel like I'm all he needs. Or how bad I want to believe he's all I need.

But I can't.

Not yet.

I bring my hands to his face and gently turn it toward me. Jace looks so tired of waiting.

"I still need time," I whisper.

I'm not sure why I'm saying this because I want to be with him, so badly. But I owe it to the both of us to be prudent, to take it slow.

Jace pulls me into a hug, resting his chin on top of my head. "Take all the time you need, Lola. I'm not going anywhere."

Well, Jace is making it really easy to believe I am out of love with Aiden and very much in love with him.

* * *

The next morning, I wake up alone in our bed.

I run my hand over the sheets, feeling the soft fabric slip between my fingers. I roll onto Jace's side of the bed, burying my face in his pillow. The scent of his soap and shampoo still lingers on the fabric. I close my eyes and take a deep breath, imagining he's still lying next to me, his arms around me.

I roll back to my side, letting out an exasperated growl. If all we did last night was sleep in each other's arms, I'm to blame. But this thing between us is too precious. I don't want to ruin it by being in a hurry. I want to savor every moment I am with Jace, every brush of skin, every kiss.

I sit up on the bed, unable to suppress a smile at the stack of neatly folded clothes piled on a chair. Even my dress, which I discarded on the floor last night eager to get under the covers after a night of partying, is now strung on a hanger, dangling outside the wardrobe.

The little neat freak probably couldn't help himself. Is it weird that I suddenly find his obsessive need for order adorable?

The question has barely popped into my head when the room

door opens and Jace walks in, looking impossibly handsome in gym shorts and a sleeveless hoodie.

He's holding a coffee tray and a paper bag in his hands and comes toward the bed, dropping both on the mattress.

"Breakfast in bed, uh, Barlow? We're not pulling any punches, I see."

"Shut up and eat before the croissants go cold."

I squeal like an over-excited child and grab the bag. The freshly baked fragrance that wafts up as I open it is heavenly, as is the first bite of pastry.

"I've never tasted anything so good," I say with my mouth still half full.

Jace smiles but looks kind of nervous. I hope he isn't still upset about last night.

"Is it all for me?" I ask, dangling the bag. "Or you want in on the breakfast action?"

Jace's eyes darken for a second before he snatches the bag from me and gives his croissant a ridiculously large bite.

I can't help but giggle and relax a bit. He's okay. We're okay.

I stretch out on the bed, savoring my croissant and sipping coffee.

The bedroom is silent except for the sound of our chewing and the rumbling of our stomachs. Jace's got the biggest grin on his face, watching me eat.

"What?" I ask, after swallowing.

"You're cute when you're scarfing down food like you haven't eaten in a week."

I roll my eyes, pretending to be annoyed. I'm really not—I want to see that grin on his face every day of my life.

I give him another playful scowl. "What time did you get up, you annoying morning person?"

"It's almost noon, Lola."

"What?" I stare out the window. The sun is shining, the sky is clear, and the birds are chirping happily from the trees. It really looks like full-blown daylight. "I haven't slept in so late since forever."

Jace raises a cocky eyebrow. "Well, when was the last time you stayed out dancing all night?"

"Good point. You think Aiden is still wasted? They kept making him drink last night."

"Yep, Dr. Collymore is sporting a pretty terrible hangover. But don't worry, I stopped at the pharmacy and dropped a recovery pack in his room."

"You had a busy morning. Any more impulse buys?"

Jace's gaze shifts to the side, shyly almost. "As a matter of fact, yes." He rummages in his hoodie front pocket and takes out a small box. "I saw this in a shop window and thought of you."

I stare at the box, torn between elated and terrified.

"What's in it?"

"Open it."

I open the box to reveal the most gorgeous antique band. White gold inlaid with a sophisticated floral design accentuated by tiny diamonds.

I stare up at him, my heart beating in my chest at a thousand beats per minute.

"Don't worry." Jace smirks. "I'm not proposing."

"You aren't?"

He shakes his head, taking the ring out of its case. "It's a promise ring."

I frown. "What's a promise ring?"

Jace full-on smiles, making my heart drop to my stomach. "From what I gathered, it's a way for dudes who aren't ready to propose to gain a little extra time... or, like in this case, a way for me to give you something without completely scaring you off."

"Jace, I—"

"Nuh-uh, shush, it's my turn to talk."

He gently grabs my hand and slips the band on my ring finger. "I promise to wait for you for as long as it takes for you to be sure. And to love you, your four cats, six hens, and thousand rescue books for as long as my heart shall beat. I promise to love you even when you finish all the hot water in the shower and sing Taylor Swift at the top of your lungs for half an hour non-stop."

My heart melts a little with each new promise.

"I promise to love you even when you kick me under the covers at night and hog all the blankets."

"That's not true," I protest. "I'm a very still sleeper. The cats would never let me kick around the bed."

"And that might be true when you're sleeping with *them*, but when you sleep with *me*, it's like you have to make up for all the nights of stillness. I could get motion sick for how much you thrash."

He's looking at me with those big light-blue eyes and the heart-melting smile, and I know he's not lying.

Jace leans closer, his nose brushing against my cheek. "I promise to always be there when you need me and be strong when you're vulnerable. I promise to never lie to you, to always tell you the truth, even when it hurts."

Jace trails light kisses along my cheek, making me shudder. I wish he would stop being so sweet and so serious. My head is spinning and I can hardly breathe, and it's not just because he's so close I can feel his heat against my skin.

"I promise to keep on loving you every day, until my last breath, even when you get gray hair or when you lose your teeth, because you are the love of my life, Lola Archibald, and I will never stop loving you."

"Jace, I—" I croak, clearing my throat. I'm saying it, I'm going to tell him I love him. "I—"

Bang. Bang. Bang.

A loud pounding on the door makes me jolt on the bed.

"Come on, lovebirds," Aiden's brother yells from the other side of the door. "We're leaving for lunch in fifteen minutes."

"Ouch," Jace says, kissing my nose. "Guess you'll have to cut your shower short today, babe."

I whack his beautiful face with a pillow. "You're the worst."

And I love you, I add in my head.

I'll say it to him out loud... soon...

28

LORI

I wait until Tuesday evening to knock on Aiden's door. Jace left early since he sees patients in the morning on Tuesdays while both Aiden and I receive them in the afternoon. I finished my consultations a while ago, and even if it's been a long day, I stayed back, leaving my door open to keep track of the comings and goings of our practice.

Even if I checked the time of Aiden's last appointment—Mrs. Davenport at five thirty—with our receptionist, I wanted to make sure he wouldn't leave before I could talk to him.

So the moment I spotted Mrs. Davenport cross the hall, I dashed out of my office to knock on his door, barely leaving Aiden time to drop his white coat.

Now, as his calm voice utters a polite, "Come in," from the other side, I nervously enter.

Aiden is at his desk, white coat still on, typing on his keyboard. When I get in, he looks away from the screen and greets me with a big open smile—one that used to cause all kinds of flutters in my belly. Only lately, it seems I'm more into crooked grins.

"Lori," he says. "What's up?"

"Do you have a moment? I need advice."

"For you, always. Do you need help with a patient or..." he trails off.

"No, Dr. House, my patients are fine. It's personal." The irony of going to Aiden for advice on how to navigate my relationship with Jace is not lost on me...

"The juicy stuff, then." Aiden playfully waggles his eyebrows. "Let me finish writing this note in Mrs. Davenport's file and I'm all yours."

Five minutes later, Aiden swivels in his chair to face me, giving me his undivided attention. "Spill the beans, Dr. Archibald, I'm all ears."

I hesitate only for a second before asking, "How did you know Kirsten was the one?"

Aiden low-whistles. "I suppose we're really talking about you and Jace?"

I nod because, at this point, I'm pretty sure I love Jace. But with him, I don't have the chance to explore things and see how the relationship would go. The kind of all-in commitment he's asking of me is comparable only to taking wedding vows, and the only person I'm close to who's about to do just that is Aiden. Hence why I'm sitting in his office having the most awkward conversation of my life.

"Any particular reason you're asking how to recognize The One?" Aiden smirks. "Do you want to propose or something?"

"No, no," I say. More I can't keep my hands off my best friend any longer without risking auto-combustion every five seconds, but I also don't want to mistake lust for love and ruin something with the potential to be my forever. How do I explain that to Aiden?

He keeps staring at me questioningly.

I need to share the truth, or at least part of it.

"Okay, I might need to make a small confession."

Aiden chuckles. "You mean *another* one? Hit me."

Blushing tomato red head to toe, I say, "I might've slightly overplayed how... sexually active my relationship with Jace is..."

Aiden frowns uncomprehendingly.

So I continue, "You know..."

He shakes his head. "I actually don't."

Turning even more crimson, I blurt, "We haven't done it yet."

Aiden's eyes widen. "So the knocking boots morning, day, and night..."

"Never happened. We only kissed."

"Okay." Aiden seems to digest this development and not be exactly displeased by it. "Why? How did you get Jace to be with you for two months without sex?"

Because in reality, it's been only a few weeks and he's had years of practice. Of course, I can't say any of that, so I go with another partial truth. "Actually, he's the one who wanted to wait."

"He did?"

"Yeah. Before we do anything, he wants me to be sure he's *The One*! He said we can't risk our friendship for anything less."

Aiden's grin turns foxy. "Is the only reason you came in here today that you want to..." He waggles his eyebrows again.

I grab a medication flyer, crumple it into a ball, and throw it at him. "Don't be a jerk."

Aiden dives left to avoid the projectile. "Okay, okay, Lori, no need to resort to violence. I guess I'm just not used to you coming to me for love advice."

No, because I always went to Jace for my love advice, mostly about you.

"Please be serious. How do I know for sure?"

"Sorry, Lori, the skies won't open to send you a missive stating you've found your soulmate."

"Sucks." I pout. "How did you know with Kirsten? How did you go from I love you, to I'm in love with you, to I want to spend the rest of my life with you?" And if a month ago hearing the answers to these questions would've killed me, now I'm just eager to get an insight.

"The more we dated, the more Kirsten became a priority for me. I started rearranging, re-prioritizing, and reimagining my life around her."

Despite myself, I snort, "Yeah, we noticed the dropout from our usual hangouts."

"Come on, guys, we still hang. Just less. That's what happens when you're in a good relationship, and it never feels like a sacrifice."

Okay, I'm definitely spending more time with Jace and reimagining my life around him. I'm even vacuuming my house regularly. *Check.*

"Then there's the attraction," Aiden continues. "Only, it's more like a craving, a physical, inescapable need. It's a constant yearning at the back of your mind and that feeling almost like a rush when you think of them."

Check and *check.*

"That can happen with any new relationship." Aiden ponders for a moment. "You know you're really in trouble when you start to even find their quirks attractive. Like if you ever thought Jace's neat-freak tendencies were cute, I'd say you're toast."

I blush. I believe I said adorable, even so, *check.*

"And last but not least." Aiden pins me with a stare. "You want to say those big three words. Like, they want out, and you can hardly keep them to yourself anymore."

Check.

In New Orleans, I almost blurted it out at random a thousand times.

Aiden shrugs. "But I guess you know when it just feels right."

It does. It so does.

Last check.

"That sound like what you have with Jace?"

I swallow and give him a tiny nod.

Aiden sags back in his chair. "Then I guess you have your answer."

We share a loaded stare. Once again, I'm not exactly sure what's crossing his mind.

"Can I ask you something?" he says.

Guess I'm about to find out.

I nod again.

"It's about a night ages ago," Aiden starts.

Instinctively, I know at once what night he's talking about. The night of Never Have I Ever. Still, I play dumb. "Oh, which one?"

"We were at some stupid house party near campus..." he continues, and I've never been more glad I'm not sitting near a polygraph machine.

I shrug. "We've been to a million house parties in college."

"That night we were playing Never Have I Ever."

Yep, he's talking about *the* night!

"I can't remember who said never have I ever been in love with my best friend."

Tracy Dillon, I want to say, it was Tracy Dillon. I can remember every second of that night because I've replayed the DVD a million times in my head.

"So?" I just brought "playing dumb" to the next level.

"You took a shot," Aiden says, and the world stops for a minute.

I look at him, unable to speak. How many times have I imagined him asking me exactly this question? I legit thought he'd forgotten about that night the following day after listening to my rambled excuses. But if he's bringing it up now, it means the game must've stuck at the back of his mind all this time, too. Why? And what's the point of asking me now?

Since I'm not giving him anything, Aiden goes on, "The next morning I came to your room to ask you about it, but you said you couldn't remember anything of the night before... But was the shot about Jace? Even that long ago?"

Our eyes lock, a million unspoken words passing between us. As I stare into his gentle blue eyes, an entire other life passes before me. A life in which neither of us had chickened out that morning. A life in which we'd be together.

No, the shot wasn't about Jace back then. I suspect we both know it. But it would be now. And no good would come out of admitting the truth, so what's the point? There's no reason to dig up old, unexpressed feelings between Aiden and me. We've left the topic buried for fifteen years and now it has actually, inexorably died in its tomb.

I look Aiden straight in the eyes. "Yes, it's always been about Jace."

Aiden nods, accepting the lie. "Well, I guess all is well what ends well. You know, I suspect he's had a thing for you forever as well. But I got the impression that somehow he was convinced you were more into me. I bet that if he knew, he would've dropped the pact a lot sooner."

I'm nodding my head along happily, basking in the glory of Jace's undying love for me until the last part of Aiden's speech sinks in and the lovebirds' singing comes to a screeching halt, like a broken disk.

"What pact?" I ask.

Aiden blinks, with a deer-in-headlights look on his face, repeating, "What pact?"

Yeah, nice try, buddy. "You just said if Jace had known about my feelings for him, he would've dropped the pact a lot sooner. What. Pact?"

"You must've heard me wrong."

"Nu-uh, my eardrums are in perfect shape, Dr. Collymore. Out with it!"

Aiden shifts uncomfortably in his chair and then he starts talking...

29

JACE

At home, I've just gotten out of the shower and I'm in my room, pulling up a pair of boxers and sweatpants getting ready to commute to Lori's house, when my phone pings on the bed with a message from Aiden:

FROM AIDEN:

Man, I screwed up

Multiple scenarios play in my head.

Did he cheat on Kirsten after we left the bar on Saturday? Nah, that doesn't seem like Aiden.

Is he having cold feet and said something stupid? Could be... for all his good qualities. Sometimes Aiden speaks before he thinks.

But the next message clarifies the screw-up has nothing to do with him or his upcoming nuptials.

FROM AIDEN:

I accidentally let it slip with Lori about the pact

I don't need to ask what pact.

The next text arrives just as an incessant pounding starts at my door.

FROM AIDEN:

Just a heads up, she might be coming your way, fuming

Yeah, no kidding!

I pull on a white T-shirt and brace myself as I go open the door.

"Tell me it isn't true." Lori storms into the apartment, eyes blazing, hair wild. She wheels on me, gesticulating like a mad person. "Tell me you're not single-handedly responsible for the last fifteen years of heartbreak and misery."

I sigh. "I'm not responsible. If Aiden really wanted to get with you, he would have. Pact or no pact."

"So you're not even trying to deny it."

"What? That Aiden and I made a stupid pact freshman year and never spoke about it for another fifteen years?" Barring the last time Aiden brought it up two weeks ago.

"Don't give me that." I hate to see how Lori's lower lip trembles. *Loathe* it. Despise myself for being what caused the hurt. "You knew Aiden would take a promise like that seriously and stick to it, no matter what. All the times I thought something might happen between us, and he pulled back at the last minute as if he'd suddenly remembered he wasn't supposed to be romantic with me. It drove me insane. I could never understand it. And when I spoke about it to you, you just stood there and said nothing! Not once. Did you have fun? Did you enjoy watching me cry?"

Heat rises on my neck all the way to my ears. "You think I had fun? I was in love with you, Lori, and all you ever wanted to talk about was how much you loved Aiden."

"And you just stood there, knowing you were the only thing

keeping us apart. What kind of love is yours? The selfish"—now she makes a ridiculous dude voice—"'I'll have her or no one else will' kind?"

"Do you really think that if at one point, Aiden had fallen in love with you, a stupid pact would've stopped him from coming onto you?"

"Well, you made darn sure that possibility never even crossed his mind. Or that if it did, he'd think twice before acting on it. Take the option off the table. Why? Why would you've done such a cruel thing to me?"

"Because seeing you two together would've killed me," I shout.

Lori jumps, taking a step backward, and I try to calm down.

I take a step toward her, putting my hands forward, signaling I mean no harm. "Lori, I'm sorry. I know what I did was selfish but —"

"No buts." Lori points a finger at me. "Don't think you can stand there looking all sexy with your damp hair and sweatpants and mollycoddle me into forgiving you. If you were so into me you thought you might die if I got with Aiden, you could've done a million other things—"

"What things?" I snap.

"Tell me how you felt, for starters. Let *me* choose who I wanted to be with."

"You would've chosen him."

Lori stares at me without speaking. Without denying it.

Her silence slices into my heart like a knife.

I chuckle bitterly. "At least I guess we have our answer now. For you, it's always been him, it's still him, it'll always be about Aiden."

"No," she says in a whisper. "This hurts so much because it is about *you*. The person I trusted for years with my innermost secrets, the person I was about to trust with my heart. But now...

how can I? Knowing what you did? Knowing how cold and calculating you can be?"

"So this is over?" I point between us.

"No," she says, only ice and steel in her voice. "It never even started."

Lori grabs her purse and walks past me, not sparing me a second glance. The door slams shut five seconds later, and I know she's gone. I've lost her.

* * *

Two full glasses of vodka later, a soft knock on my door makes me jolt. I disregard the sound, it must be the alcohol that's making me hallucinate my hopes coming true. Lori coming back to forgive me, for her to tell me she can't be without me and that the past is in the past.

But that's impossible. I saw the look in her eyes. Lori isn't forgiving me any time soon. Maybe one day, we will go back to being friends, but everything else? Nah, I spoiled that for good.

When I hear a second knock, I sit straighter on the couch. I didn't make that up—the knock was real.

"Dude, I know you're in there," Aiden's voice comes from the other side of the door. "Open up."

Real knock... still no girlfriend.

I groan. "Go away."

"Not happening. Either you let me in or I'll ask Denzel for the spare key, claiming it's a medical emergency."

"Then I'll press charges for breaking and entering."

"Come on, man, let me in."

I don't respond.

"I'm not going away until we talk. I'll stay outside your door, pleading, all night if necessary. I'm sure your neighbors would be thrilled."

Still, I say nothing.

"I'm serious," Aiden yells. "Not gonna leave."

My head is already throbbing, and all this yelling is making the ache worse. Cursing under my breath, I stand up and stumble to the door.

I fling it open. "Happy now?"

Aiden is standing on the other side holding a six-pack of beers, looking as well put-together as always in his elegant blue coat. But as he takes in my appearance, his eyes widen, and Mr. Perfect loses some of his composure. "How much did you have to drink?"

I shrug.

"I see these aren't necessary," he says, raising the beers and pushing his way past me into the kitchen.

Aiden puts the six-pack into the fridge and asks, "You'd be better off with a soda or a cup of strong coffee. Which one would you prefer?"

"I'd actually like one of those beers," I say, making my way to the fridge.

"Nu-uh." Aiden steps in front of the door, blocking the way. "You can have a soda or you can have a coffee."

I grunt. "Coffee, then."

Aiden messes with pottery in the kitchen, and I go back to the couch to stare at the void my life has become.

Five minutes later, Aiden drops by my side with two steamy mugs of coffee.

"Here, man."

Aiden lets me take a sip before pressing on. "That bad, uh?"

"Worse."

"I get Lori was mad. She gave me an earful, too, but nothing too bad. She'll come round."

"No, dude, you and me, we're in a very different boat. Lori might forgive you right away, but she won't forgive *me.*"

"Why? What's the difference? We made the same pact, didn't we? And I get you guys have deeper feelings involved now... but..." Aiden scoffs. "Listen, man, she's probably just mad you didn't hit on her sooner."

At that, I let out a bitter chuckle. "Yeah, right. Quite the opposite, I'm afraid."

Aiden frowns. "What's that supposed to mean?"

It might be the heartbreak, the vodka, or the fact that I've nothing left to lose, but I don't feel like lying to Aiden anymore. I should confess all my sins, lose both my best friends in one go, and be done with it.

"She's always been in love with you. It's never been about me."

"No, you're wrong. Lori was sitting in my office not two hours ago, telling me how she thought you were the one."

I don't let my heart soar. "She might've been in lust with me for a minute to get over the fact that you're getting married. But trust me, Lori has been holding a torch for you since the night we stole those stupid garden gnomes together. And the reason she's so mad at me is that I knew how she felt about you and I used the pact to keep you two apart..."

Aiden is silent for a long moment. "So it was deliberate?"

I nod.

"Why?"

"Because I'm a selfish dirtbag and I've always been in love with her. But for her, it's always been you. Bet without the pact, you two would already be married and with a couple of toddlers."

"You're wrong. Earlier in my office, she told me she had a crush on you even in college."

"Well, she was lying."

"So, if she's in love with me, how come she's in a relationship with you?"

"Ah. You're going to love this next part, dude. The relationship is fake, a total sham. She made it up to make you jealous."

Aiden presses a hand to my forehead. "How much did you have to drink again?"

I swat his hand away. "I'm perfectly lucid, man."

"But you're not making any sense."

I take a deep breath and stare Aiden in the eyes as I confess, "Remember that morning you found Lori here and assumed we'd slept together?"

Aiden nods.

"Well, she was only here because she'd received your wedding invitation the day before and she wanted to vent. Then, she told me she felt too sad to go home alone and asked me if she could sleep here—*just* sleep. But when you showed up the next morning, she felt like you were acting jealous about me and her being together, so she made up the entire relationship on the fly."

Aiden frowns now. "To what end?"

"I don't know." I shrug. "You suddenly realizing she was the love of your life instead of Kirsten and calling the wedding off?"

My best friend massages his temples, trying to take this all in. "And why did you go along with it?"

"Lori barged into my room, begging me to confirm the story... saying that she'd already told you we were together and that if I said no, then how could she explain to you why she'd lied? Plus, you know I've never been able to say no to her."

Aiden sags back against the couch raking both his hands through his hair. "Man, that's a lot to take in."

"Yep." I take another sip of coffee.

"I still don't understand something, though..."

"Yeah, what? How she's never going to forgive me for standing in the way of true love?"

"No. The fact that I've seen you together these past few weeks, and nothing about it seemed fake to me."

"Lori thought she might've been catching feelings for me, but that was before she realized I was the only reason she couldn't have you." A long beat of silence passes before I find the guts to ask, "Was I?"

"Aw, man, I don't know. That is such a mind-bending question... Would I have gotten with Lori at some point if not for you or the pact? Probably..."

His words confirm just how doomed I am.

"But..." Aiden starts and stops.

"But?" I prompt.

"But there's no way to know if it would've lasted, and, frankly, I'm glad nothing ever happened with Lori."

This last statement gives me pause. "Oh?"

"Kirsten makes me happy, and I want to marry her. Looking back, I've no regrets because all the choices I've made in the past have brought me to where I'm standing now."

"Which is?"

"About to marry the woman of my dreams."

I push his shoulder. "Get out of here. Of course, all women fall at your feet, you soppy, cute puppy."

Surprisingly, Aiden takes me seriously and stands up. "I am going on one condition..."

"Shoot."

"Promise me you won't drink any more alcohol tonight."

I make the boy scout salute, then say, "Or should we pinkie promise?"

"See, making jokes already. Quick recovery, Barlow. My diagnosis is that you shall live."

I walk him to the door. "Thanks for not biting my head off, man." We slide hands and bump fists.

Aiden nods. "See yah at the office tomorrow," he says, getting out of my apartment.

I wait for a few minutes after he's gone before I grab my phone and wallet, and put a coat on.

I promised I wouldn't drink, not that I wouldn't do something stupid.

30

LORI

I'm in bed, eating ice cream straight from the carton, submersed in cats.

In the last hour, I've been replaying in my head all the times I thought Aiden was about to kiss me over the years and didn't.

The night we were walking home from the bus station, I can't remember where from. Instead of heading straight for our dorms, even if it was November and chilly, Aiden started humming a tune and pulled me to him. We started dancing and messing around with spins and dips, giggling and laughing. Then, all of a sudden, we were slow dancing, and he was holding me close. I could feel his warmth even in the night's cold and we were holding hands, and he was looking at me *that* way... until suddenly he wasn't.

"I should take you home before you catch a cold," he said, taking a step back and leaving me confused and shivering.

In retrospect, I can practically see the bulb that went off in his head: ALARM! Pact, I can't kiss her, take her home instead.

Or that night I tried to *Notebook* him, feeling sure watching the most romantic movie in history together would shift something in him. We were cozied up on his bed, watching the movie on his laptop, his arm draped over my shoulder. After the kissing-in-the-rain scene, Aiden turned to me, looking all intense. There was no doubt in my mind he was about to kiss me; the look in his eyes, his expression, and the way he nervously swallowed as he kept looking at my lips. Now all that was needed to seal the deal was true love's first kiss. I waited for him to move as we gazed at each other, the tension mounting. I was sure I was sending all the right kiss-me signals. I even licked my lips at one point. Yet, he never moved. Not a single inch.

Again, the alarm went off and he got off the bed, asking me if I wanted more popcorn.

Or again, that time I was stung on the neck by a bee and Aiden was more than ready to play doctor, bringing me over to his room and applying an ointment to the puncture. Despite the pain, I couldn't help but shudder a little under the gentle pressure of his fingertips on my skin. As the throb of the sting eventually subdued, I looked up at him and we stared into each other's eyes, hesitating for only a split second before almost kissing. Suddenly remembering himself, Aiden pulled away and practically ran from the room, leaving a very confused, dismayed, and bee-stung me behind.

On reflex, my hand goes to the spot on my neck as I feel the ghost of the sting—both physical and emotional. The doorbell rings, interrupting the reverie. I jolt on the bed, sitting straight up while the cats flatten their ears—as they should. We're facing a common enemy.

For a moment I consider pretending I'm not home, but the light in my bedroom is visible from the doorstep, and anyway, what would be the point? Jace and I work together. If not tonight, he's going to corner me tomorrow at the office—a much less private environment. So we might as well get down to round two of our fight straight away and be done with it.

I throw the blankets off my legs, dislodging the cats, and trudge down the stairs just as the doorbell rings again.

Impatient prick.

"I'm coming, I'm coming," I yell as I make my way to the door. I fling it open, ready to attack, but the words die on my lips as I find Aiden on my doorstep instead of Jace.

"Hey," I croak out, trying to swallow my disappointment.

"Hey you," he replies, leaning against the doorframe.

I'm chewing on my lower lip and I probably have chocolate on my face. I'm a mess. I've been crying, my eyes must be puffy and swollen, and my hair is a rat's nest.

I'm still so surprised to see him, that I barely have time to take in his clothes. Under the navy coat, he's still wearing the same olive-green sweater he had on earlier at the office.

But it's definitely too late for him to have come straight from work. Has he gone to see Jace after we talked? Is he here as some kind of peace ambassador to butter me up on Jace's behalf?

I narrow my eyes and swing the door wider, almost expecting to see Jace waiting in the shadows, but my street is empty.

"What are you doing here, Aiden?"

I'm still mad at him. Not as mad as I am at Jace, but still... Aiden was a willing participant in the pact, too.

"Can I come in?"

We stare at each other for a few long moments before I decide I don't care what he's come to say and step aside, letting him in. If he wants to apologize, he's welcome to, as long as he keeps the apology personal and doesn't mention He Who Shall Not Be Named.

"So? To what do I owe the late-night visit?" I prompt.

"I came to forgive you," Aiden says as he enters my house.

My jaw drops. I close the front door and wheel on him. "*You* want to forgive *me*?"

We square off to each other across the hall.

"Yes, Lori. I'm here to forgive you."

I cross my arms on my chest. "And what for?"

Aiden mocks my gesture and crosses his own arms over his chest. "Oh, let's see," he says with a hardly contained smirk.

Does he think this is funny? The two of them playing with my feelings for years? I'm about to go ballistic when he adds, "How about I forgive you for lying to me every day for the past month? For making up an entire relationship with Jace just to make me jealous. And for not coming clean with me, not even when I point-blank asked you how you felt in college, or after I confessed about the pact?"

I'm floored. I have no words.

Aiden watches me intently, his eyes twinkling in the light from the living room lamp. The guilt about all the lies I've been telling him resurfaces with a vengeance.

"Jace told you?" I ask at last, softly. That vindictive prick. I can't believe Jace ratted on me out of spite. That piece of poo on a stick!

Aiden's cross-armed stance drops. "Before you go on a mental rant about what a jerk Jace is for selling you out, he didn't tell me in a malicious way."

"No? How then?"

"Jace only wanted to explain why it'd take you more time to forgive him over me, and I guess he was also tired of lying to me."

That shuts me up all right. I've been a horrible friend to Aiden these past few weeks.

Aiden walks up to me, eyes still twinkling with a sort of amused mischief. I expect him to give me a pat on the back and forgive me, but he doesn't. Instead, he smiles, drops his arms, and takes both my hands in his.

"Lori, can we have an honest talk, heart to heart, no more lies?" he asks.

I nod and let him pull me to the couch. Aiden drops his coat on the backrest and we both sit.

"How about I go first?" he suggests.

I nod again, I couldn't speak if I wanted to.

"That morning I saw you at Jace's house. I *was* jealous."

I frown.

Aiden shrugs. "I guess I've always been a little possessive of you with no right to be at all. I'm not perfect. And, yeah, the thought of us getting together crossed my mind over the years"—he lowers his gaze—"more than once if I have to be honest." Our eyes meet again. "But I don't think we were ever meant to be, Lori. I've found my person, and it's Kirsten."

A month ago, a frank speech like this would've gutted me. Destroyed me to smithereens. Now, it brushes off me, not even bruising my ego too much. I tend to agree with him instead.

"And finding Kirsten," he continues, "is the reason why I have no regrets, why I wouldn't change a single thing about my past because it all led me to being with her."

I smile despite myself. "Oh my gosh, you're cheesier than a Labrador puppy."

Aiden smirks.

"What are you smirking at?"

"Jace told me something along the same lines when I explained my feelings to him."

At the mention of The Unmentionable Number One, the smile gets wiped from my face and my cheeks flush.

"Don't be mad at him, Lori," Aiden pleads. "Love makes you do crazy things, stupid things... you should know." He pointedly raises an eyebrow at me.

"I know, but I never intentionally hurt you. My fake relationship was just a moment of insanity and didn't cause anyone any harm. But Jace saw firsthand what consequences his choices brought. How hard I had it for you and what misery those unrequited feelings caused me."

Aiden grins despite himself. "And I'm flattered to have inspired such awe. But, Lori, what you felt for me, was it ever real? Or was it all in your head? A fantasy?"

"What do you mean?"

"How does it compare to what you feel in here"—he bumps a fist over his chest—"now, for Jace?"

Not. Even. Close.

I look at my best friend and he must read the answer in my eyes because he adds, "See? You came into my office today asking how to recognize if you've found the one for a reason."

I keep looking at him with a mixed expression of confusion and surprise. "I love him, Aiden. I love Jace with all my heart, but I'm still so mad."

"So angry you won't forgive him ever? Because if it's only a matter of waiting a week instead of doing it right away, could you spare the poor guy a lot of heartbreak and just do it now? When I went over to his place earlier, he was a total mess."

"A mess how?"

Aiden slings an arm over the backrest. "He had a glass on the coffee table without a coaster, a half-drunk bottle of vodka abandoned in the sink, leaking, and an empty packet of Cheetos discarded on the floor."

I smile, despite myself. For such a neat freak as Jace, those are capital offenses.

"He was drinking?"

"Yep, while simmering in self-pity. But I made him a strong black coffee, and he was in slightly better shape when I left. But really, there's only one thing that would make him feel whole again... knowing he hasn't lost you."

"Don't you think he deserves to stew, at least for a night?"

"Poor guy, no. Jace's been stewing for the past fifteen years."

I self-consciously pull a lock of frazzled hair behind my ear. "Well, I'd better go make myself presentable if I'm about to have my big romantic moment. Do I have chocolate on my face?"

Aiden laughs. "You most definitely do, Lori."

"And you let me sit through this whole pep talk without mentioning it once?"

"Why? Chocolate looks really cute on you."

Playfully outraged, I ask, "You think Jace would agree?"

Aiden nods, satisfied.

"I'm still washing my face before I go put him out of his misery."

"That's a shame." He gets up from the couch and opens his arms. "Can I have a hug?"

"Yeah, you can."

I take his hand and he pulls me into a warm embrace.

Fear has been simmering in my insides for the past few weeks, and now, in Aiden's arms after his stupid, soppy, sweet pep talk, it evaporates.

"I'm sorry I tried to make you jealous by using Jace," I whisper. "It was silly, and it didn't even work. You were never jealous of us and you really are the best of friends."

"And I get accused of being the soppy puppy. Enough with the schmaltzy fest." Aiden puts a finger under my chin and lifts my head up. "Now go and make up with your boyfriend. I'm gonna go home and spend some time with my bride-to-be."

I smile at Aiden's overly casual tone. "Yes, Jace and I, we're really together now. Or at least we will be after I sort this whole mess out. I'll walk you to the door."

Aiden draws away, smiling. He slings one arm over my shoulder, grabbing his coat as we go.

I open the door and we pause on the doorstep to say goodbye.

"Lori," Aiden says, giving me an uncharacteristically serious look. "You deserve to be happy. And Jace is a lucky guy."

"I'm really happy for you, too, Aiden, Kirsten is..." I don't really know what to say.

Aiden pushes a finger to my lips to silence me. "Get to know her better before you decide. I promise, if you give her a real chance, you're going to like her."

I can't deny I've been prejudiced against Kirsten from the moment Aiden announced she was his new girlfriend. But now that we're no longer rivals, I don't see why we couldn't become friends... in time... we'll see...

Aiden drops his hand away from my mouth, and I say, "I will."

"Thanks." Aiden bends down and plants a soft kiss on my cheek. "Now go to your guy. I think he's still alone with his booze and Cheetos."

"Will do." I reach a hand up to cup his cheek. "Thanks, Aiden."

"Don't thank me." He grabs my hand and kisses my knuckles. "I really did nothing. Goodnight, Lori."

"Night, Aidenberry."

I watch him go, unable to wipe a silly smile from my face. I'm in love with Jace, and he loves me back. I can't wait to tell him...

31

JACE

I step out of my building and walk. I walk and walk and walk until I can't feel my hands in the cold and my feet go numb. Unconsciously—or very consciously—I head north toward her house. Chicago is unforgiving around me, bleak in the dead of night with the February wind working its icy fingers under my coat, against my face, while a clammy humidity dampens my clothes.

I welcome the discomfort. I've earned it. I let my thoughts run free with no intention of stopping them because I don't deserve peace of mind.

So I walk.

My eyes ache from the cold. And I walk.

I see a group of men walking down the street and I step aside. Luckily, they pass without incident.

They look like they are heading to a bar. Probably to drown their sorrows in alcohol and oblivion. I envy them. They are the lucky ones. They don't have to live with the knowledge they've harmed someone they care about.

I walk.

I walk until I'm at her house and then I stop dead in my tracks. Aiden's car is parked across the street from Lori's loft.

What is he doing here? Why did he come to see her?

It might be innocent, I tell myself. He's come to help me out, plead my case with her.

But then the devil of jealousy, the one that's been rotting and festering in my guts for the past fifteen years, hisses a warning in my ear, *"Or he's here to finally make her his. You told him all he needed to know."*

No. Aiden wouldn't. He said he was in love with Kirsten, and that he was glad Lori was only a friend.

"People lie," the devil whispers. *"How many times have you lied to him... to her... It's only fitting they'd get their happily ever after now... after another lie."*

I stay rooted on the spot, on the curb opposite Lori's house.

Without moving, the cold gets even worse. If I stay here long enough, I'm going to get frostbite. A suitable punishment alongside the fact I'll have to live knowing I've lost everything.

The devil's whispers are getting unbearable, and my thoughts are unrelenting. I can't block them out anymore. I can't deny the truth. I lied. And I deserve to lose everything.

I killed love.

I killed the only thing that ever really mattered.

I deserve all her anger and her hate.

I deserve to be alone and miserable.

I deserve the cold.

The minutes trickle by and still, Aiden doesn't come out. Are they together right now? Finally unleashing years of unrequited passion?

No, he wouldn't. Aiden is a decent man—contrary to me. If he wanted to be with Lori, he'd break it off with Kirsten first. I know him.

I keep my eyes glued to the door, willing him to come out. The city around me is silent with an indifference that befits a night like this one. The cold makes me shiver. A splitting headache is building at my temples. I haven't eaten and I'm running on an empty stomach and vodka fumes. All I want is to lie down and sleep... to sleep and forget everything.

I try to move, to go back home, but I can't. Maybe I'm frozen stiff. The blood has frozen in my veins, and I'm paralyzed.

I don't know how long I stand hiding in the shadows of the streetlight. The perfect lurking spot. If she comes to the door, she won't be able to see me.

The cold doesn't seem to get any worse. Maybe it's not the cold at all, maybe it's my own heart. I'm so numb I can't tell the difference.

The door to her house finally opens, and Aiden steps out. I lean further into the shadows as I watch them.

Aiden is talking, his face serious, committed. I can't hear what he's saying, but he sure looks like a lover promising to go home to dump his fiancée. Lori is saying something back, but Aiden silences her, pressing a finger on her mouth.

The gesture makes my blood sizzle. It's too intimate, too familiar for any old friends. He shouldn't touch her like that...

Aiden and Lori aren't just friends. They're more. I clench my hands into fists but stay put in my shadowy corner.

Aiden removes the finger from her lips and she says something, then he bends down to kiss her. From the distance, I can't tell where he's kissing her. On the lips or on the cheek? I can only sigh with relief that the kiss is brief. At least until Lori reaches a hand up to cup his cheek. He leans into the touch and then kisses her hand.

Not that I needed any more proof of their new status, but it still hurts worse than I could ever imagine.

Then he finally leaves.

I don't follow his progress across the street. My eyes stay glued to Lori, to the doting expression on her face as she watches him go.

That's the face of a woman in love. Only not with me.

It's never been about me.

32

LORI

By the time I get to Jace's building, it's already past midnight. I wanted to take a shower, get dressed, and leave the house. But then, as I blow-dried my hair in front of the mirror, I told myself, well, if I'm about to live my big romantic moment, I might as well do it in style and give my hair a shape. Makeup came next. And then a wardrobe crisis.

How do you choose a dress for a you're-the-love-of-my-life declaration?

In the end, I opted for a sensible, winter-in-Chicago black wool skirt, a long-sleeved dark green sweater, and black calf-high boots. I hope Jace will like the outfit. Or even better, hate it and rip it off me.

The guest parking spots in the garage are taken, so I search for street parking, and finally get out of the car, pulling the faux fur-lined hood of my jacket over my head against the icy night wind.

With my coat zipped up to my chin, my heels click loudly against the concrete as I cross the street.

I take a deep breath before pushing open the door to his building.

"Good evening, Dr. Archibald," the night doorman greets me.

"Night, Denzel, could you tell Dr. Barlow I'm here to see him?"

"Oh, I'm sorry, Dr. Barlow left a while ago and hasn't come back yet."

My bright smile falters and I lose most of my momentum. Frazzled nerves take over. Already, coming here, wearing my heart on my sleeve, hasn't been easy, but having to wait after all the anticipation is nerve-wracking.

"Are you sure he's gone, 'cause I saw his car in the garage."

"Yes, Dr. Barlow left on foot."

"How long ago?"

Denzel checks his watch, raising his eyebrows. "A couple of hours, actually."

Oh my gosh, I broke him. Jace went out in the freezing cold because of me. Because of the horrible things I've said to him. And Aiden said he'd been drinking. What if something happened to him?

Denzel must read the worry on my face because he says, "I'm sure Dr. Barlow is fine."

I fish my phone out of my bag and call him. The line goes straight to voicemail.

A thick lump grows in my throat. "Do you mind if I wait for him in the lobby, Denzel?"

"No need, Dr. Archibald. I'm allowed to let you into Dr. Barlow's apartment at any time; he left us a spare key. So you can wait for him upstairs."

"Thank you, Denzel."

I enter Jace's apartment, feeling weird standing in the crime scene by myself. I hang my coat in the closet behind the door and remove my shoes before walking into the living room.

The house still smells of coffee. Aiden was here not long ago. I collect the two empty mugs from the coffee table and the bag of Cheetos from the floor. The bottle of vodka Aiden told me about is still in the sink, now almost entirely empty. Did the liquor leak out or did Jace drink more? I empty the rest of the bottle in the sink and put it in the glass recycling bin. Next, I wash the sticky glass Jace must've used to drink the vodka, the mugs, and wipe the coffee table in the living room.

There's nothing else to do. The rest of the house is as pristine as always.

I check the time again, past 1 a.m.

I try Jace's number one more time, knowing he won't pick up. He doesn't. I get sent to voicemail.

Worry wrings my stomach into tight knots. I pace the living room aimlessly, then sit on the couch, then get up and pace again, my mind racing with what-ifs. What if something happened to him? What if he's hurt?

He's hurting. I did that myself, but what if he got mugged, hit by a car, or thrown in jail for public intoxication?

I call the police to inquire about any accidents or arrests. Nothing. I try all the major hospitals in the city next, and still come out empty-handed.

Jace isn't in jail or at the hospital. But even if he's still just walking, it's so cold outside, he'll catch his death.

I try calling him again, to leave him a message, but as the beep sounds, I can't get the words out of my mouth. I can't tell him I love him over a voicemail message.

My broken heart is squeezing so hard it might just stop beating. I want to run out of the apartment and search for him. Find him and hold him in my arms until he's warm again. Tell him how sorry I am.

Instead, I walk into his bedroom. I drop onto the bed and inhale his scent on the pillow.

The mattress is so soft, and Jace's scent is so familiar, so reassuring... I close my eyes just for a second...

When I open them again, light filters in through the blinds, and I'm still alone in Jace's bed.

I jolt awake with an electric shock.

What time is it?

I reach for my phone and see it's already 7 a.m.

Darn it.

My heart sinks.

Jace, where are you?

I try his number again—voicemail. The police. The hospitals. Nothing.

I call Aiden next.

"Lori, hi," he picks up, sounding surprised—to hear from me this early, presumably.

"Have you heard from Jace?"

"Ah, yes." My racing heart slows down to a slightly less tachycardic tempo. Jace is alive. He's okay. "He sent me a weird text message last night, but I read it only this morning."

"Can you forward it to me?"

"Sure, just a sec."

I chew on a nail while I wait for the text to arrive. When my phone pings, I quickly switch apps and read the message with my heart in my throat.

FROM AIDEN:

Fwd: Man, I can't make it to the office tomorrow. Or all of this week. Please cover for me. I'll see you at the wedding on Tuesday. If you're still getting married?

I read the text again, then bring the phone back to my ear.

"What does he mean, if you're still getting married?"

"The hell if I know."

"Have you texted him back?"

"Yes, but the messages still appear undelivered. I called him, but his phone was off."

"Yeah, same here. What do you make of this?"

"You told him you wanted nothing to do with him, and he's disappeared off the face of the Earth to avoid dealing with his broken heart."

I chew on more nails. "Okay, but why ask you if you're still getting married?"

"That, I've no explanation for." A voice calls his name in the background, presumably Kirsten. "Listen, I was about to grab breakfast. Talk later at the office?"

"Sure, thanks, Aiden."

We hang up, and I stare around Jace's bedroom, undecided on how to proceed. My eyes fall on a smear of black mascara on his otherwise pristine white pillow. The stain makes me equally sorry and satisfied. On the one hand, I regret saying those awful things to him last night. I was merciless. But I was so angry. On the other hand, is this how he'll react whenever life gets tough? By running away? He kind of deserves his pillow to be tainted by my tears and melted makeup.

This brings me to the next practical aspects of starting my day: fixing my face and going to work. If Aiden and I have to cover Jace's patients while he's gone, it'll be a hell of a week. Especially since Aiden will be busy with the last pre-wedding arrangements, which means most of the extra work will fall on me.

I move into Jace's bathroom and check the trainwreck of my face in the mirror. Not good. A rabid raccoon would look more reassuring.

I turn on the faucet and try to wash the hurt away. Of course, that only worsens the mascara damage, spreading a blackish tint all over my features.

I never brought toiletries over to Jace's place, so I search the cabinets for any kind of lotion I could use in place of a proper makeup remover. I only find a tube of aftershave. I squeeze a little on a cotton disk. It's white and creamy and looks a lot like a moisturizer. Should do.

I shrug and squeeze more product on the disk, then rub it all over my face and my eyes. In five seconds flat, I feel like my head has been teleported to the North Pole during a volcanic eruption or locked into a burning ice cube. My skin feels freezing and on fire at the same time. I quickly splash myself with more water, trying to rinse the dreadful aftershave.

I blindly reach for Jace's towel and dry my slightly less white-hot face on it. When I meet my gaze in the mirror, I almost laugh… I thought the rabid raccoon look was rock bottom, but add blood-shot eyes and a flaming complexion and I look like one of the red monsters from *Labyrinth*, but one who had an epic mascara fail.

I stare at the tube of aftershave accusingly and read the label.

> Menthol aftershave for a refreshing effect, apply only in small quantities. Test for skin sensitivity before using.

Guess I should've read that first.

The face fixing will have to wait until I can get to the emergency kit in my desk at work. Since it's so much closer to work, from Jace's apartment, I go straight to our practice, skipping breakfast. My stomach is too knotted for food, anyway.

I'm still wearing the same outfit as last night. But at least it's work-appropriate—as opposed to my face.

As I storm into the clinic, I ignore the receptionist's shocked expression as I enter my office and get to work at once on cleaning up my face. Once I'm a little less scary, I walk back into the reception and ask to be alerted as soon as Dr. Collymore arrives.

"If you could also cancel all of Dr. Barlow's non-urgent appointments and redirect the rest to me or Dr. Collymore."

Betty nods. "Is everything okay, Dr. Archibald?"

"Peachy," I say, then go to hide back in my office.

I sag on my chair, silently cursing at the ceiling.

I can do this. The wedding is on Tuesday, a week from yesterday. So, at worst, I'll only have to wait six days before talking to Jace.

Six short, impossibly long days.

33

JACE

My phone dies when I arrive at my parents' lake house in the middle of the night. I don't have a charger, I don't even have a change of clothes, only my wallet and my dead phone.

But the little charge I had left is all I needed to book an Uber to get me here from Lori's house.

I use the spare key under the mat to unlock the door. The security keypad beeps a countdown. I punch in the code, disarming the alarm.

The house is dark and freezing. I kick off my shoes and turn on the heating. It'll take all night for the house to warm up and maybe some. In the darkness, I find my way up the stairs and then to my old room.

I don't get undressed because of the cold. Instead, I open the closet, searching for a warmer hoodie and a few extra blankets.

Sitting on the edge of the single bed, I close my eyes and inhale the familiar smells around me. Old wood, pinecones, and the faint hint of dust the house always has when it hasn't been used for a while.

My room is a loft with a tall ceiling and wide windows overlooking the lake. Jessica always bugged me to no end for having the bigger room. She was right. The view is wasted on a loser like me.

Moonlight glints on a bunch of framed photos on the wall. The beam of light going to die in a corner where a few scattered toys lie abandoned—forgotten, just like me. The same teddy bear I used to sleep with as a child is sitting on top of the dresser. I grab it. Its soft, worn fur does nothing to ease the tension in my neck or the ache in my chest. I'm home, but my life is still falling apart.

My head falls forward and I sigh.

On the car ride over, I've had enough time to accept that I shouldn't be mad at Aiden. If he and Lori want to be together, there's nothing I can do about it. I have no right to be upset. While he has every right to hate me for keeping them apart for as long as I did. I should consider myself lucky he still calls me his friend. If I'd given up years ago, they wouldn't have wasted so much time, and I would've stopped hanging on to a hopeless dream a long time ago. I'd be far better off now.

So what am I doing hiding in here?

I just need a few days to fully come to terms with what's about to happen. I couldn't bear to walk into the office tomorrow and see them exchange worried stares as they prepared to make the announcement. Nope, definitely not ready for that.

But I will be. I just need a bit of peace and quiet first.

I crawl under the covers, silently thanking my mom for always keeping a clean set of sheets on the beds.

As I close my eyes, I try to remember the last time I slept in this room. It must've been during our residency that week Aiden, Lori, and I came here as a sort of study retreat to pass our in-training exams. I vaguely remember staying up all night revising with Lori in this room while Aiden had already gone to bed. How we fell asleep on my bed among a sea of flashcards. Me waking up the next morning, getting rid of the flashcards and enjoying the weight of Lori's body pressed against mine in the tiny bed. This bed.

We all passed the test with flying colors, but that wasn't the point. It has never been for me. I would've taken a thousand more exams if it meant I could study with Lori.

And I thought I finally had her. I could almost touch the dream until it slipped through my fingers.

And maybe that's all the last month has been: a dream. Tomorrow I'll wake up knowing I imagined Lori kissing me. Telling me she wanted more. Practically begging for it.

I imagine Lori and Aiden in their own fictional room, laughing together, talking about their future. I picture Lori asking if Aiden wants kids, and him answering that he would love to have a half-dozen babies with her.

No jealousy, no burning rage, no sadness.

No pain.

I'm numb.

I slowly drift to sleep, my bear clutched to my chest.

* * *

The next morning, I walk into town to buy food supplies and grab breakfast. Passing a hunting and fishing store, I decide to gear up for ice fishing. Not much else to do around the frozen lake in the dead of winter. I also buy a charger, but I don't charge my phone. I'm not ready to go back to the real world yet.

After a quick lunch, I sort through my new equipment and head outside to drill my perfect hole. I stack the new plastic sleigh with all the equipment—tackle, bait, auger, scooper, and ice fishing rod—and set off for the lake. A fresh coat of snow makes it difficult to tell where the shore ends and the frozen water begins, so I walk a little further. At midday, the sun has climbed high into the sky, making the ground glare so bright it hurts to look at it.

No one is in sight. The world is silent, except for the occasional snap of a twig under my feet and the sound of the sleigh sliding behind me. When I've walked far enough to be sure I must stand on ice, I set up camp. I remove the safety cover from the auger—the large metal hand drill used to pierce the ice—and start drilling. The auger is easy to use and I work it into the ground until the ice below me gives way with a pop. Struggling to hook a waxy on the jig with my snow gloves on, I take them off until I've succeeded. Then the gloves come back on and I start jiggling to bait the fish.

I like the repetitive task and enjoy the peace of the deserted lake. It's only me, my thoughts, and my memories...

Maybe I should try not to think about anything.

Yes, I'm just going to stay up here and revert to a primordial lifestyle. Eat, sleep, hunt for food, and repeat. Forget I have a ruined life waiting for me back in Chicago.

* * *

That works well for the following few days, but come Monday night I itch to recharge my phone. Aiden's wedding is supposed to be tomorrow and I'm the best man. Has he canceled it? He must have after what I saw happening on Lori's doorstep. I just need to turn on my phone and get definite proof.

Still, I hesitate.

I'm trapped in a quantum mechanics paradox.

Until I don't check, both scenarios involving Aiden's wedding could still be true. The ceremony could still be on and my reading on Tuesday night's rendezvous wrong. Or the wedding could be canceled and Lori and Aiden be together.

But if I open my texts and find the cancelation notice, I will have effectively sealed my fate.

I'm being silly, I know. Nothing I do will impact the situation. Either the wedding is canceled or it's not. I might as well check my messages.

With a deep breath, I plug the charger in.

34

LORI

An entire week with no texts, no calls, not even a smoke signal or a stinking like on my Catstagram!

"Doesn't Jace know that even through a fight, he's supposed to send daily proof of life?" I ask my hens as they roam the backyard. It's a sunny, not-as-freezing day and they've left their luxury heated henhouse to get a little fresh air in the warmed midday weather.

Gemima clucks at me.

"I know, right? Asking for a selfie next to the day's paper isn't too much, is it?"

I hate being left in the dark. The waiting is the worst. Trying to decipher Jace's thought process feels as random as reading tea leaves. Everything could mean something and its opposite. Is Jace ignoring me because he's still hurt by what I said? Or is he using the silent treatment to punish me? Or maybe he's re-evaluating our relationship and, in all his wisdom, has decided it's best to break up with me. Round one was painful enough, and he doesn't think he can take another.

I'm going crazy. I don't know what to think anymore.

Patience I must have, I know. But my Jedi skills are evading me right now. I'm so not at peace with the universe, the opposite, I want to rip my hair out. I'm doing my best to hold on to my sanity, but it's hard. And I'm tired of being patient, tired of being mature. I just want to shout.

I want to hug him, hit him, and kiss him. Maybe do all three at once—that would require some serious coordination.

At least now the wait is over. Today is the day of Aiden's wedding and, as best man, Jace will have to attend. Or at least, so Aiden said. After Jace skipped the rehearsal dinner last night, I was losing hope. But Aiden reassured me they texted yesterday, and that Jace promised he'd be by his side today. And willing or not, he will have to talk to me, too.

"All right, ladies," I tell the chickens. "Mommy has to go get ready. Wish me luck."

The girls answer with reassuring croaks and clucks. Hens are so much more supportive than cats. I swear Leia has been giving me pitying looks all week for being so pathetically strung up about a male. Easy for her to judge when she has three handsome tomcats doting on her twenty-four seven.

The wedding is at four, but I have to be at the hotel by two. My instructions for the day from Kirsten are clear. I have to shower and wear pretty underwear suitable for my bridesmaid dress. But under no circumstances should I try to style my hair or apply makeup. Professionals will take care of that in the bridal suite before the ceremony.

I'd usually hate the fuss, but today I'm happy I'll be looking my best for the reunion with Jace. So I do as I'm told. I shower, towel-dry my hair, put on a pair of not-too-threadbare yoga pants, and throw on an old sweater. I grab my cellophane-covered dress from the closet, put my new Sergio Rossi shoes in a tote, and slip into a pair of old sneakers for the journey. My new pumps are gorgeous, but I'm not sure how long my feet will handle the high heels before killing me.

I won't drive to the wedding. Aiden and Kirsten chose a convenient location for the ceremony: the Palmer House Hilton Hotel. But even if it's only a fifteen-minute drive from my place, I booked a cab. I could've taken the metro, but I didn't want to have to drag my gown down and up a million flights of stairs among a bunch of strangers.

The driver is already waiting for me outside my house. I wave at him and cross the street to get into the yellow cab. I drape the gown across my lap, close the door, and nod to the driver, signaling I'm ready to go.

"Where to, miss?"

"The Palmer House Hilton Hotel, thank you."

Ten minutes later, Jace's building comes into view. My heart jolts in my chest as I zone in on his windows with sniper precision. Is he there now? Or has he already left? The hotel is so close to Jace's place, he could walk. Since he's been such a fan of long walks lately.

I still don't know where he disappeared to for the last week. My best guess has been at his family's lake house, but I can't be sure. I was half tempted to drive up there and check, but Aiden talked me out of it. He told me to give the guy some space.

Well, he's had enough space now—time to dock back on Planet Earth. I wonder what he'll do when he sees me. Ignore me? Pretend nothing has happened? Something else?

And what am I going to do when I see *him*? What should my best strategy be?

I tap the leather seats at a red light, pondering. I sure don't want to have our talk in front of other wedding guests, so I should definitely try to corner him on his own. Before the ceremony?

Probably it'd be better after, at the banquet... but I don't know if I can wait that long.

As the driver pulls up in the center of The Loop, I thank him, pay, and shimmy out of the back seat, trying not to wrinkle my dress.

The moment I set foot on the curb, I wonder if Jace has already arrived. Should I try to find him? Text Aiden for intel?

Similarly to the bride, the groom should have a private suite for him and the groomsmen to get ready. I could join them and ask Jace to talk. I belong more on the groom's side, anyway.

Then I stare down at my old, baggy clothes and suddenly panic. I'm definitely going to run into him now while I look like the before version of a makeover in a rom-com.

I'd better find that bridal suite right away. I hurry into the hotel but stop again after my first step in, gaping in awe at the lobby. The large room has a magnificent high domed ceiling decorated in gold and with frescos of ancient mythology. Golden chandeliers adorn the marble walls. And the room ends in a grand marble staircase, where, atop the box newel posts, two majestic bronze winged angels oversee the entire space.

This place looks like the Sistine Chapel.

"Impressive, huh?" Erin, one of my fellow bridesmaids, asks, pausing next to me to admire the room.

The question shakes me out of my haze, and, shockingly, I'm happy to see a fellow member of the bridal party.

I can't wait around the lobby like a sitting, un-pampered duck.

"Erin, hi," I say. "Do you know where we're supposed to go?"

"Yeah, Kirsten texted me a second ago." My phone vibrates in my pocket and for once I don't jump up thinking it'll be Jace. In fact, it is Kirsten sending me the same info. "The bridal suite is in Room 405. Shall we go?"

"Sure."

I repocket my phone and follow Erin to the elevators.

"Is the groom's suite near Kirsten's?"

"No," Erin chirps. "Aiden and the boys should be in the opposite wing of the hotel. So as not to risk the groom and bride seeing each other before the ceremony."

I sigh inwardly, so no risk of the best man and the bridesmaid bumping into each other either. As per my new normal, I'm gripped by contrasting emotions: relief and disappointment.

Erin and I are the only two persons in the elevator, and I get lost in thought staring at the little numbers lighting up for each new floor we climb.

"You look worried." Erin peeps at me from the corner of her eye.

I shake my head. "No, I'm fine. Just tired. I had a long week."

What feels like the longest week of my life.

We exit onto the fourth floor, quickly finding the bridal suite near the end of the hall.

We enter the room and find Kirsten, in a white sparkly robe, and her mother and sister sitting on a couch. Kirsten turns to us and smiles. "Ladies, you made it."

The bride stands up, and she and Erin air-kiss. I awkwardly smile at the bride, sending strong, don't-even-try-to-air-kiss-me brainwaves. They must reach Kirsten because she only smiles back.

"Here." Kirsten passes each of us a flute of champagne. "Help yourselves."

"Thank you." I grab a glass and observe the room. It's not nearly as opulent as the lobby, but it's still pretty grand. More one-bedroom apartment than a hotel room.

The bridal party is assembled in the living area where two women and a man I don't recognize are working on the maid of honor's hair and makeup. The tall man pins and sprays, curls and fluffs, while the two women try to work around him on Britney's face.

I'd laugh if it weren't for the fact I'm going to be next.

I've never met Kirsten's mother. I saw her for the first time last night at the rehearsal dinner, but I was in such a bad mood, I avoided all social interactions with strangers, hiding in the close circle of Aiden's family.

Now I approach her to introduce myself while simultaneously trying to steer clear of Kendall. I didn't like the smirk on the bride's sister's face at the mention of Jace's absence last night. She's smelling blood, and I wouldn't put it past her to try something funny. Not that I'm really worried Jace would fall for it. Although, if she got to him before we had a chance to talk, he might do something impulsive—a sort of self-destructive rebound.

"Hello, dear," Kirsten's mom says a few bits after I've clearly made an approach and then stood silently planted in front of her without saying a word. The mother of the bride stands up from the couch. "I don't believe we've met."

"Hi, Mrs. Cunningham, I'm Lori, one of Aiden's oldest friends."

"Oh, please call me Kimberly," she says.

Ooh. So you really can't be a woman in the Cunningham club without a K-starting name.

"Okay, Kimberly." I take the hand she offers me. "It's really nice to meet you."

We exchange a few more pleasantries and make more polite chit-chat until my turn comes to go under the knife—I mean under the curling iron.

Then in no time at all, an usher comes knocking on the door, informing us that all the guests have arrived and the groom and groomsmen are already waiting for us in the Red Lacquer Room.

This is it. I'm going to see Jace for the first time after our fight.

I collect the hem of my long skirt and march out of the bridal suite like I'm about to enter a war zone.

35

JACE

A few hours earlier...

I arrive at my apartment mid-morning on Tuesday. At once, as I step past the threshold, something seems odd. I peek into the kitchen. There are two washed mugs and a clean glass on the counter. No bottle of vodka in the sink. Did Aiden get rid of it when he was here? I can't remember.

I move into my room and stop dead in my tracks when I see a black stain on my pillow. Is that mascara?

I sit on the bed and grab the pillow to then bring it to my nose. It's faint, but I can still smell the scent of Lori's shampoo: coconut and shea butter.

Was she in my house? When? Did she sleep in my bed?

I rush back into the hall and buzz the day doorman.

"Dr. Barlow, how can I be of assistance?"

"Hi, Peter, I just wanted to check if you let Lori into my apartment?"

"When?"

"Anytime in the past week. Please check since last Tuesday."

"Hold on a moment, sir." A brief pause and then, "Yes, Denzel logged her in as a visitor on Tuesday night at seventeen past midnight. Is there a problem?"

"No, Peter, thank you. No problem at all."

I let go of the intercom button and get back into the living room, sinking onto the couch, raking both hands through my hair.

She came back. That same night. After talking with Aiden.

Lori must've fallen asleep while waiting for me. But what had she come to say?

Aiden is getting married today, so it's clear they're not together… and if she isn't with him… I squish the hope in my chest before it can rise.

Why did she stay the night here? Was it only to talk?

I check the time on my phone. I should be getting ready; I'm still wearing yesterday's clothes—old sweats ransacked from my closet at the lake house.

I shift out of them and take a quick shower. Then I'm in front of the mirror, putting on my best man's uniform: a stark white shirt and three-piece black tux.

By the time I'm done, I still have an hour before I have to be at the hotel. So I decide to walk. It's only a mile and a half from here. It won't take me more than half an hour.

It's a beautiful day, not too windy, and I could use the fresh air to clear my head. All I've been assuming in the past week seems to have been turned on its head. Aiden is marrying Kirsten. He and Lori aren't together. And the night she came to tell me we were over, she returned a few hours later and slept in my bed—or at least she lay down on it. Why was the mascara running down her face? Was she crying?

Now I feel so stupid for going incommunicado all this time.

As I approach the hotel from the corner of Wabash and Monroe, a yellow cab coming from the opposite direction glides to a halt next to the sidewalk. The door opens, and Lori steps out, wrestling with a shimmering gown covered in cellophane—the one she sent me a selfie in.

I freeze in place when I spot her. A rush of adrenaline makes me flatten against the wall so as not to be spotted, but in a position from where I can still see her.

Lori looks beautiful. Breathtaking with her hair wild and not a drop of makeup on her face. I want to walk up to her, hug her, kiss her, and tell her I'm sorry. Just as she's about to turn her head my way, I bolt instead. I hide behind the corner, still flattened against the wall, panting.

Not cool, Barlow.

I'm a fool. A coward and a fool.

I wait for a long time in the same position until I'm positive Lori must've left the lobby.

I walk into the hotel and ask a bellhop for directions to Aiden's room. Across the impressive lobby, I step into an empty elevator just as the doors are about to close.

During the short upward ride, I pull myself together. I straighten my tie and get ready to face the music. Aiden is going to be kind of mad at me, too. I bailed on him the week before his wedding, dumping a load of extra work on him and even skipping the rehearsal dinner. I'm the worst best man.

But now I'm here. And if I'm doing this, I have to do it right. When the elevator pings open, I stroll down the hall, counting the numbers until I reach Aiden's room.

When I open the door, I stop on the threshold as everyone turns to look at me. Aiden comes to me and locks my hand in a brotherly handshake, saying, "Hey, man," with a proud smile, which makes me feel even more shameful for having doubted him.

I push the thought aside and pull him into a bro hug, smiling. "I'm happy for you, man."

"Thanks."

I step into the room and try to put the other disturbing thoughts out of my mind, so I can do my job and be the best man of the situation.

After I say a brief greeting to the others, Aiden takes me aside and leads us to the far corner of the room.

"How are you, bro?"

"Hey," I say. "Shouldn't I be the one curing your last-minute jitters?"

"No jitters here, man." He studies me for a second. "Not sure I could say the same about you, though."

If this is our all-cards-on-the-table moment, I need to clarify a few things. "Can I ask you a question?"

"Sure, dude." Aiden widens his arms. "It's not like I have anything else important to do, like getting married or whatnot," he adds, teasingly.

I ignore the banter. "Where did you go after coming to see me on Tuesday night?"

"Ah." Aiden contemplates me for a few seconds. "If you're asking, I bet you already know the answer, don't you?"

"Okay, why did you go to her house?"

"To talk some sense into her and give her some of her own medicine." Aiden fake-punches himself on the cheek. "Because I'm such a good doctor."

So he went to see Lori to advocate for me. I feel like such a lousy friend for immediately jumping to the conclusion that he was there on his own agenda.

"And did you... talk some sense into her?"

Aiden gives me a fish-eating smile before making a zipper-over-mouth gesture. "My lips are sealed. If you want to know where Lori stands, you're going to have to talk to her."

"Aww, man, I bet running away didn't help my case."

"No, she's been a Nervous Nellie for the past week. But I told her you were coming today." He pats me on the shoulder. "So be ready, she knows you're here."

I smile and shake my head, muttering, "I love you, man."

Aiden laughs. "Love you, too, bro."

We hug just as the groom's brother comes to call us. It's time to get to the altar.

The hotel's wedding coordinator escorts us to a grand ballroom with red velvet wall panels and dangling chandeliers. Each side of the room has been filled with chairs where the guests are already seated. Plentiful flower arrangements and scattered lanterns surround the seating areas, turning the ballroom into a mix between an enchanted forest and a European Palace.

We walk down the aisle and take our places beside the ivory-draped altar. I'm right by Aiden's side to the left of the minister, my hands behind my back, trying to avoid eye contact with the guests below.

I care about only one guest, and she's about to make her entrance.

After a short while, the wedding coordinator motions to a loud fanfare, and all heads turn to look at the ballroom door. Aiden takes a deep intake of breath, but probably not as deep as mine.

I think I spot Lori standing in the doorway. But it's such a brief glimpse before she disappears behind the curtain, I'm not sure it was her.

Then the first notes of a classical tune begin to play. A flower girl walks into the room. She is a miniature version of Kirsten, with big green eyes and long blonde curls—must be a cousin. She's wearing a white dress that makes her look even cuter. The girl throws white rose petals along the aisle as she walks to the delight and appreciation of all the guests until she takes her spot in the front row.

The maid of honor is next. My heart thumps against my chest as the bridesmaids each make their entrance into the room. Until there's only Lori left.

I hold my breath until she's at the doorway, and then the air hitches in my throat as she looks up—right at me.

36

LORI

I wait behind the curtain with my nerves on edge, my heart pounding in my chest. From the other side, I can hear the murmurs of appreciation as the flower girl makes her entrance—she's the cutest little bunny. Britney is next. I stare at the points of my shoes, avoiding everybody else's gazes.

Kendall goes in a short minute later.

Then Erin until only Kirsten and I are left standing behind.

My hands are slippery on the small bouquet I'm holding, and if my pulse speeds up any further, I might need a trip to the emergency room.

The wedding coordinator motions for me to hurry out of the backstage. For a moment, I'm tempted to flee. Ever heard of a runaway bridesmaid? This would be a first.

The coordinator beckons me again, and I hesitate only an instant before I walk past the curtain right in the center of the aisle.

On instinct, my eyes dart straight to Jace's, and I'm startled to find his icy-blue, direct gaze on me. Eye contact is a streak of fire sizzling through me from the tips of my hair to my toes. My cheeks heat.

I want to blink away, but I can't. Slowly, I make my way down the aisle.

I'm suddenly so nervous that everything around me seems to blur except for his face.

I want to run away and never see him again.

But I also want to run up to him and throw myself into his arms.

The music swells, and I neither run away or toward him. I bravely put one foot in front of the other, making my way to the altar until I reach my place in the row of bridesmaids.

Being still and no longer having to walk doesn't help. My heart is pounding in my chest, and the air feels thin. But most of all, Jace hasn't stopped looking at me.

The bridal march starts, but I don't look away. I can't. Jace looks devastatingly handsome in a black tux, so good-looking I could cry.

He was mine, and I pushed him away before he even knew I was his as well.

My thoughts might be all over the place, but his eyes are steady on mine.

"Dearly beloved, we are gathered here today to join this man and this woman in matrimony..."

I hardly listen to the minister. My attention is focused on the best man and the way his eyes are locked on my face.

* * *

The next hour is a blur. Present and past mix in an unfocused new dimension. Instead of the groom and bride reciting their vows, I hear the echo of Jace's words in my head from that morning in New Orleans.

"I promise to love you, your four cats, six hens, and thousand rescue books for as long as my heart shall beat... I promise to love you even when you finish all the hot water in the shower and sing Taylor Swift at the top of your lungs for half an hour non-stop."

"I promise to love you even when you kick me under the covers at night and hog all the blankets."

"I promise to always be there when you need me and be strong when you're vulnerable. I promise to never lie to you, to always tell you the truth, even when it hurts."

"I promise to keep on loving you every day, until my last breath, even when you get gray hair or when you lose your teeth, because you are the love of my life, Lola Archibald, and I will never stop loving you."

Wasn't that just the best declaration ever? How could I think even for a second to let him go? And we might both have to work a little on how we handle ourselves in a fight, but everything else was perfect between us... and I threw it all away in a moment of blind rage.

Present and past keep mixing when the bride and groom exchange rings. I can't help but fidget with the promise ring still on my finger. I never took it off. Jace's gaze drops to my hand as well to then bounce back to my eyes more intense than ever.

Aiden kisses his bride for the first time, and the only thing I can focus on is the phantom of Jace's lips pressing on mine.

When the ceremony ends, I can't wait to rush to Jace and finally talk to him. Instead, I'm herded away from the altar into a smaller side room by the wedding coordinator. Before I even have time to realize what's happening, I'm swarmed away in a tidal wave of chiffon and giggling women.

Apparently, we have to make a separate entrance to the reception ballroom, and each of us will be escorted to our sitting place by one of the groomsmen.

Unfortunately, I'm lower in the bridal party pecking order than

Jace. When he gets ushered into the same small room, he's immediately snatched up by Britney, the maid of honor, and they go to the head of the queue. I'm at the bottom, paired with Aiden's cousin.

It's not that bad. I've waited this long. Another ten minutes won't kill me.

Except it's not ten minutes. Before going to the reception, we have to pose for a million staged photos where every possible combination is explored—bridesmaids and bride, groomsmen and groom, only bridesmaids, only groomsmen, every bridesmaid with her escort, etc....—except one that would bring Jace and me close enough to utter two words to each other.

Once the photo shoot is over, we're marched into the reception ballroom and after making our gracious entrance, we sit at our assigned tables.

I'm at the same table as Jace, which is good. But he's seated on the opposite side, which isn't ideal. I can't yell to him across the table, "Hey, Jace, would you mind passing the bread? By the way, are you still in love with me, or have I screwed it up for good?"

Aiden and Kirsten have a small, rectangular, one-couple-only table at the head of the room, while Jace and I are by the windows with the rest of the bridal party plus Aiden's and Kirsten's parents. Really not the best setting or audience for a love reunion.

This is ridiculous. I make to stand up, meaning to excuse myself to go to the restroom, hoping Jace will follow my lead, when two hands press down on my shoulders shoving me back on my chair.

"Please, wait to move, dear," the wedding coordinator instructs me. "We still have to take a few pictures of the room with all the guests seated and the plating still intact. We don't want any holes, especially not at one of the most important tables."

"Oh, okay." I sit back down, mortified, and sneak a peek at Jace.

His eyes are on me like they've been all day. But this time... there's a new glint of solidarity in them. Like he gets what I was trying to do.

I let out a breath of relief I didn't know I'd been holding inside all week.

We're on the same page. He wants to talk, too.

When the photographer has finished taking the millionth picture of glass stems no one will ever look at, I'm about to excuse myself again when Aiden's mom turns to me, asking, "Did you know the Palmer hotel was built as a wedding gift?"

No, I didn't know and I couldn't care less.

Still, I plaster a polite smile on my face and pretend to find the nugget of information riveting. "Really? For who?"

"Potter Palmer, a Chicago business magnate, built it for Bertha Honoré, a wealthy socialite twenty-three years his junior. It was quite the scandal at the time. Someone even said their marriage was cursed."

"Cursed, why?"

"Because only thirteen days after its grand opening, the hotel burned down in the Great Chicago Fire."

Uselessly, I search the room for signs of fire damage. "How are we sitting in it now, then?"

"Because Palmer rebuilt it right away, making it one of the nation's longest continually operating hotels."

"Not so cursed, then."

"But to lose all that money and for the hotel to be destroyed precisely thirteen days after opening its doors for the first time. Have you noticed they don't have a thirteenth floor?"

Like half the hotels in America, I'm tempted to reply, but keep my mouth shut. Aiden's mom is being nice, she can't know her chit-chat is effectively keeping me from telling the love of my life how I feel for the first time. So I keep quiet and listen to her story.

By the time I'm finished discussing the century-old love affair with Aiden's mom, the appetizers arrive, and at that point, I don't attempt to leave again. Everyone else at the table seems glued to their seats, and I don't want to appear rude, unappreciative, or uninterested in the wedding banquet.

Plus, Jace could excuse himself first. He saw what I was trying to do earlier. If he wanted to talk as badly as I do, all he'd have to do would be to get up, prove we're allowed to use the restroom, and I'd follow.

But he doesn't. Not after the appetizer, nor after the first course.

When a server drops the second course in front of me, I pale, and for a moment I forget all about Jace as the man announces, "Our entrée is an Amish breast of chicken in a marsala reduction with a side of mushrooms."

An image of Gemima lying bloodied and deprived of her body parts stares back at me from the plate. I swallow hard, trying not to gag. The room spins around me and I might start to sweat cold any minute.

They forgot I asked for a vegetarian meal. I didn't notice with the appetizers and first course because the tomato garden basil soup and pesto and goat's cheese risotto were basically vegetarian for everyone.

What do I do now?

I'm not eating this, but I hate making a fuss. I don't want to complain and point out someone, somewhere messed up my meal, especially not when I'm sitting next to Aiden's mother. The Collymores must've spent a fortune on this wedding.

I could just leave the food untouched on my plate, even if every extra second I stare at the cooked corpse of a once-beautiful chicken, I die a little inside.

But then Aiden's mom would probably just ask me if something was wrong with my food—at which point I'd either have to admit I'm a vegetarian or eat the darn thing.

I'm not eating the darn thing.

And I might be getting better at handling confrontations, but it seems only when it's Kendall making a move on Jace. The servers haven't done anything to me, and I don't want to make a scene, especially since Kendall has already been rude enough to the waiting staff for all the people seated at this table combined.

What do I do, then?

As I look across the fancy dining room table, desperately searching for an alternative solution, my gaze lands on the open window just over to my right. And it's one of those moments where a cartoon light bulb pops over my head.

The window behind our table overlooks a back alley, whereas the city backdrop is reserved for the newlyweds' table. All I have to do is wait until everyone is distracted and throw the meat out. No one is bound to be in the back alley, so it's not like I risk hitting anyone over the head with a chicken breast projectile.

And I know someone could argue wasting food is just as much of a crime as chicken murder. But even if I send this back to the kitchen, they're just going to throw it away all the same. At least in the alley, I could make a few city rats happy.

I basically have no choice.

I inconspicuously fidget with my knife and fork, suppressing another gag reflex as I impale the whole chicken breast on my fork.

Now I only need to pick my moment and be decisive. As if on cue, Kirsten stands up, clicking a fork on her champagne glass to get everyone's attention. In response, all heads at the table turn to the bride. No one's looking my way.

Now or never. I loosen the grip of the fork on the meat a little, and with a powerful swing of my arm, I execute the perfect throw right through the center of the open window.

Except the window isn't open. Apparently, I'm just sitting next to the cleanest flipping window in the history of hotel windows. Or at least, it was the cleanest one until my chicken breast slams up against the glass and slowly slides down, leaving a trail of marsala reduction in its wake.

Of course, the window isn't open. It's forty degrees outside. If the window were open, we'd all be freezing.

At the loud chicken-on-glass thud, Aiden's mom turns, her jaw dropping as she takes in the smeared window. Next, she stares at my empty plate and finally at me like I'm a two-headed, three-eyed, alien from outer space.

Her gaze turns back to the window disaster one last time to then settle on me. With an inquisitive, puzzled look, she asks, "What happened, dear?"

I stare at her for a second before my gaze flickers toward Jace. He's looking my way—like the rest of our table, I should add. His eyes dart from me to the chicken breast now sitting on the windowsill, the sauce trail, and my empty plate. I can practically see understanding dawning on him as his lips curl at the corners.

Aiden's mom is still staring at me, waiting for an explanation when I really have none to give. I feel like I've been keeping silent forever while in reality, it must've been only three or four seconds, tops.

"S-sorry," I stutter. "I'm such a klutz... I-I was... mmm... cutting the meat... and, I don't k-know, I must've hit a bone... it just slipped off my plate... I mean these plates are so slippery..."

"Totally slippery," Jace's voice booms from across the table. "I almost just threw my meat right across the room as well." Jace gives me a quick, I've-got-you stare before turning all his charm on Mrs. Collymore. "It must be the fine china. I've never seen a finer set in my entire life."

Among the still-perplexed stares of the other guests, Aiden's mom seems mollified. "Oh, yes, you know this is the original Bertha Palmer 1879 Havilland bone china place setting. It's valued at over thirty thousand dollars." Aiden's mom touches the rim of her plate. "The trim is actual gold." Then, covering her mouth with a hand as if she was telling a secret, she adds, "We had to pay extra to get it."

Still looking very perplexed, Aiden's father waves a server over, then pointing at the window Armageddon, he says, "I'm sorry, we've had a little flying chicken incident."

The server raises an eyebrow but doesn't look too shocked—as if this wasn't the craziest thing he had witnessed at a wedding.

I watch, mortified, as the poor fella smears the sauce around the window with a cloth napkin, attempting to clean the glass.

That window will never be the same.

Another server comes to my side, asking, "Would you like a replacement brought out for you, miss?"

"NO!" I yell, earning a few other she's-just-escaped-from-the-looney-bin side glances. "I mean, no, thank you." I theatrically rub my belly. "Everything else was so delicious. I'm full. Totally full. Except, I'm saving a little space for dessert because it's terrible luck to leave a wedding without having tasted the cake. Did you know?"

Lori, please stop talking.

If I had to diagnose the server's expression, I'd call it a case of being on the receiving end of TMI ramblings from a crazy wedding guest.

Ever the most polite, he replies to me with a simple, "Very well, miss, enjoy the rest of your meal."

I quietly keep my head down, staring at the white tablecloth in front of me for a long time before I dare raise my gaze again.

At once, my eyes dart to Jace's, and he winks at me.

A wave of relief washes over me. We're okay... we're going to be okay.

37

JACE

Lori's eyes are locked on mine. I'm drowning in her gaze. In her brown irises.

The people around us are a blur, and I can't hear what anyone is saying. I only have eyes for Lori. My eyes, my mind, my heart, my body, and my soul are all focused on her.

There's a smile on her lips, and I can almost see the love reflected in her stare.

I want to kiss her.

But I know we have to talk first. No running away this time, no lies, no untold truths. Just us. Our souls bare.

But still, we have to wait for this blasted meal to be over.

No, not even then.

As the dessert buffet opens and I think Lori and I will finally be able to sneak away, the wedding coordinator is back to haunt us.

She appears behind Aiden's brother, clapping her hands. "Members of the wedding party, please stand up. I'm going to need all of you for the first dance."

Guess I would've known that was one of my duties if I had attended the rehearsal dinner.

Once again, I'm paired with the maid of honor. We're making our entrance from the opposite corner of the room to Lori and her escort. But first, Aiden and Kirsten have to open the dances. The music starts, I don't recognize the song and I couldn't care less, I just want it to be over fast.

As the wedding coordinator prompts me and Britney to join the newlyweds on the dancefloor, we waltz alongside the bride and groom. But as we swirl around the room, my gaze keeps seeking Lori. She's dancing too, now, also ignoring her partner. Her eyes focus on me, searching for me after every spin.

The music changes and finally we're allowed to change partners. I don't waste any time. I drop Britney's hands and cross the room toward Lori.

"May I have this dance?"

Aiden's cousin steps aside. "Yeah, sure, man."

And finally, I'm in front of her.

We're facing each other. Not touching.

Our eyes are locked on each other's, and the world around us seems to disappear. It's just the two of us.

As the music starts again, I take her in my arms and pull her body flush against mine. Her scent, her soft body pressed against me, is all I need to know this is real. Her body fits mine perfectly as if we were made to be together.

We hold each other, too close, too tight—not close enough.

The way it should be.

I never want to let her go.

And then we're dancing.

As we're moving in rhythm with the music, I can't help but wonder if she feels the same way.

Lori's gaze on me is just as intense, her eyes full of emotions. Neither of us speak. We just dance, eyes locked.

Our steps are in sync, our bodies following each other's lead.

I guide her around the floor, but I'm only following her every move, every breath, her every blink.

The song ends too soon.

As the music stops, I keep holding her. I don't want to let go of her. Not yet. Not ever.

The silence stretches as if we're both thinking the same thing.

We need to talk.

Around us, everyone claps, celebrating Aiden and Kirsten.

This is not the place.

I know what I have to say. What I have to tell her. I need to make her understand, but not here. Not in front of all these people.

"Not here," I mouth.

"Let's get out," she mouths back.

I nod, and we slip out of the reception hall undetected.

I pull Lori down a corridor before someone else can stop us. I open a door at random and stumble upon another grand ballroom cloaked in semidarkness.

It's perfect.

I usher Lori inside and seal the door behind us.

The last thing I expect when I turn is for Lori to hit me in the chest. Not so hard that it hurts, but still a blow. "You left me," she accuses. "You disappeared on me."

I grab her hand before she can hit me again. "Only after you said you never wanted to have anything to do with me."

"When will you learn never to listen to a thing I say?"

I kiss her knuckles. "I take it I'm forgiven?"

Lori snatches her hand away. "Don't kisstract me. And forgiven for what? For the pact? Or for bailing on me?"

I shrug, making a cute face. "Both?"

She might still act indignant, but I knew I had her after she let me help her out of Chickengate.

Lori puffs her cheeks, letting out an exasperated sigh.

"We should talk a few things through first."

"Okay."

I smile at her. I'm in no hurry.

I take Lori's hand and lead her deeper into the opulent ballroom, to a hidden alcove. We sink together onto a plush couch in a dark corner.

Lori crosses her legs, tugging at her dress as if she suddenly realized the height of the slit.

My pulse picks up at the sight of the inch of extra skin. I muster up a cocky grin, but I can't keep it up for long.

Lori tracks my stare to her legs, and I must look feral because she blushes.

"What happened after I left your house on Tuesday?" she asks, her voice barely a whisper.

I take a deep breath, trying to slow my racing heart. I have to get this right. She has to understand. "I drowned my sorrows in a bottle of vodka, then Aiden came to see me, then I walked to your house and I saw you together."

She frowns. "You mean Aiden and me?"

"Yes..." My stare is intense, shameful, and maybe still a little hurt.

Lori does the math before I have to explain. "And you assumed the worst and bolted."

"Yep, from where I stood you looked like two long-lost lovers reunited. The look on your face... I swear—"

She pushes two fingers on my mouth to shut me up. "Was about you. I was excited to come to see you after Aiden had talked some sense into me."

I gently pull her hand away. "What did you want to tell me?"

A stretch of silence follows, the only sound that of my heart pounding behind my rib cage.

"That I'm sure..." Lori looks up, her eyes shiny. "It's you, Jace, it's only you."

Even if I'm already seated, I have to steady myself. These are the words I've dreamt of hearing since I set eyes on her for the first time fifteen years ago. Lori was strolling across the Main Quad, earphones on, dark hair up in a ponytail, too many books in her arms, and her lips synching to some unheard music as she swayed her head in time with the music.

I was struck dumb on the spot. Mesmerized. Even more so when I found her sitting in the same classroom I was headed to.

I remember the moment our eyes met across the rows of chairs lining the lecture hall. Then her gaze moved past me and settled on Aiden, her cheeks flushing.

Now, I clench my jaws. "What about Aiden?"

"I don't see him that way, not anymore. He's a good friend, nothing more."

"You've been in love with him for years. How are you suddenly over him?"

"Because I—I..." Lori falters, then looks me straight in the eyes. "I fell in love with you. Jace, I love *you*."

I want to believe her. I do with all my heart, but... years of self-doubt coil in my stomach. I want to kiss her but I'm frozen on my side of the couch.

"Okay, I get it." Lori sighs. "If you'd spent the last fifteen years pining with me over another woman, I'd have my doubts, too. That's why I bought you this." She rummages into her clutch to take out a small velvet box. "I saw it in a shop window and it seemed like the twin to the one you bought me in New Orleans." Lori opens the box to show me an antique white gold ring with an intricate geometric pattern. She pulls it out of its stand. "This is an orange blossom pattern, but the antique dealer assured me it has a very masculine feel."

We both stare at the ring, then at each other.

"What is it?" I ask.

"Supposedly a vintage wedding band, but I thought we could use it as a promise ring?" She gestures at my hands. "May I?"

I give her my left hand, and she slips the ring on.

"Jace, I love you. Everything about you. You're my best friend, my person, my rock. I know it's soon, but I want you to know that I want to be with you, only you. I want to spend the rest of our lives together. And I promise to love you every day that we're together, and not to use all the hot water in the shower." Lori smiles. "But I'll keep singing Taylor Swift at the top of my lungs. That's non-negotiable."

I grin like the dumb idiot I am.

Lori keeps holding my hand and continues, "I promise to limit the number of pets I have and to never exceed having a thousand rescue books in our house if you'll ever find the courage to come live with me." Lori pauses for breath. "But I can't make any promises about the number of kids I'll want—it's going to be a high number. And I promise to be the best mother I can and love them with all my heart, even if they turn out to be little neat freaks like you."

I chuckle at that.

"I also promise never again to yell hurtful things without thinking, even if you've made me super mad. But I also want you to promise me you will never, ever again bail on me and run away *ever* again."

I mock-pout. "Those are more evers and nevers than in a Taylor Swift song."

"I'm serious, Jace. This past week has driven me crazy. Not knowing where you went, what you were doing or thinking, if you were okay or not... And I don't want us to make some impossible promise like never going to bed angry, but I want to know that even if we're mad at each other, you'll be in bed with me, quietly sulking under the covers."

"If you haven't already hoarded them all." I bump my forehead to hers. "I promise, Lola. I'll never disappear on you again. Anything else?"

"Only that I can't wait to make the rest of the journey with you until we're old and crusty and will spend all our days complaining about the 'young people' and how things used to be better in the olden days."

Lori's out of breath, and I'm still trying to process what she just said. A lump forms in my throat. My heart feels like it's about to burst.

Then I get up, pulling her with me. I take her in my arms and kiss her as if my life depended on it.

The kiss is warm and soft, full of life and promise, the promise of a future, of an entire life together. Pressed against me, she feels like the heat and light of the sun. Like the freshness of the first breath of spring. Like a ray of hope, like the promise of a whole new world to explore together.

I drink her in, my heart racing, my hands shaking. Our kiss is both sweet and electric, a touch at first, a mere brush of lips that soon turns into something more.

My lips part. With a soft moan, her lips do the same, allowing me to deepen the kiss. I place my arms around her, pulling her closer, and I don't want to let her go.

A tear falls from my eyes, and another. I'm kissing the woman I love, and who loves me back—for real this time.

"Gosh," Lori finally whispers, her voice thick with tears as well. "I've missed you so much."

I can't help it. I laugh and I kiss her again. Then kiss her some more.

We only pull apart when we're desperate for air.

"I love you, Lori," I say.

"I love you, too, Jace."

I break into the widest, most carefree grin.

This is how I want to spend the rest of my life.

I put my forehead on hers, still afraid to believe I'm not dreaming. I take her hands and ask, "Will you marry me?"

Lori's eyes bulge. "What?"

"Will you marry me?" I prompt again.

"You want to get married?" she repeats in a daze.

I shrug. "We've already made the vows. Plus, getting married is what people do when they love each other and want to spend the rest of their lives together, isn't it?"

Lori laughs, squeezing my hand. "Yes, I want to spend the rest of my life with you."

"Yeah?"

"Yes," she says, her voice full of laughter. "I want to marry you."

38

LORI

Jace squeezes me into the tightest hug, then pulls back, looking a little manic.

"Okay, we already have the rings, all we need now is a minister. Do you think the pastor from Aiden's ceremony is still around?"

"You want to get married *now*? Like right at this moment?"

Jace's determined expression doesn't waver.

I smile. "You're not joking, are you?"

He flashes me a radiant grin that pulls all kinds of strings in my chest. "I know it's only been a month for you, but I've waited fifteen years, Lola, and I don't want to waste another minute."

"But we don't even have a marriage license."

Jace is already busy on his phone. "We can get it online." He's tapping furiously on the screen. "Aaaand... We have a virtual appointment in fifteen minutes."

Excitement bubbles up in my chest. "Are we really doing this?"

"My mother is going to kill me for eloping."

I pat Jace on the chest. "She'll forgive you after the first grandbaby."

Jace leans down and nuzzles my neck. "I can't wait to make babies with you."

His words ignite a fire in my belly. My hormones have been raging since the moment he kissed me for the first time. And now they're shifting into high gear.

Jace pulls back, looking at me with a mischievous twinkle in his eyes. "I'm dying to get you home. But first I have to make an honest woman out of you," he jokes, and kisses me again.

We kiss again and my fingers itch to touch him, to feel his skin, but I can't find a point of access. This tux that I found so sexy only moments ago, now has turned into an impenetrable barrier.

Jace doesn't have the same impediments, my dress is way more generous with the amount of skin he's allowed to touch, kiss, bite.

He trails soft kisses down my neck and collarbone and I'm about to throw all patience out the window and begin unbuttoning his blazer when his phone vibrates with a reminder.

"We're on," Jace says.

He efficiently pulls up his phone and connects with the marriage license office through a video link.

The interview is brief, over in less than fifteen minutes.

"Go wait for me in the Red Lacquer Room," Jace says. "I'll come with the pastor."

***

The ceremony is done and over in less than ten minutes. The pastor leaves us immediately afterward, eager to get back to the dessert buffet, I suspect. So Jace and I are alone in the grand room.

I hold his hands, my husband's hands, saying, "This must be the shortest wedding in the history of weddings."

A wicked grin lights up his face. "Then I'll make the wedding night the longest of your life." He winks at me, and I want to drag him down to the hotel lobby, book a room, and get started on that project right away. But we can't, not yet.

I shake my head, grinning. "We have to be there for the cutting of the cake."

Jace nods. "Let's go back to the party."

We sneak back into the reception ballroom, alone in knowing that we're husband and wife.

Jace makes a mock bow before me. "Would you do me the honor of a first dance, Mrs. Barlow?"

A thrill runs down my spine. Jace and I are married. I still can't believe it.

"I would be delighted," I say, offering him my hand.

Jace slips an arm around my waist and pulls me close.

We sway together to the music. Jace's hand is warm and firm on my waist, I rest my head on his chest, feeling his heart beating under my ear. I relish the sensation of his arm wrapped around me, of his hand tenderly resting on my waist.

Jace kisses my hair, then my temple, turning my mind fuzzier than it already is. I'm only following the rhythm with my body, barely able to concentrate on anything besides the feathery touch of his lips until he whispers, "I love you more than anything, Lola."

"I love you, too, hubby." Now that I've said I love you once, I can't stop repeating it.

Jace smiles a secret smile and pulls me even closer to him. We sway some more. I'm not sure how long we dance, or how many songs pass, but too soon, the music stops.

The wedding coordinator takes up a mic, announcing we have to clear the dancefloor as the wedding cake is about to arrive.

All the guests make room for the massive five-layer white cake being rolled in on a white-clothed cart.

Aiden and Kirsten get behind it. Our friend catches sight of us huddled together and his smile becomes even brighter. All three of us exchange a nod, and Aiden winks before turning his attention back to his bride. They share a glance, then Kirsten says, "Let's do the thing."

Aiden nods and they join hands over a huge knife.

The crowd holds its breath as they cut through the white fondant, then a collective sigh spreads around the room as the first slice falls away, revealing a red filling—giving me serious "I Bet You Think About Me" vibes. Kirsten must be a fellow Swiftie, maybe we could get along after all.

Jace and I pull away from each other. He makes a bow and kisses my knuckles. "I'm going to go get us a slice of cake." His gaze turns teasing as he adds, "Seeing how apparently it's terrible luck to leave a wedding without having had a bite of cake."

"Maybe the server didn't know," I say. "I could've saved him from years of misery and awful luck."

Jace winks at me, striding off in the direction of the buffet.

I track his progress across the room, admiring the way his behind fills out his tux as he joins the other guests already gathering around the cake table, chattering compliments about the white sugar roses and edible pearl decorations.

Jace returns with a plate of cake in each hand and a smear of frosting on his upper lip, which makes him look so darn cute I could melt.

"Couldn't resist, huh?" I ask, stealing one of the napkins in his hands to wipe his cheek.

"You know red velvet is my favorite."

"I thought I was your favorite?"

Still balancing two plates of cake in his hands, Jace somehow manages to pull me into him. "You are my favorite," he says, "and my second favorite is red velvet cake." Jace kisses me. A deep kiss that tastes like sugar and paradise and only ends when my knees have turned into jelly.

"Come on," Jace says, leading me to our table to eat the cake. Servers are meandering through the guests with glasses of champagne on trays, I grab two flutes and bring them to the table with us.

We're the only ones back, and Jace steals Mrs. Collymore's seat to be next to me.

Jace's gaze is full of promise as he grabs one glass and lifts it. "To the most beautiful bride I have ever seen."

Our eyes lock, and time slows down. His gaze pulls me in, filling me with warmth, and I know he's thinking the same thing I am.

This entire day is surreal, dream-like.

Jace and I are married.

39

LORI

Once the cake is gone, the party begins to wind down. The guests start saying their goodbyes and preparing to leave.

On the dancefloor, we watch Aiden, who's had a few too many drinks, sway our way. He wraps his arms around Jace and me and teases, "You guys are going to be next."

"Deal," Jace agrees, grinning.

"I mean it," Aiden insists, and for a moment, he looks serious. "I can't be the only old married dude."

My husband and I share a complicit smile, but also a subtle message. Today's not the day to tell Aiden. It's his day, his party, and it should remain about him and Kirsten. We will surprise them with the good news once they're back from their honeymoon.

Jace gives me an understated nod and pats Aiden on the chest. "You won't be, man. Not for long."

Aiden lets out a loud whoop. "I like the way you think, brother. This calls for another round of drinks."

Aiden grasps three glasses from a passing tray, struggling to hold all three in his hands. Jace relieves him of the bubbly and plants a solid glass of water in his hands.

"Hey," Jace says, "My role as best man compels me to point out you have some marital duties to attend to later that you don't want to be too wasted for."

Jace's eyes flicker to me as he says this, and my cheeks catch fire.

Aiden gives us his best shocked look, but the hint of a grin quirks the corner of his mouth. "You could be right, man." The groom puts up his hands. "Speaking of... how long do you think I have to wait before I steal the bride?"

Jace shrugs. "Your wedding, dude, your call."

Aiden nods. "I'm going."

The groom skirts across the room and tackles Kirsten into a hug, dragging her toward the exit door.

Kirsten protests at first, but then he whispers something in her ear and she blushes, following him willingly.

Two months ago, seeing them so happy, so in love, and so randy, would've eviscerated me, but now only happiness spills in my heart.

Strong arms wrap around me from behind. "So." Jace's warm breath tickles my neck as he whispers in my ear, "If the bride and groom have discreetly fled their own wedding, does that mean we're free to go, too?"

"I suppose so..." I turn my head to stare up at him. "Did you come in your car?"

"No, I walked."

"I took a taxi, should we call one?"

Jace's eyes darken a little and he nibbles at my earlobe. "I'm not sure I can wait that long. Want to see if the hotel still has free rooms?"

"The cats will murder me, but yes."

* * *

"Welcome home, darling," Jace announces fifteen minutes later as he kicks the hotel room door open, struggling to get past the threshold while carrying me in his arms—wedding-night style.

I chuckle before a thought hits me. "We haven't even decided where we're going to live. My place or yours?"

Jace kicks the door shut behind him. "I can't fit six hens in my apartment, so it's probably going to be your place for now... but it doesn't really matter..."

"Why not?"

"Because wherever you are it's home." We cross the room, and he gently lowers me onto the bed, scooting next to me—more half on top of me. Pushing aside a lock of my hair, he whispers, "It's been a long road, but we're finally here."

"I'm glad Professor Quilliam made us steal garden gnomes," I say. "I would've never struck up the courage to talk to the coolest boys in our year otherwise."

Jace quirks an eyebrow. "Anything else you're glad for, I mean, besides my thieving skills?"

"Everything about you," I whisper. "And I'm glad you made the pact with Aiden."

Jace's eyes widen at this. "Really?"

I nod.

"Why?"

My fingertips trace the edges of his bow tie as I say, "Because it made us wait until we're both mature enough to see this to the end. Because it made this love possible, uncomplicated, pure, real."

The expression of unaltered joy on Jace's face melts my heart.

My husband kisses me, long and slow. "You're with me."

"Always. And there's no one else I'd rather have by my side than you," I tell my husband again and again because I know he'll still need reassurances. I love him all the more for it. For sharing all his vulnerabilities, for being an open book. And there's nothing I look forward to more than telling him times and times again how much I love him. Only him.

EPILOGUE

LORI

On the hotel room bed, Jace kisses me. We're alone. We're sure. We're married. Nothing is standing in the way anymore. Except maybe our clothes. I swear, I've never loathed three-piece suits more than at this moment.

What's the purpose of a blazer? I mean, other than keeping me from getting to feel my husband's chest against mine, skin to skin.

We're kissing and touching, and I'm all about tearing off his tuxedo, but the rotten buttons won't budge.

Jace is suffering the same frustration with my bridesmaid dress. He's fumbling with the tiny pearl buttons, unsuccessfully trying to pry them open. Soft, impatient grunts escape his lips as he loses the battle with fancy haberdashery until I whisper in his ear, "The buttons are fake, my darling." I tilt my body up, giving access to my back. "There's a clasp at the top and a hidden zipper."

Jace's fingers are swift. He flicks the hook free and pulls down the zipper. Slowly, ever so slowly, his eyes lock on mine in a way that threatens my sanity.

As the zipper bottoms out and I think we're about to solve the first part of our hang-up—getting me naked, Jace pulls back, leaving me still fully clothed.

He shifts slightly to the side, holding his weight on his elbow in a way that can't be comfortable, but that only makes me think of the level of muscle definition ready to be uncovered under that darn tux.

I search his eyes. "What's up?"

He pushes a wayward lock of hair behind my ear. "I don't know what to do."

I consider the affirmation. From the way he has been kissing me over the past month, I'm pretty sure Jace Barlow knows his way around a woman's body. So I don't suppose he's talking about practical lessons here.

"How do you mean?"

My husband trails a finger over my collarbone, leaving a trail of icy cold fire in its wake. "I've dreamt of this night for so long... now I don't know which fantasy I want to live first."

A wide, randy smile creeps across my face. "Maybe if you shared a few of those fantasies, I could help you sort through the most promising ones..."

The hint of a grin plays at the corner of Jace's mouth. "That's not something I had considered, but you make a good point, Princess."

Princess. The nickname causes a warm flood to spread across my body as if instead of blood, melted honey was coursing through my veins.

I can feel my heart pounding in my chest. The thump-thump-thump so loud, I'm certain Jace can hear it too.

"Mmm... We could take it slow... or fast?" I suggest, starting with the basics.

He shakes his head. "I don't want fast, I want slow."

Jace gives me the sweetest, most genuine, most loving smile.

His doting expression makes him look so vulnerable. So open-hearted, so sweet, so different from the "can't touch this" Jace I've been picturing for all these years. In my head, he used to be all danger and cockiness. The bad boy. I couldn't have been more wrong. His projected confidence has always been a shield to protect the exposed heart underneath. A heart that's always been beating for me.

I'm still overwhelmed by how much I love him, by how much he loves me back.

Jace twirls a loose lock of my hair around his finger and a breath hitches in my throat.

"I want to savor every second of this night," he continues.

I'm tempted to reply that he should get down to it. That all this talking and not doing is torture, sweet anticipation. But he's waited for me for so long, I can be patient for a few more minutes.

"I want to memorize the shape of you, the scent of your hair, the feel and taste of your skin," Jace says, his voice low, rasping, grating on my very soul. "I want to remember the way you're looking at me right now, that sparkle of love and desire in your eyes. It drives me crazy, Lola."

I can sympathize with the sentiment. My breath is coming in quick gasps, his words smothering me with their intensity.

"I want to know every inch of you," Jace continues. "Every secret spot, every quirk and turn of your body and soul. I want to kiss every inch of your skin and trace every curve with my hands..."

Listening to his plans is enough to threaten to melt me in my skin. Gosh, if the guy can get me so worked up by just talking... what will happen when he finally does all those things?

"I want to take my time with you, so I will remember every moment of our first time, our wedding night."

His words send another warm rush through my body. Jace's

voice washes over me, smooth and soft, but with a hint of steel. Not for the first time, I become aware that Jace Barlow is made of so much more than good looks and an amazing body.

I clear my throat. "You should take up public speaking. I'm feeling pretty inspired. Real rallied up."

Jace's icy blue eyes twinkle with amusement and… something else. Love? Lust? All the above?

I reach forward, threading my fingers through Jace's hair, drawing his face close to mine. Our lips meet, tentatively at first, and then, like a dam breaking, we're kissing as if our ability to breathe depended on it.

This time, I'm the one who pulls back. I cup his face, his beautiful, sexy face.

"I love you." Searching his eyes to make sure he truly understands me. "It doesn't matter what we do tonight, how we do it, or how many times. You won't wake up tomorrow discovering this has all been a dream. We're here. I'm yours…"

My husband doesn't say a word, but his lips are on mine again in an instant, crushing, devouring all at once. I'm kissing him back, hungrily, and pulling his tuxedo jacket off at the same time.

I stumble backward on the mattress and Jace tumbles on top of me, still kissing me, our hands tangling and tripping over each other's clothes. He quickly gains control of the situation. The tuxedo jacket flies off the bed, and, now that the back zipper of my dress is undone, he tears my corset down my front with a single yank.

I guess that's how "slow" we're going at it—not that I'm complaining.

The gentle, sweet smile is gone from my husband's face. In its place is a look of primal hunger.

"You're the most beautiful woman I've ever seen." Jace's breath is warm on my skin, and his voice is a husky whisper.

I'm not sure if he's talking to me or himself, but I'm pretty sure I don't care as long as he doesn't stop doing all the wicked things he's doing.

"You have too many clothes on," he assesses.

"Pot... kettle... black," I manage to say between labored breaths.

His hand travels up my leg, tickling its way to my hip and up my stomach. He's excruciatingly gentle, and my body strains against his touch until he finally pulls my skirt off.

Never taking his eyes off me, he undoes the buttons of his blazer. And I know I should probably help him, but it's like all the bones have left my body and I've lost the ability to move. So I just watch, enjoying the show.

The button-down shirt goes next, and I'm struck by how much more of him is on display now. His muscular chest and shoulders are now revealed in all their ripped masculinity.

I only have a moment to admire the magnificent view before my husband is back on top of me, kissing me.

"I love you so much," he says in my neck.

"I love you too," I reply.

It doesn't matter what will happen next, I feel so complete already. I'm so full of love for Jace, my husband, the man I love.

* * *

Afterward, we lay in bed, spent. I can feel him still trembling next to me. His face buried in my neck. He's breathing heavily.

"I love you," Jace tells me again. "You're my entire world."

"I know." I kiss his temple, wrapping my arms more tightly around him. "Stay with me."

"I will, sweetheart. I'm not going anywhere."

I'm overwhelmed by the whole thing.

"So this is what it feels like to make love," I marvel.

Jace's head snaps up, eyes searching mine. "What?"

Oh, guess I said that out loud.

I cup his face. "I've never been in love with any of my boyfriends, not that I had that many."

Jace bites my palm. "I hated every single one of them."

I brush his hair. "Well, I never loved any of them, not the way I'm in love with you..." A tender smile curls on my lips. "This hasn't been my first time making love to you, it's been the first time I made love to someone."

Jace seems overwhelmed by the admission as if he can't express in words what he's feeling. So he does with his mouth, showering my face in tiny kisses. Until he crushes me into a bone-cracking hug.

Neither of us speak again. We lie still in each other's arms. Until, after a while, Jace rolls off me and lies on his back. His hand immediately shoots to the side, seeking mine, as if not to lose contact. Fingers interlaced, we lie on the bed in silence, side by side, spent but still panting slightly. I'm about to pass out when Jace, eyes closed, says, "I have a question."

"Okay?"

"The cat, Ben, is he named after Ben Solo or Obi-Wan's alias?"

I roll to face him, propping myself up on my elbow to look at him. "After what we just did, that's what you want to talk about?"

"They're my cats, too, now... I need to know."

I yawn and then laugh a little. "I couldn't decide, so I left it undetermined."

Jace opens his eyes then, grinning at me. "Mmm... and why have the chickens got regular names?"

"As opposed to?"

"Galactic names?"

"If that disturbs you, I promise we're naming all our future pets after Star Wars characters."

He rolls toward me and kisses my sternum over the sheets. "What about real babies?"

I chuckle. "Perhaps we stick to normal names?"

"You're right." Jace nods, accompanying the statement with a yawn. Then he snuggles into me and I hold him close.

"I love you."

"I love you," I whisper into his hair.

"Now, what were you saying earlier about making a baby? Because I'd be totally on board with resuming that topic," he says —lids heavy with sleep.

"Really? Because you look more ready to pass out." I gently stroke his hair. "How about we reopen the discussion in the morning?"

"Deal." He kisses me on the cheek, then closes his eyes. "Good-night, Princess."

I'm about to reply when I hear him snoring softly. I can't help but laugh and turn off the lights, feeling more at peace than I have in forever.

* * *

I wake up first. Jace is still asleep, naked, and sprawled on his stomach, hugging a pillow. His hair is messy and there's a sexy, one-day's worth of stubble on his chin.

He's my husband.

Yesterday's events swirl in my head as a vortex of joy, love, and naughtier stuff...

I run a finger over his shoulder blades, and Jace stirs in response. His eyes flutter open, and he looks around dazedly.

When he sees me, he smiles, his voice still thick with sleep. "Good morning, beautiful."

"Good morning," I answer, my heart singing.

Jace turns to face me, cocking his head to one side, tracing a finger down my jaw to my collarbones.

We're still naked and tangled in each other's arms. "You want to...?" he whispers, his hand moving down my back.

"I would love to, but..." My stomach churns with a spectacular grumble, answering for me.

"But I'd better feed you first," Jace assesses. "Should we order breakfast in bed or do you want to go out?"

If I could, I'd never leave this bed. I peek out the window. It looks like Chicago is in a mood today.

Jace follows my gaze to the window. "Room service, then."

"That would be fantastic."

He turns to grab the room's phone, and I slip out of bed and into the bathroom to freshen up.

It's only after I'm done washing my face and brushing my teeth that I realize I forgot to put on any clothes. I'm about to step out of the bathroom when Jace steps in, dressed in a T-shirt and boxers. He takes one look at me and his lips part in surprise.

I throw him a towel. "Stop staring."

"Impossible," Jace says, picking up the wet towel I just threw at him. "You're too beautiful, Princess." He approaches me slowly, leaning in to kiss me on the shoulder.

My entire body breaks into goosebumps.

"Did you order breakfast?" I mumble, distracted by his mouth moving up my neck.

"Yeah. Room service should arrive in twenty to thirty minutes. But I wanted to take a shower." He slides the glass doors open and looks back at me.

"Do you want to join me?"

"You know I do," I say. "Are we going to have a Taylor Swift singing contest?"

Jace tilts his head and utters a single word, "No."

* * *

Room service arrives just as we're stepping out of the shower. Jace pulls on a robe and goes to the door. I wrap myself in a towel and wait for him on the bed.

When Jace returns with our breakfast, I'm already half dozing in the giant bed, my head resting on the pillows.

He places two covered plates on the mattress and then hops on the bed next to me.

"You look so peaceful, Princess," he says, wrapping me in his arms.

"I could stay here forever... I can't believe we have to be at work in less than"—I peek at my watch—"three hours."

Since Aiden decided to get married on a weekday, we moved all patient appointments for the day after to the afternoon, foreseeing Aiden's wedding reception would end late. But we hadn't anticipated just how late we'd actually end up going to sleep last night. And I still have to go home to change, feed the cats and hens, and then drive to work. We'll have to go soon, *too* soon.

"Let's worry about work later. We still have a few free hours." Jace frees the plates from their coverings, the delicious smell of pancakes and French toast invading the room.

"I just wish we had all day. Couldn't Aiden and Kirsten get married on a weekend like normal people?"

He grabs a strawberry and offers it to me, chuckling.

"Why are you laughing?" I ask.

"I just realized we got married on Valentine's Day... do you still think that people who get married on Valentine's Day are overcompensating for lack of real romance?"

I shrug and take a bite of the strawberry. "I thought so once."

Jace leans closer to me. "And now?"

I chew my food thoughtfully and then sing-song, "All I know since yesterday... Is everything has changed..."

"Is that another Taylor Swift song?"

"Yep! Thought you'd missed me singing in the shower..."

"Nope, I'm very into the new shower activities you've taken up."

He winks at me and I blush, which is ridiculous considering all the things we've done in the last few hours.

Jace takes a bite of French toast, dusting his upper lip with powdered sugar.

As I reach out to wipe his lip, I think of another Taylor Swift song: "You Belong with Me." No words ever sounded more true. Only I'm the one who never realized that what I was looking for had been right in front of me the whole time.

ABOUT THE AUTHOR

Camilla Isley is an engineer who left science behind to write bestselling contemporary rom-coms set all around the world. She lives in Italy.

Sign up to Camilla Isley's mailing list for news, competitions and updates on future books.

Visit Camilla's website: www.camillaisley.com

Follow Camilla on social media:

- instagram.com/camillaisley
- tiktok.com/@camilla.isley
- facebook.com/camillaisley
- x.com/camillaisley
- bookbub.com/authors/camilla-isley
- youtube.com/RomanceAudiobooks

ALSO BY CAMILLA ISLEY

The Love Theorem

Love Quest

The Love Proposal

Love to Hate You

Not in a Billion Years

Baby, One More Time

It's Complicated